WINTER'S BLOOM

Readers are encouraged to go to
www.JohnWemlinger.com to contact the author
or to find information on how to buy this book
in bulk at a discounted rate.

Published by Mission Point Press
2554 Chandler Lake Rd.
Traverse City, MI 49686
(231) 421-9513
www.MissionPointPress.com

ISBN: 978-1-943995-06-6

Library of Congress Control Number: 2016906902

Printed in the United States of America.

WINTER'S BLOOM

a novel

JOHN WEMLINGER

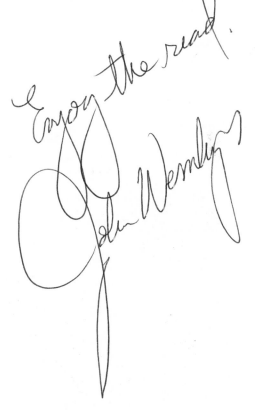

Enjoy the read.

John Wemlinger

MISSION POINT PRESS

CHAPTER ONE

Flint
6:00 a.m., September 28, 2008

Sleep had been elusive to the point that trying to find it was more exhausting than just getting up. Untwisting the covers entwined around him, Rock Graham rolled his legs over the side of the bed, grimacing in anticipation of the pain he knew would bark at him. Indecision had never before been an issue, yet it kept him awake nearly all night. It started the day before when Patti rather off-handedly, or maybe not, said to him, "So, tomorrow you're going to leave us." There was a certain finality in her voice that he had not challenged at the time. He hadn't wanted to get into it with her. He was coming back to Flint in the spring. He'd made sure both of them understood that, and, what the hell, they were going to Florida for the winter. So why couldn't he go wherever the hell he wanted to. Nevertheless, she could practice a kind of Catholic guilt on him like no one else he knew, and her comment had stuck with him. He never wanted to hurt Russ or Patti Sluwinski.

He glanced at his cell phone on the nightstand and then at the clock. If it hadn't been so early, he might have called and cancelled. Instead, he stood, wobbling slightly as he slowly applied weight to his right leg. In this pre-dawn hour his loft above the four-car garage was still dark, the only illumination coming from a night-light located next to his bed. Limping, he moved with familiarity through the open loft into the kitchen, flicked on the gentle under-counter lighting, put water on to boil, deposited a packet of Earl Grey tea in his favorite mug and leaned back against the counter slowly stretching out his bad leg. Whatever pain he might have felt was pushed from his mind, a tangle of indecision. He couldn't have said how long he had stood there. It was the teapot's whistle that pulled his mind back into the room.

Mug in hand, his right leg starting to stretch itself more, the limp slightly less noticeable, he walked into the living area, sat down in his leather easy chair, took a sip of the hot tea and laid his head back into the chair's buttery soft-ness. His eyes closed, he let his mind's eye recall the room, bookshelves lining the walls, filled with books he had read or was planning to. *Why go away?*

Thirty-five years ago, Patti Sluwinski suggested she and Russ build a big, four-car garage at the rear of their newly purchased home. And she suggested above that garage they plan a loft for him. At first Rock thought they were only feeling sorry for him. He was fresh from a divorce that he hadn't seen coming, but he didn't need or want anyone's pity. He caught his wife in bed with a co-worker on the only day he'd ever come home from work sick and that had been the end of that. But Patti and Russ had been patient and persistent with him. Along the way they made good arguments on why the arrangement made sense as all three of them were working an average of sixty hours a week on various General Motors' assembly lines around Flint. Six months later the garage and his loft were com-pleted. He'd lived here ever since.

This place was his retreat. Lately, however, he had come to see it as the eye of a hurricane, that sweet center of tranquility surrounded by chaos. GM was shuttering every one of its Flint plants. He, Russ, and Patti were forced to retire, but all three considered themselves lucky. They, at least, had pensions. They had been careful, invested some of their earnings outside the company that was now crumpling around them. Even though the market was completely in the dumpster right now, they'd seen cycles like this before. They could afford to wait it out, which was not so with too many others they knew.

All Rock had to do was walk a few steps to the front yard and look up and down their street to see the toll the economic downturn was taking on his hometown. The four new *For Sale* signs this week brought the number of houses in a three-block segment to eight. Of these eight, six contained the additional banner *Foreclosure* across either the top or bottom of the sign. He knew all eight of these families. All had young children and either one or both of the parents had worked with him in the plants. No one knew exactly what the unemployment rate was in Flint. The published figure was "over 50%", but anyone who had worked for GM knew it had to be higher than even that fantastic number. Then there was Bill Kaufman and Larry Sherman, two guys he'd worked with for over fifteen years. He had cried at their funerals. Their wives had been left with mountainous debt, their children without fathers to help raise them. Both had committed suicide shortly after being laid off. He was one of the biggest donors to a memorial fund that would help the two families, but he never felt he had done enough. He wanted to do more; he wanted to help in some way those eight families up and down his street who were living behind those For Sale signs. But what could *he* do? His desire was infinite, his resources were not.

Just as he felt the anger rising in him again, he heard the footsteps on the stairs first and then the knock. "Rock?" There was a pause and then another knock, "Rock, you awake?"

He took a deep breath and turned his head toward the door, "Yeah, Russ, it's open."

Dressed in his usual bib overalls, Russ Sluwinski filled the open doorway, his T-shirt stretching over massive shoulders and biceps. He stepped in.

Rock Graham stood, turning to face his old friend and grimaced again. "You're up early."

Sluwinski, who had been there when the leg was injured nearly forty years ago, looked past the grimace, "Yeah, Patti and me, we couldn't sleep. Today's the day, right?"

"Yeah, today's the day."

Sluwinski just nodded and rubbed his chin. "Patti's making breakfast."

Rock moved toward him, "She doesn't need to do..."

Sluwinski's big right hand went up. "C'mon, Rock. If I go back over there and tell her you're not coming, she'll just be up here. You know how she is, especially today."

Rock smiled and held up his hands in resignation. "Got a point, buddy. Let me get dressed and I'll be right over."

"Rock..." Sluwinski paused, looking for the right words.

Graham finished his old friend's thought, "She's going to grill me, isn't she?"

Sluwinski hung his head, nodded affirmatively and said, "You know how she is."

"Russ, you know I'll be back in the spring. This isn't the end of anything."

Russ nodded, "Yeah, Rock, I know, but Patti, she..."

Rock looked helplessly at his old friend who had an even more helpless look on his face.

"Yeah. I know. Patti's being Patti. Thanks for the warning."

Sluwinski turned rapidly on his heel and reached for the door. Rock saw him take a swipe at one eye the way a bear would brush away a bothersome fly. "She said about fifteen minutes and breakfast will be on the table. She told me to tell you to hurry up. She doesn't want it to get cold."

They both chuckled as Sluwinski again said, "You know how she is."

Chapter Two

Holland
9:00 a.m., September 28, 2008

The dramatic violins of Brahms's Symphony No. 4 in E minor swept across the bedroom like the wind across prairie grass. Though the piece had immediately driven Flower, her two-year–old yellow lab, from the room, the music perfectly fit her mood. Through teary eyes she glanced at the clock on the mantle above the cold fireplace. *9:02 a.m.* "Uh-oh," she muttered under her breath. Blotting her tears with one hand, she reluctantly closed *The Last Lecture,* stood and reached for the remote control on the table next to her. The push of a button opened pale teal blinds built into an expansive wall of windows, revealing a brilliant morning. With the press of another button on the same remote, she silenced Brahms and stood, taking in the vista. The sun shimmered off Lake Macatawa as if a billion diamonds had been strewn in front of her. Heavy dew lingered on the grass of the manicured lawn, edged with well-tilled, weed-free flowerbeds. The 50-foot Sea Ray rocked alongside a dock that thrust out into the lake. Reluctantly she pulled her eyes away from the view and checked the mantel clock again.

Late was very much unlike Claire Van Zandt, but as she took stock of herself, she knew she was not going to make her 10 a.m. appointment on time. She found her cell phone on the nightstand and speed-dialed her youngest daughter. Four rings later, Beth's lilty voice told her to leave a message. "Beth, it's Mom. Sorry, but I'll be a bit late. You and Ingrid get started and I'll get there as quick as I can."

She showered quickly, just dampening her hair enough that she could give it some shape. She thought she'd put the top down on the BMW and drive it into town. The breeze would dry her hair and also give her a good excuse for it not measuring up to its usual level of perfection. Stepping from the shower to the sink, she noticed a waiting voice mail.

"Mom, I hope you're not answering this because you're already on the road. Don't make me do this by myself. I'm going to call Brides-To-Be and tell them I'm going to be a little late, but that we will still be there. Ingrid will be pissed...sorry...upset... you know how she can be. C'mon, Mom. Please hurry. I love you."

Claire chided herself for her tardiness, but, almost perversely, she found the desperation in Beth's voice to be humorous. Ingrid would be pissed. Ingrid Van Zandt Hoffman, Claire's eldest daughter, five years older than Beth, was every bit as driven as her father had been. An attorney married to an attorney, she and her husband, Ethan, were ambitious junior partners in a large Grand Rapids law firm, their lives driven by their work schedules. Everything had a start and an end time. Beth had joked once that Brian, her five-year old nephew, had the audacity to be born two weeks early and that had caused a ripple in Ingrid's life that took two years to work itself out.

In the huge walk-in closet, Claire selected a casual slacks outfit and complimented it with a long, silver necklace with garnet-colored glass beads. She finished the look with a light green and dark red, plaid, loosely woven scarf artfully doubled over and placed around her neck with the ends pulled through the loop. It would ward off any chill that might still be lingering in the mid-morning breeze during the top-down trip into downtown Holland. Finally she chose a pair of dark gray, calf-high boots, but as she bent over to pull them on a sudden shortness of breath and dizziness caught her. She straightened up and put her hands behind her, feeling for something solid to stabilize her, but found only hanging clothes. Stumbling, she managed to grasp the shelf behind her on a second try. She took a deep breath. Whatever it was, it was gone as quickly as it had come, and she was late. *9:45 a.m.* She shrugged it off, tardiness trumping any reason for concern. She walked over to the full-length mirror that stood in one corner of the closet, looked herself over, patted a few curls back into place and headed downstairs.

Even before she walked into the kitchen, Claire smelled the freshly cut roses in the vase on the dining table. "Good morning, Maria," she said to the woman at the sink washing some dishes from dinner the evening before. "Good morning, Jesus." Pointing to the roses, she said, "They're beautiful. I could smell them from the foyer." In addition to his current duty as dish dryer, Jesus, Maria's husband of fifty years, was also the gardener, handyman and former chauffeur. "Good morning, Flower." The big dog got up and walked over to Claire, tail wagging, looking for a rub on the head.

"Good morning, Ms. Claire," said Maria with only a hint of an accent.

Jesus, concluding that she was on her way someplace, asked with an edge of eagerness that only made his thick accent even more difficult to understand, "Ms. Claire, would you like me to bring the Mercedes around?"

Claire caught Maria's quick glance and slight shake of the head.

Back in the day, chauffeuring had been one of Jesus' primary duties. He'd always taken Alan to the airport and been there to pick him up. When Claire had been working as a middle-school counselor and had to squeeze into her schedule the many duties of an up-and-coming Holland/ Grand Rapids socialite, she would have Jesus deliver her to school, pick her up at day's end and then run her around both towns on errands for this or that charity. She had served on a dozen or more boards and chaired many of them. Alan had encouraged her volunteerism.

There was little chauffeuring to be done now. Alan died in 2005. In that same year Claire retired from public education and from nearly everything else as well. Nothing was as it had been, including Jesus. Never a big man, even in his prime, he now bore the bend of a man who had worked hard at manual labor for most of his seventy years. His eyesight was also dimming. It was almost comical to see him behind the wheel of the big Mercedes Benz S600 or the huge Rolls, with hands fixed at ten and two on the steering wheel, pulling himself forward and up enough so that he could see the road beyond the massive length of hood stretching in front of him. Maria had told Claire, "He looks like Mr. Magoo. He shouldn't be driving at all, much less these big cars, Ms. Claire." Each had told the other hair-raising stories about trips they had taken with him over the last few years. Both agreed that it was in everyone's best interest if Jesus' chauffeuring responsibilities could be significantly curtailed if not eliminated.

"No, Jesus, but thanks. I'm just going into town, and I'm not sure how long I will be," Claire said nicely, but firmly.

Maria handed him a plate to dry. "I fed Flower," Maria offered in a good attempt to change the subject. "She came down about 8 a.m. and seemed hungry."

"Thank you," Claire said, very much aware of what Maria was trying to do. "I was playing a CD from the symphony. Flower isn't a fan of Brahms, or any classical music for that matter." They laughed as Jesus knelt down in front of the gentle lab and rubbed her ears while reassuring her that mariachi music, he thought, would be more to her liking. The two women exchanged knowing glances. "I'm going to town to meet with Beth and Ingrid about the wedding. There's no need for you or Jesus to wait for me. Why don't the two of you enjoy a day with your grandchildren." Claire saw the sparkle come into both of their eyes.

"Are you sure, Ms. Claire?" asked Maria. "What about your supper? I will…"

Claire interrupted her. "Maria, I'm not sure what I'm going to do this evening. Don't worry about me. You two go enjoy your family."

Maria turned to Jesus and said something in Spanish that Claire was able to loosely translate as, "Finish with the roses and cut some for the bedroom. We are so lucky to work here."

Jesus replied simply with, "Si," and then turned to Claire and said, "Thank you, Ms. Claire."

Claire checked her watch. 10:04 a.m. "I have to go. I'm late." As she turned to head to the front door, Flower followed her. "No, girl, you stay with Maria. She'll let you out after I leave."

Maria nodded. This was Claire's way of avoiding those eyes. Though Flower rarely went with her mistress in the car, it was her habit to sit outside at the intersection of the walkway to the front door and apex of the semi-circular driveway and watch with drooped ears as Claire drove away. No matter which way Claire exited the drive she couldn't help but see the big dog's disappointment. It was the eyes. Those eyes could melt cold steel.

She'd loved the dog almost from the moment Beth had walked in the front door with her as a ten-pound puppy. Beth was certain Flower had helped her mother through some desperate days. Claire, on the other hand, had never considered whether or not Flower was a remedy for her grief. All she knew was that Flower loved her and she loved Flower, and those sad eyes could riddle Claire with guilt in a second or less. At the front door Claire patted her broad head and said, "I'll see you this afternoon."

As she walked to the five-car garage that was separate from the house, Claire stayed on the walkway and the concrete drive to avoid the heavy dew on the grass. In an hour or two it would be gone, dried by a brilliant sun in a cloudless sky. She estimated the temperature to be about seventy degrees, a perfect, late-September, Indian-summer day. At the middle garage door she punched in the code and the door rolled up revealing the black BMW 650i convertible, her favorite of the five cars garaged there. It was immaculately clean. If Jesus couldn't drive, his next favorite work, after the roses, was to keep the Van Zandt cars spotless, inside and out. Claire located the key fob in the console, slid it in the slot and pushed the start button. Instantly the V-8 engine roared and then settled into a dynamic hum. As she held the button down to lower the Beamer's top, she looked up and down the row of cars and shook her head. *"I've got to do something about this."*

Pangs of social conscience like this had been bothering her for most of the year as the country seemed to swirl further and further down the economic toilet that was *recession*. It also didn't make sense to her that two wars were raging in the Middle East. While people were losing their jobs, savings and homes inside the U.S., still others were losing their lives in far-away places like Ramadi, Fallujah and other areas no one had ever heard of before 2003. Yet she was surrounded by opulence everywhere she turned. On her left, in the garage's first bay was the Mercedes 600S. The second bay contained a Rolls Royce Silver Shadow. On her right was a Range Rover Evoque and the last bay was home to Alan's 2003 50th Anniversary Edition Corvette. It was the one car of the bunch that she wouldn't drive because the 6-speed manual transmission required too much effort, in her opinion.

She looked at the 'Vette and, for an instant, thought she could see Alan sitting in it, smiling at her. She put her head between her two hands on the BMW's steering wheel. She would have given it all up just for one more moment with him. Her heart racing, she lifted her head and looked back at the empty 'Vette. All that was left were the *things* that had been their life together. Now, three years after his death, she couldn't let go of even just one of these things. It would be like letting go of him again.

She glanced at her watch. *10:10 a.m.* *"Oh, no! Ingrid is really going to be angry."* As she pulled from the garage and hit the remote to close the door behind her, Claire caught her own reflection in the rearview mirror and cracked a mischievous smile. *Ingrid... pissed... Beth trying to calm her down...* the mental picture cheered her mood so much that she laughed out loud.

Chapter Three

Rock

Descending the steps from the loft to the garage floor below, he pulled the car cover off of the vintage Sting Ray parked there. "Ready for a road trip, old girl?" He took a rag from the shelf next to the car and wiped off a water spot from the last time he washed it. A few minutes earlier, while pulling on his jeans and sweatshirt, he'd made the decision that he wasn't going to let Patti guilt him into something. He was frustrated, even angry about the economy, about GM, about the abysmal future that Flint faced without the company. No, he was going to go and that was all there was to it. "Looks like a great day! I won't be long," he said over his shoulder as he strode toward the back door of the house.

When Patti made breakfast, nine times out of ten there was an agenda, something she wanted to discuss or get off of her chest. In fact, it was at a breakfast like this that she and Russ had first suggested the idea of building the garage with his loft above. In the past, such breakfasts hadn't happened often because there simply had not been time when they had all been working. Now, thanks to the free-fall that General Motors was in, time was hardly a factor in their lives. All three were still adjusting, even after six months, to their more carefree lifestyles. In fact, Rock thought it was proving to be hardest for Patti. She had built in her mind's eye a picture of what it would be like, the three of them, romping through their retirement years. That picture had not included Rock's current plan for the upcoming fall, winter and early spring. Patti had already made it clear to him that she thought he was nuts. He knew breakfast was a last-ditch effort to change his mind about leaving today for the Lake Michigan shore.

It was her habit at these gatherings to lay out more food than a dozen people could eat as if her power over the matters at hand might be increased proportionally by the amount of food leftover after everyone had eaten their fill. He suffered no illusion that breakfast this morning was going to be easy. He and Russ had been best friends for five decades now, ever since high school. The three of them had been close friends for three and a half decades. So many things had bound them together for so long. Rock knew, though Patti had never said it out loud, that she had convinced herself his time away from them over the upcoming months was some kind of precursor to the end of their friendship. Though he had tried to reassure her otherwise, breakfast this morning was proof to Rock of his failure in this regard.

He knocked lightly on the back door and let himself in. Patti met him with tears in her eyes and a bear hug. Rock put his arms around her and looked across the kitchen at Russ, who stood there shrugging his shoulders as if to say, *"You know how she is."*

"Hey, what's with the tears?" Rock asked.

She pushed away from him and pawed at her cheeks. "Sit down. Breakfast is getting cold. We can talk about this while we eat. Nothing worse than cold eggs."

He and Russ commiserated about the miserable condition of General Motors while Patti scurried around
making him a mug of Earl Grey and serving their breakfasts. When she finally sat down, the two men stopped the
small talk.

Her opening gambit left no doubt about where she stood.
"So, you're really going to do this crazy thing?"

Trying to sound confident, he responded quickly, "Yes.
Green Girl and I'll be heading out about eleven o'clock this
morning."

"And how long are you going to be over there?" She knew
the answer to this one. They had discussed it. She was just
warming up.

"I'll be back just before Memorial Day."

Patti acknowledged his answer by shoveling a forkful of
scrambled eggs into her mouth. Both men knew this was
her show now, so they sat quietly while she ate. When she
was ready, Patti asked, "And exactly why in the world are
you going to the frozen edge of nowhere when you could
be coming to Florida with us this winter?" Patti Sluwinski
was a tough, direct woman who had worked in the man's
world of GM assembly lines for as long as either of them.
"C'mon, Rock. Think about it. You've got enough money
you can go anywhere you want, so why in the world did
you choose this Little Point Whatever the Hell the Name
of the Place Is?"

"*Sable*, Patti, the name of the place is *Little Point Sable*."

"OK. Just tell me *why there*? I don't get it."

Now it was Patti's turn to wait while he took a bite of his
eggs. Her question was the crux of his earlier indecision
and, while he hated to admit it, maybe this breakfast and
her questions were exactly what he needed at this point to
help him, once and for all, resolve any indecision. When he
was finished with the bite of eggs, he took a sip of tea and
answered, "I've got to get out of Flint. This place is dying

right along with GM. I can't sit around and watch that happen any longer."

Impatiently, as if she were dismissing his answer, she waved her fork in the air. "You've told me that. But you still didn't answer my question. Why there on the frozen edge of nowhere? I have this picture of you holed up in this cabin with only a wood fire to keep you warm, the winter winds howling across Lake Michigan like a banshee, you can't get out of the place because you are snowed in and..."

He laid his knife and fork down.

Patti continued, "... and I don't know what other miserable things might befall you over there," waving her hands around for emphasis.

He slowly swiped his napkin back and forth over his lips, stalling. She was getting worked up and it would be easy for him to get angry at her, but he couldn't. Her motivation was purely out of concern for him and concern for their friendship. All he could do was answer her questions. He waded into the fray, "Patti, stop it," his voice holding a firm, yet gentle edge. "You've seen the pictures of the place. It's beautiful."

"Those are summer pictures, Rock," she countered. "What's this place like in the dead of winter? Can you get out to see a doctor if you need to? Or here's a better question: Is there even a doctor anywhere around there that could see you?"

Russ, who'd kept his head down and was trying to avoid the line of fire, looked up and offered, "She's got a point, Rock. It may be heaven in the summer, but you ain't gonna be there in the summer, buddy."

"Look, you two. I will be fine. I'm going to Little Point Sable, not the North Pole. The Jeep's in Silver Lake in a storage locker. I'll put Green Girl away for the winter there and take the Jeep out to the cottage. That thing is built for two-tracking. There's a hospital in Shelby, ten miles away. I'll be fine," he repeated.

Russ took a different tack, "You know, Rock, Green Girl is worth a lot of money these days."

Russ was right. Rock had paid just under six thousand dollars for her as a new car thirty-six years ago. The Fathom Green, '72 Corvette Sting Ray was now worth ten times or more that amount at the right auction. Rock had kept her in mint condition. "You gonna just throw her into some storage locker for the winter? I'll drive you over and bring her back here. How about that?"

Patti harrumphed something unintelligible, having neither an appreciation of vintage cars nor an understanding that Russ' suggestion was some sort of weak compromise.

Rock appreciated what his old friend was trying to do, but easily recognized the flaw. "Russ, I know you're trying to help, but the guy at the storage locker is going to supply me with electricity so I can hook up her battery tender. I'll clean her up, hook her up and put the bag over her and she will be just fine. I can even go into town and check on her periodically. Who's gonna do that here after you guys leave for Florida in November?"

Patti wasn't going to give up. "It's winter, Rock. What the hell are you going to do all day over there when it's fifty below zero?"

Calmly, as if to imply they should not be surprised, he said, "Read and think."

Patti shook her head. Russ tried to hide behind a forkful of eggs. As good of friends as they were, as much as they had all helped each other through the good times and the bad over all of these years, there was a distinct difference between them. That difference had placed them on opposite sides of this great divide before. He knew it was their friendship that was driving them to make him change his mind and he loved them for it. But when it came to things like the Great Recession, Rock's DNA contained an extra chromosome that most working-class stiffs didn't have to contend with. It wasn't that stuff like the recession didn't make Russ and Patti angry. It did. He had never seen either of them as riled up as the day all three got their notices of mandatory retirement. Between them there were over a hundred years of experience on GM's damned production lines. How could the company just blow off that kind of experience, that kind of loyalty and dedication? But over the last six months their rhetoric had softened, maybe even his had, too. Yet the rhetoric that kept sifting through his thoughts had not softened. Rock Graham always wanted to know, *"Why? Why did 58,000 have to die in Vietnam? Why hadn't he been one of them? Why didn't we know what Osama Bin Laden was planning? Why did we invade Iraq?"* He had come to his own terms with these questions by reading everything he could get his hands on about them. Now with this Recession bearing down on the country, the *whys* were mounting up again. *"Why had credit been so easy to get? Why had the financial markets put so much stock in such risky business? Why hadn't GM planned better? Why hadn't Chrysler... or Ford?"* And the big one that was really bothering him, *"Why wasn't someone being held accountable?"* It looked to him like the middle class was taking it on the chin while the fat cats on Wall Street and in the Board Rooms around the country were still living pretty well. As for the politicians, the government officials, they really got his dander up. Since the Monica Lewinski scandal, public apology seemed to be the accepted cure for malfeasance. But no one was even trying to apologize for the economic mess the country was now in.

Softly, Patti offered, "Rock, you know you can't change what's already happened." It didn't help. He was in his *Why?- m*ode, and she knew that the only way out for him was to *read and think.* Patti gave Russ her look that said, *"OK, I give up. He's your best friend. Say something!"*

"Listen, buddy, you could 'read and think' in Florida and, then, when you got tired of doing that you could go fishing with me. You could take your meals with us. It would save you time if you didn't have to cook."

Rock shook his head. It wasn't working.

Russ tried one more time, "You could help us look..."

"Russ, don't..." Patti cautioned.

Rock looked up to catch Patti shooting Russ her killer look. "Help you look for what?"

Russ dove back into his pile of eggs. Patti was glaring at him.

Rock smiled and took a guess. "You guys are going to look for some property down there, aren't you?"

Their sheepishness was all the answer he needed. "Hey, look, I think that's a great idea. I've heard Florida is as bad off as Flint, so that means they must be giving real estate away down there." He glanced back and forth between the two of them.

Patti didn't miss a beat, "OK, so call off this cockamamie freeze-your-ass-off idea of yours and come to Florida and help us look for a place."

For as long as he'd known her, Patti always played hard-ball, and today was certainly no exception. He leaned back in his chair, forced a smile, shook his head and stuttered weakly, "I...I can't do that. It's not you guys. I'd just be bad company."

Chapter Four

Claire, Ingrid and Beth

For most of the twenty-minute drive into downtown Holland Claire pondered Alan's apparition she'd seen in the garage and whether or not she should mention it to her grief counselor. In Claire's mind it was a setback after nearly a year of progress. She knew that two days from now, on Monday, the first question the counselor would ask would be, *"How was your week?"* As she pulled into a parking space about two blocks away from Brides-to-Be, any decision on how to answer that question was overtaken by the reality that she was very late.

She stopped at a Bigsby Coffee Shop on Holland's main street, waiting in line ten minutes before walking out with three tall, skinny mochas to take as a peace offering.

At 10:45 a.m. she opened the door and stepped into Brides-to-Be and Ingrid's wrath. "Mother, what is going on? Beth called and said you were going to be late and that she was delayed as well. That was an hour ago. I have been here waiting all this time. I have to be ..."

Claire blocked out the rest of the lecture. She was sure Beth would have been here by now and would have diffused Ingrid somewhat, but apparently that task was going to be left to her. "Darling, I am so sorry, but I overslept..."

Impatiently, Ingrid shot back, "Where's Beth? My God, Mother, this is *her* wedding! It seems to me that she could be..."

The door opened and Beth stepped into the shop.

"Well, it's about time..."

Beth looked at Claire and then at her sister. "I... I'm sorry, Ingrid, but..."

"Don't tell me you overslept. Am I the only one in this family that has an alarm clock?" One of the store's consultants approached the three just as Ingrid fumed, "I have to leave at twelve. If we can't get this done between now and then, the two of you will just have to do without me. I wasn't the one that was an hour late."

Tactfully, the consultant hung back, waiting to see if there were to be any more exchanges. Claire handed them a mocha and said, "Ingrid, we're both sorry. Now let's not ruin a beautiful morning over this..." she wanted to add *triviality*, but knew that would cause Ingrid to erupt again, so she stopped.

Brides-to-Be was not the bridal shop for those looking to do a wedding on a budget. It was well known across west Michigan as the place to go for all your wedding needs, if your wallet could withstand the strain. The impending nuptials between Beth Van Zandt and her fiancé, Dr. Nathan Hathaway, would be one of the more lavish events of the year, but one that Claire Van Zandt's wallet could easily handle. The consultant waiting to help them was one of the store's owners, and she had become wealthy herself by handling these kinds of weddings and catering to every whim of the over-indulged clients who sought her services. Stepping forward, she addressed Claire, assuming she had the money backing the wedding, "Mrs. Van Zandt, welcome to Brides-to-Be. I'm Mary Jane Bielama. Please call me MJ."

Taking the proffered hand, Claire said, "Good morning. I'm sorry we are so late, but it couldn't be helped." In the corner of her eye she saw Ingrid shaking her head, but cut off any further eruption by beginning introductions, "This is my daughter, Ingrid Hoffman, the Matron of Honor." Claire then turned toward her youngest. "And this is the bride, Beth."

MJ shook each of their hands, artfully choosing whom to call by their more formal names. "Well, Mrs. Van Zandt, Mrs. Hoffman, Beth, shall we get started? I have taken the liberty to lay aside a dozen or so dresses that I thought you might like, but certainly if none of these are what you are looking for, we have a much more extensive inventory for you to look through. I see you have coffee, but if you'd like something else just let me know. I have made a pitcher of mimosas this morning if you'd like."

The three demurred. MJ led them through her collection of wedding gowns. An hour later, Beth stood on an elevated podium in an exquisite gown imported from Paris. Ingrid fussed with the neckline while a seamstress listened and nodded dutifully. Beth, from her perch, looked over Ingrid's head at her mother, who was watching all of this with tears in her eyes.

By the time the seamstress had finished this first fitting, Ingrid glanced at her watch and announced, "It's 11:50 a.m. We could have gotten more done today. Next time, be on time." She grabbed the light jacket she had taken off earlier, pecked her mother on the cheek and said, "Next weekend the firm is celebrating its twentieth year in partnership. Ethan and I would like you to go with us to the party. It's at the Country Club. I'll call you with the details. It's important, Mother. We think they are going to offer Ethan a full partnership." Over her shoulder as she flew out the door, she added, "We could use your support."

Beth looked at her mother, who smiled at her and nodded, "It's a beautiful gown, honey."

MJ escorted Beth back to the dressing room and helped her out of the dress. As Beth finished dressing, MJ asked,

"Is there anything else you'd like to look at today, my dear?"

Beth thought for a moment and replied, "Not today, MJ. We'll be back another time and work on picking out dresses for Ingrid, the bridesmaids and Mom. The wedding is December, 13th. There will be six bridesmaids. How much time will you need to get the gowns fitted?"

MJ thought for a moment, "As long as we have everything picked out and first fittings finished by November 15th, we will have plenty of time. Does that work for you?"

Beth nodded, "I will make sure we have everything done by then." They shook hands, and Beth walked over to Claire, who was looking into the mirror of a compact and blotting her eyes. "You OK, Mom?"

"Yes, just fine."

"Would you like a bite of lunch? I could sure use some. There's a Panera near here. They have wonderful salads."

Claire nodded. "I'll drive."

"How about if I meet you there? Nathan and I are leaving for Detroit at four. He has tickets to a Red Wings game tonight... some skybox thing he wants me to see."

"I didn't realize you were a hockey fan."

"I'm not, but remember those golf trips you used to go on with Dad?"

Claire nodded, "Enough said. I'll meet you at Panera."

It took Claire about twenty minutes to walk to her car and drive to Panera. Beth was waiting for her inside. "They have a great Asian chicken salad here, Mom."

Claire nodded, "Sounds good. What do you want to drink?"

"Oh, no you don't, I invited you to lunch, remember? This is my treat."

Beth stepped up to the counter and ordered two Asian chicken salads, a green tea and asked Claire, "What would *you* like to drink?"

Claire gave a smile of concession, "The same. Thanks, honey."

They picked up their teas on the way to their table. As they sat down, Beth apologized, "I'm sorry you had to take the blast from Ingrid this morning."

"It's OK. I wish she wasn't so driven..." Parents aren't supposed to have favorites, but truthfully Claire so much more enjoyed Beth's company over Ingrid's.

"Are you going to go?"

Claire looked at her quizzically.

"To the thing at the Country Club with Ingrid and Ethan," Beth clarified.

"Oh, that. Yes, I suppose so. If she thinks it will help Ethan."

Beth smiled and shook her head, "You used to do a lot of stuff that you really didn't like doing when Dad was alive, didn't you?"

"No, honey. What makes you think that?"

"C'mon, Mom. I'm not a little girl anymore. The golf trips? Remember? Those dinners with clients at the Country Club? You didn't even play golf."

Claire laughed. "No, I didn't, but your father thought it important that I be there, and I was always glad that he included me."

Beth paused somewhat apprehensively and then asked, "Well, what about all the times he didn't include you?"

The question made Claire grimace. "What do you mean, dear?"

"I mean all that time you spent alone, raising us girls, while Daddy was off someplace around the world building some bridge. All of that had to be tough on you."

Claire didn't respond, unsure of where this was coming from and what was triggering it. She caught a brief reprieve when their salads arrived and they busied themselves with napkins, utensils, salt and pepper.

"I don't know if I can do it, Mom."

Claire sensed a deep foreboding in Beth's voice, but avoided overreaction. "Do what, honey?"

"Marry Nathan."

Claire laid her fork on her plate and looked across the table into her daughter's eyes, where the first tears were welling up. "Beth, honey, what's wrong?"

"I don't know, Mom. When I'm with him, I love him; I love everything about him. He's so gentle with me. But..."

Claire sat quietly and let Beth frame her thoughts. Beth, on the other hand, was having trouble finding a way to say what she had to say without hurting her mother's feelings.

"There's a side to Nathan that is so much like Daddy and Ingrid, it makes me think I can't spend the rest of my life with that part of him. It's a part that I see more and more. I take second place to everything in his work life. I find myself waiting on him to call... and he does... but usually it's hours after I was expecting him to. Then when he tells me what he was doing, some lifesaving operation or something, I feel guilty, but I also have this overwhelming sense of having been cheated somehow. It's like you and..."

Claire completed her daughter's thought, "It's like it was with your father and me."

The tears were streaming down Beth's cheeks now as she nodded. Claire reached across the table and took one of Beth's hands in hers. "Bethie," Claire had not called her that in a very long time, "I loved your father with all my heart. He was wonderful to me and he was a good father to you girls, but he was also a brilliant engineer and he built a world-wide business with that brilliance. God, I miss him now that he's gone." Then as if reassuring both herself and Beth, Claire repeated, "I loved him with everything I had inside of me."

They reached for their napkins at the same time and blotted their tears. "If you had it to do all over again, would you marry Daddy, knowing how much he was going to be gone?"

"Absolutely," Claire answered without hesitation. "Yes, I would."_

Beth just looked into her eyes, smiled weakly and said, "I'm just not sure I can give away so much of myself."

Claire thought how very different her two daughters were. They ate in silence for a few minutes before Claire said, "Beth, I can't make this decision for you, but I want you to understand how important it is. I can tell you this, look at yourself and who you want to be and what you want to do, as much as you look at Nathan and who he is. If you want to talk about it, then you know I'm here for you, but only you can decide. I will support whatever decision you make. Know that. Never doubt it."

When they finished eating Beth looked at her watch, "I'd better get going."

"Enjoy the evening, darling, even if it is hockey." They laughed.

"There will be some other docs there tonight. They want Nathan to join their practice in Detroit and to apply for hospital privileges at a hospital over there. I don't know where he will find the time to..." She hugged her mother tight. "I'll call you," she said as she let go and headed out the door.

Claire waved good-bye, knowing that she would be true to her word. Beth stopped home all the time and called her almost every day. Ingrid seldom did either.

Chapter Five

Little Point Sable

Rock Graham knew that Patti understood him as well as anyone, but Patti Sluwinski had misjudged her efforts at breakfast that morning. There was a stubborn streak in him and by over-arguing her points about why the lakeshore in the winter was a bad idea, she was actually appealing to his stubbornness. So while trying to persuade him not to go, she had actually pushed him in the opposite direction. It was one of the few times in thirty-five years of friendship she'd gotten it wrong with him.

As he hugged her to say goodbye, she whispered, "We've got two bedrooms down there, so if you change your mind..."

He smiled at her, "Thanks, Patti. Good to know."

Somewhere around 10:00 a.m. he heard Russ pull the truck from the garage. Patti said they had shopping to do. Maybe they did, but he was sure Russ had gone with her under some duress. He hated shopping. Or, maybe it was simply that neither of them wanted to be around when Rock left.

An hour later he turned the key and Green Girl's big V-8 roared to life. As he headed down the driveway, he watched the garage door close behind him as if separating him from all of the earlier drama. The drive from the loft to Interstate 75 was short, but long enough that he could tell the vintage Vette was ready for the quicker accelerations and higher speeds he was about to demand of her. No one knew better than he that cars are mechanical things; he'd built a million of them. Cars didn't have hearts, minds, emotions, feelings or any of those elements that make humans so complex. But as she gobbled up the miles of asphalt ribbon between Flint and Silver Lake, he fell in love all over again as she performed for him. In one particularly empty stretch of US 10 between Evert and Reed City, a part of the state that an old Michigander like him would call "*the sticks,*" Rock spoke to her, "OK, girl, let's see if you've still got it." Steadily, evenly, he pushed the accelerator toward the floorboard. The car leapt at her opportunity. As the speedometer's needle touched 120 miles per hour, he held her there for a minute, marveling that he still had more gas pedal to give her, but backed down to a more sensible and legal 65 mph. "You've still got it," he murmured and smiled.

Just east of Ludington, he hit US 31 and turned south. Glancing at his watch, he couldn't believe how fast the time had gone. At 3:20 p.m. he pulled into the parking lot of Silver Lake Storage and struggled with his bad right leg as he tried to pull himself up and out of the old Corvette.

"Can I give you a hand?"

"Naw," Rock replied with accustomed nonchalance. "I just have to get the juices flowing again." He stood up on both legs, rubbed his right leg, and limped awkwardly over to the owner. "Good to see you again."

"You, too, Mr. Graham."

"Call me, Rock."

"OK, Rock. The locker is all ready for you. I took the liberty of starting the Jeep yesterday. It fired right up. I've got an extension cord run in there for your battery tender." He pointed to Green Girl, "You said you had an *old* Corvette." Admiringly he walked around Green Girl,

"But this one looks like you just drove her off the show room floor. "

Rock smiled, "Well, I did ... thirty six years and eighty thousand miles ago."

"So you're the original owner?"

"Yes, sir, I am," Rock said with pride of ownership obvious in his tone.

"And except for about a thousand miles when I was teaching my nephew how to drive, all of those eighty thousand miles are mine."

Rock checked his watch and grimaced. "Listen, I've got to get going. I'm supposed to meet my landlady at 4:00 this afternoon out at Little Point Sable." He opened the Jeep's door and slid in behind the wheel, turned over the engine and backed it out of the storage locker. The owner helped him load from one car to the other. When they were finished, Rock tossed him the keys to the classic car and said, "I'll be back to clean her up and hook up the battery tender. Want to put her away for me?" Rock could tell he had caught him by surprise.

"You sure?"

"If I wasn't sure, I'd be storing her someplace else this winter. I'll see you soon."

The storage locker's owner was beaming as he waved goodbye to Rock and opened the Vette's driver's side door.

In the summer, making a left hand turn onto Silver Lake's main street could take as long as five minutes before one found that little break in north- and south-bound traffic. But this time of year, Rock stopped only long enough to fish an email out of his pocket that he'd printed out earlier.

"You can try a Garmin, but mine craps out just as you turn onto the gravel road at the Cherry Point Farm Stand. No satellite coverage, I suppose. No cell phones after that point either. It's kinda' remote, Rock," had been Jan Fremeyer's words to him. So she'd provided him with written directions via email. They read like a scavenger hunt:

"Take the main drag out of Silver Lake past the State Park to Mac's Dune Rides and turn left. You are on County Road B15. Follow it. It will turn sharp right. Stay on it. It will then turn sharp left and on your right will be a farm stand. Straight ahead will be a gravel road. Take the gravel road and turn left at the stone church. Stay on the two-track past the stone church until you come to Lake Michigan and follow the road to the left. Far-Far-View is about a half mile on your right. Look for the sign that says, 'Fremeyer'."

He had no trouble finding it, which was a good thing, because after he turned onto the gravel road, he saw no other signs of life except for the occasional squirrel scampering here to there. At 4:10 p.m. he pulled into the hard-packed sand driveway and up the backside of the dune atop which Far-Far-View was perched like a silent sentinel. One woman was sweeping the walkway to the cottage while another was shaking some rugs. The one sweeping waved at him.

"Jan?"

She nodded.

He extended his hand, "Hi, I'm Rock Graham."

Smiling, she shook his hand, "Well, nice to finally meet in person." The other woman had joined them. Jan Fremeyer introduced her as Madeline Murphy.

He shook her hand and said, "Nice to meet you both. This is some day, isn't it?"

They both smiled and Madeline said, "They don't get much better than this." She pointed, "There's hardly a breath of wind. I'm not sure I've ever seen the lake so calm."

The view was magnificent even from the back side of the cottage, which jutted out on a promontory along the shoreline, thus allowing a virtually unobstructed view north, west and south across the vast expanse of Lake Michigan.

He regretted wasting time ever thinking that he shouldn't do this.

Jan headed for the door. "Come on in, Rock. I'll show you around." All he'd ever seen of the place were the online pictures Jan had posted. "Then we can go over the paperwork."

Though not huge, the place was much more than he needed. In the summer when Jan rented it week-to-week, it could accommodate eight people comfortably. What had drawn him to Far-Far-View, however, was a picture of one room in particular.

"This room is why I bought the place," Jan said from behind him, pointing to the expanse of windows.

Speechless, he stood in the middle of the sunroom admiring the view of the vast blue-green lake in front of him. After a moment he turned to her, "It's not hard to see why."

She pointed, "Go around the north end of the cottage and there are steps; twenty-five of 'em to be exact. They will take you right down to the beach."

He'd turned back to the view. "It's ..." he paused while he scanned his eyes from left to right, south to north, "It's just incredible."

She left him there while she stepped back into the kitchen and shuffled her paperwork. Reluctantly, Rock joined her. "I've put together this lease. Pretty standard stuff, I think." She handed him three pages. He scanned through the boilerplate until he got down to the dates of occupancy, September 28th, 2008 through May 28th, 2009; the security deposit, $1000; and the monthly rent, $1000; all of which were as they had verbally agreed earlier.

"Rock, I know you can read, but I want to emphasize the no pets clause."

He hadn't paid much attention. "Sure, Jan. I understand. I don't have a pet, anyway."

She pointed to the carpet in the living room. "That's brand new this month. I just had it installed because a renter in August brought a dog in here without asking me, even though the no pets clause is standard in my summer rental agreement. Long story short, the dog ruined the carpet. I wasn't happy, the renter wasn't happy with me when I kept his security deposit. He got really pissy with me, but..."

"I understand," he reassured her, but apparently she felt the need to be very explicit.

"I love dogs. I have one at home waiting on me right now, but I just can't..."

Rock reached for the pen on the counter and scrawled his name on the line on the last page of the lease and pushed it over to Jan. "I understand completely. This place is beautiful and you want to keep it that way."

Madeline walked in and announced, "It's all clean. Hope you enjoy it this winter, Rock. Pretty desolate up here."

He nodded, "So I'm told." Pointing toward the lake, he said, "I can't wait to get down on that beach and take a walk."

"Well, don't let us stop you," Jan said. "I just need to pack up a few things from the closet in there and we'll be gone. Go ahead, Rock. Enjoy the sunshine while you can."

Five minutes later he was headed north up the beach toward the Little Point Sable Lighthouse, which Jan had told him was about two miles away. He'd gone, he estimated about a mile up the beach, and could see the lighthouse looming ahead of him. He checked his watch and saw he'd been walking about twenty-five minutes. His limp, though it appeared painful, over the years had worked itself into an awkward gait that was not pretty to watch, but was not painful once the leg had stretched itself out. He pressed on, determined to make it to the lighthouse.

By the time he'd walked the four miles to and from the Little Point Sable Lighthouse, Rock's stomach was growling, but he pulled a plastic beach chair from behind the low dune running parallel and perhaps twenty-five yards behind the water's edge in front of Far-Far-View. The sun, lower in the sky and not as warm as it had been when he had arrived, was due west. The rays shimmered off the placid lake water like a coating of gold, silver and red molten minerals. He sat reveling in the fading beauty of the Indian summer's day. A large flock of geese flew from north to south directly over him. He watched and listened until they were a speck in the sky and their honking could no longer be heard. Sea gulls swooped and soared all around him. Fifty yards or so north, a doe bounded to the edge of the lake to drink. She hadn't noticed him sitting there. As Rock leaned forward to watch, the movement caught her attention and she turned to run. Two bounds and she was over the lowest dune along the lake's edge. His next glimpse of her was as she climbed the steep bluff behind him in strong, graceful bounds. Amazed at her power, he watched her crest it and disappear into the tree line along its upper edge. Leaning back in his chair, he realized he had surprised the doe. If he hadn't moved, it's hard to know how long she might have stayed. Rock looked around him. Except for the things of nature, he was alone in this beautiful place. Far off shore, he had no way to determine exactly how far, a Great Lakes freighter was headed south, toward Chicago he presumed. *Was it as far away as Shelby? Ten miles? Twenty?* Shelby to the east and the freighter to the west were his perceived closest contacts with other human beings at that moment. He suddenly felt small and insignificant as the magnificent emptiness of his new surroundings wrapped around him like a blanket.

Chapter Six

Old Friends

Her conversation with Beth at Panera bothered Claire much more than she had let on. Now as she wandered the grocery aisles looking for she-didn't-know-what-exactly, her mind was elsewhere. It also didn't help that grocery shopping for her was about a twice-a-year experience because Maria usually did it. Fishing her ringing cell phone from her purse, Claire saw it was her friend Natalie Perkins calling. "Well, this is a pleasant surprise, Ms. Perk. How are you?"

Natalie laughed at Claire's use of the name given to her by her students. "Just fine, Claire. I'm not interrupting you, am I? How are the wedding plans coming together?"

Claire thought this call was fortuitous. She had been wondering who she could confide in and seek advice from. Now, here was Natalie, calling her at the perfect moment. "Fine. I was with Beth this morning to pick out her dress."

"How nice," Natalie paused and then asked, "Claire, I was wondering if you'd like to meet me for dinner tonight?" I'm sorry for the late notice, but I ..."

Of course, Natalie had no way of knowing how timely her invitation was on several levels. Claire had been dreading going home to that big, empty house. Flower was a good companion, but a terrible conversationalist.

Second, Claire couldn't imagine why she hadn't been the one calling Natalie. She was perfect. The two had worked together for over a decade as middle school counselors in a large inner-city public school district. They had developed a mutual respect for one another both professionally and personally. Natalie had been a great comfort to her in the days, weeks, and months immediately following Alan's death. It had been Natalie who recommended to Claire the grief counselor she was seeing. In return, Claire had helped Natalie through an ugly divorce from a prominent doctor. "No, Natalie, don't apologize. Your timing is perfect. I was just wondering what I was going to do for dinner. This is wonderful." Claire knew she must be sounding over-eager, but didn't care. She glanced at her watch. 4:00 p.m. "I have to run home and take care of Flower. How about if we meet at the Yacht Club at 6:00 this evening? My treat, Nat."

"Claire, you don't have to ..."

"I know, but I want to. Six at the Yacht Club?"

"See you there."

The Yacht Club, perched on a huge parcel of land at the edge of Lake Macatawa, prided itself on the exclusivity of its membership. Exclusivity and privacy went hand in hand with keeping the masses at arm's length. Claire made the necessary calls that would allow Natalie to get past the gated entrance, through the receptionist at the club's front door and into the dining room. Claire's membership was another one of those things remaining from her husband. She didn't need it, didn't use it much, nor necessarily want it, but couldn't make herself let it go.

As Claire pulled into the parking lot she recognized Natalie's car but was surprised to find her sitting in it. Natalie appeared to be reading. It seemed odd to Claire that she hadn't just gone into the club. They had dined here together and she knew Natalie liked the cuisine. Then it hit her. They had not dined here since Natalie's divorce. Carelessly, Claire had forgotten that her friend's ex-husband was also a member here.

As Claire pulled into the adjacent parking space, Natalie put the book down, smiled at her and opened her car door. The two embraced and Claire said, "I hope you haven't been waiting long. You should have gone in. I gave them your name."

"It was such a glorious evening, that I just waited out here for you," Natalie said, covering nicely whatever discomfort she may have felt with this little white lie.

As they walked toward the entrance Claire said, "It is good to see you. I'm so glad you called." Once inside, there was no waiting. The staff had been carefully schooled: Claire Van Zandt was never to be kept waiting. They were escorted to a waterside window by a tuxedo-clad *maître d'*, who said Penny, their waitress, would be right with them.

Small talk filled the period between cocktails and the arrival of their entrées, but Claire had just taken the first bite of her grilled whitefish when Natalie turned the conversation in a more serious direction. "I need your advice, Claire."

Claire noted her solemnity. "Sure, Nat. What is it? You OK?" With the divorce fresh in Claire's mind after finding Natalie sitting in the parking lot, she added, "That jerk ex of yours isn't giving you any more problems, is he? It's been about a year now hasn't it?"

Natalie nodded, "Yeah, and no, that isn't why I called." She chuckled, "He's lived up to every bit of the settlement. It's all in my bank. He wouldn't dare do anything less. He's scared to death of Ingrid and doesn't ever want to see her again anywhere, much less in a courtroom."

Claire smiled, "Well, good. I am so glad she was able to help. Divorce cases aren't her forte, but I think she really liked working on yours. That bunch of high-priced attorneys your ex hired didn't know what they were up against."

Natalie laughed and said, "I don't know how she ever got those pictures. She wouldn't tell me. But once the judge saw them, everything went my way after that."

After a good laugh and a sip of their cocktails, Natalie became serious again. "Claire, what I want to talk to you about is retirement."

Claire didn't respond immediately. She knew full well Natalie Perkins didn't work in the public schools because she needed the money, not after the divorce settlement Ingrid had secured for her. Claire knew how devoted Natalie was to the students she served, and, if she was considering retirement, something must really be wrong somewhere. "Things not going well at school?"

"No they're not," Natalie flung her hands up, her frustration evident. Public education just isn't what…" She didn't need to finish the thought for Claire to be able to relate, but Natalie's almost desperate fatalism was not something she was used to seeing in her dear friend. "Nothing is the same since you left," Natalie said.

Claire already knew the answer, but asked the question anyway, "Are you still the only counselor?"

"Oh, yeah. They never replaced you. So for the past three years it's been on me. Remember how we used to have two assistant principals?"

Claire replied, "Yes."

"Last year that number slipped to one. This year we don't have any."

Claire responded incredulously, "No." There was a pause and then Claire asked, "Who does discipline then?"

"Remember how we used to have to struggle with that, but could always convince the principal that counselors can't be effective if you make them do discipline?"

"It's an unspoken rule," Claire said, "Counselors can't counsel and do discipline at the same time."

"Yeah, well, then they need to change my job title from counselor to disciplinarian."

"What?"

"The principal called me in his office last Monday and told me I was going to have to help him out with the discipline. Since then the biggest part of every day has been spent doling out suspensions, detentions, and meeting with parents because of discipline issues. The fact is, even if these kids would trust me after I've disciplined them, there wouldn't be time in my day to see them, to help them get to the root cause of their misbehavior. Discipline is literally all I do these days."

"What about the union?" Claire asked.

Shaking her head, Natalie simply replied, "Gutted. I've asked for help. They've offered to help me get transferred to another school..." She put her palms down on the table. "Like that is going to solve anything. It's almost like the union has bought into the administration's party line about declining enrollment. So our enrollment drops every year and when that drops, so does the money we have to help our kids, who, by the way, are the ones that need the most help."

"Are you thinking about leaving now? At the start of the school year?"

"I am that frustrated, but you know I won't."

Claire's helplessness translated into silence between the two as they picked at their food for a while until Natalie looked across the table at Claire and said with a smile, "OK, I needed to get that off my chest, so enough negativity. Tell me about the wedding."

"But what about you?"

"It's OK, Claire. I just needed to vent. I feel better already. Now, let's talk about something more pleasant. Tell me about the wedding."

"The plans are coming along. Beth's dress is beautiful, but..."

Natalie waited while Claire picked at her food. When the pause became uncomfortably long, she asked, "But what, Claire?"

As the tears brimmed over, Claire told Natalie about the conversation between her and Beth earlier at Panera. "I don't know what to tell her. I know how she feels. I have regretted so many times over the last three years not telling Alan that I wanted him to slow down, spend more time at home, spend more time with me. Now that he's gone, I'd give away everything just to have that time back again, but you don't get that chance. I don't want Beth to feel this way a year from now or, worse yet, twenty years from now."

"Have you told her that?"

"No."

"Why not?" It took Claire a moment to think, and in that moment Natalie added, "If it's what you feel, Claire, then Beth should know. Yeah, you may have to swallow your pride. Believe me, I know how hard it can be to do that, but, if you really believe you'd do things differently if you had the chance, then don't you think Beth should know that?"

Penny, the waitress, approached. Claire was blotting some tears. Penny, well-schooled not to react to anything she saw or heard within the walls of the club, ignored Claire's distress and asked if either of them would like dessert.

Continuing to blot, Claire looked at Natalie, who shook her head. Claire declined for them, and a few minutes later Penny returned with her tab, which Claire signed. In the parking lot, they hugged and as they parted company Natalie offered her old friend some advice, "Claire, be honest with Beth. She can handle the truth."

Claire thanked her. Natalie stood there for a moment, and Claire sensed she had something else to say. "What is it, Nat?"

Now it was Natalie's turn to cry as a tear welled up in her eye, "Feel free to have her call me. I know what it's like to be married to a doctor. Sure mine liked other women, but I know what Beth is feeling about playing second fiddle to the medical profession. He was so busy, I got lost in the demands on his time. Too many others were there and willing to fill in for me, if you know what I mean." Dabbing at a tear, she smiled and chuckled, "But in hindsight, letting myself get lost like that to his work is one of my regrets. I still beat myself up about it, but, you know what?" Natalie paused and then continued, "Even if I would have tried harder, I don't know if it would have made a difference. I guess that is my real regret. I don't know if I tried hard enough. I think I did, but who knows?"

Claire decided they needed to part on a positive note and said, "Nat, it's been much too long since we've seen one another. Let's do this again, soon."

"You can count on it, Claire. Have Beth call me, OK?"

As happens often along the Lake Michigan shore, the weather can change quickly. The perfect Indian summer day had given way to a cloudy night and a rising west wind. A chilly gust blew off Lake Macatawa. Claire bundled herself against the chill and said, "It's been good to see you, Nat. Thanks."

Chapter Seven

Billy Riley

The growl in his stomach reminded Rock again that he had not eaten since early that morning. With some reluctance, he pulled himself up out of the beach chair. After the long walk and the equally long sit-down, Rock's right leg yanked at him. He didn't mind. From his vantage point the beauty of the setting sun, the blue sky that was now tinged with oranges and reds on the horizon, the gentle breeze that had just come up from off shore and the dazzling blue-green of the lake's water lessened the pain. Putting the chair back behind the dune, he stretched everything out again as he climbed the stairs back to the cottage. It was getting late, and he figured he had about an hour, maybe an hour and a half, before the sun set.

He unloaded the Jeep and put away the few things he'd brought with him from Flint, setting aside the meal he would eat that evening. Then he took the night light from the kitchen counter where he'd prominently placed it so as not to forget, plugged it in and switched it on. Every now and then he stopped to check the position of the setting sun. His goal was to be sitting at the table in the sunroom eating dinner as the sun set on the western horizon.

He put a full package of brats on the grill, thinking he'd enjoy some as leftovers later in the week. While they cooked, he opened a can of beans, poured them into a plastic container and nuked them in the microwave. When everything was done, he cut an onion and put out mustard. Though not a deeply religious man, as he sat down at the table and looked at the spectacle of nature on display in front of him, he lowered his head and said a silent prayer. He ate slowly, amazed at the light show on Lake Michigan even after the fireball was gone below the horizon.

He called Russ and Patti and gave them the cottage's landline number. There was no cell service at Little Point Sable; for that he would have to return to the farm stand at the head of the gravel road. He told them that he did have internet service, so they could communicate via email. Patti had settled down, telling him to have a good rest. He discussed Michigan State's football outlook for the year with Russ. They'd won big over Notre Dame the week before and had just won the first conference game of the year, so Russ was thrilled at their prospects for a good, no, great year.

After the phone call he took a seat in an easy chair in the sunroom and read a few pages of Thomas Paine's *Common Sense*. Even though it was an abridged version, the language was stilted and difficult for him to pull the thread of Paine's thought out. He found himself reading and rereading sentences, paragraphs, entire pages, trying to digest what the author thought must be plain *Common Sense*. When he found himself nodding off, he decided that it had been a very long, but a very good day, and it was time to turn in. He turned off the floor lamp he had been reading by and was reassured by the glow of the kitchen's overhead light and the night light he had so carefully placed earlier that evening.

He walked to the door of the sunroom and turned at the threshold to gaze one last time at the vast expanse of lake that he knew was out there, but could not see through the darkness of the moonless lakeshore night. He stood backlit by the two lights, staring intently out into the pitch black looking for the slightest point of light on the lake, but there was nothing. He reached over with his left hand to turn out the kitchen light. Whether or not it had been the electrician's intention to wire the night light's outlet to the switch was moot at this point. As he moved the switch to the off position, both lights were immediately extinguished, and Far-Far-View was plunged into the same darkness inside that surrounded it outside.

The panic began as a feeling of dizziness quickly followed by an equally strong feeling of nausea. It had gripped him so quickly that he had no time to react, and the fact that he was in new, unfamiliar surroundings only intensified his disorientation. As the dizziness grew, he staggered a few steps back into the sunroom, and then everything became a blur spinning into total black. He knew he was starting to fall and as he fell, he hit his head on the corner of the table. Unfortunately unconsciousness in this case meant only that the body was disabled. Rock Graham's mind slipped back forty years to places he never wanted to go again, to memories he never wanted to relive.

2200 hours, 14 August, 1969,
somewhere in the jungle west of DaNang, South Vietnam
Sergeant Geoffrey "Rock" Graham was walking point because he was the best point man in his platoon. It was a miserable night with monsoonal rains drenching the triple-canopy jungle over their heads, making it cold, dank and dark as hell on the jungle floor. He had an instinct for this work: a compass-like sense of direction; keen eyesight even when there was no light; and uncanny observation skills. He could sniff out booby traps like a bloodhound. He took tremendous pride in the fact that he'd never led the men who were now following not far behind him into trouble.

Tonight, however, he had walked right past the enemy lying in ambush, never suspecting their presence until they opened fire on the main body of his platoon, strung along the trail he'd laid for them. Even though he was a hundred yards or so ahead, the shots rang out like they were right next to him. Bile filled his throat as he realized his mistake. In between bursts of gunfire, he could hear the screams of his platoon mates caught in the ambush's kill zone. This was his fault. He choked the bile down, turned on his heel, and began to run back toward his platoon. All he could see were long fingers of North Vietnamese or Viet Cong green tracers crisscrossing the trail. Conspicuously absent were any red tracers that would be coming from American guns, and that told him that his platoon was pinned down hard.

"Fuck you bastards!" He flicked the selector on the side of his M-16 to full automatic and in three quick bursts emptied a magazine, reloaded, and emptied another. Green tracers came his way. He felt one round go through his left shoulder. It slowed, but didn't stop him. "Fuck you," he muttered again, slapped another magazine into his M-16 and kept firing. When he was nearly back to the edge of the beaten zone, he realized he was out of ammo. "Shit!"

"Rock, hey, Rock, over here, man. I'm hit. Oh, shit, it really hurts. Rock you gotta help me."

He strained to see, stepping in the voice's direction and there he was, Riley, lying on the side of the trail, almost cut in half. Green tracers were flying all around them.

"Get me outta here, Rock," Riley pleaded.

"You're OK, Riley," he lied to him.

Rock reached for the M-60 machine gun lying across Riley's upper half. As he lifted it he felt Riley's grip tighten on the weapon. "No, man. No, Rock. Don't. I'm goin' home soon, Rock."

Billy Riley was within sixty days of going home to his wife and infant daughter. Now he was going home early, but not in the way either of them had discussed. *Riley, I'm sorry, man. I didn't mean to...* a bullet slashed through a leaf next to Rock's ear and the sound snapped him back to reality. They were losing this fight. In the midst of their desperation, Rock knelt down next to his doomed friend, "Riley," he whispered into his ear, "You gotta give it to me, man. No one's gonna get outta here unless you give me the machine gun."

Riley's grip eased up, and as Rock took the weapon he saw Riley's head fall to the side. The weapon and the heavy chain of bullets attached to it tore at his wounded shoulder as Rock stood, spun in the direction of the curtain of green tracers and moved toward them. Riley's machine gun was now an extension of Rock's arm, the red tracers coming from its muzzle were like red, flaming fingers that were attempting to spread the green curtain apart. Oddly, he couldn't hear the rattle of gunfire around him. He heard the sizzle of the steady rain falling on the hot barrel of his machine gun. He paid no attention to the green tracers flying by him, only the red ones he was dishing out at their enemy. *Time* was unimportant. Was he in the thick of it for a minute, five minutes, an hour? He couldn't say. He was shot twice in his right leg around his knee, the two bullets hitting him in quick succession. Yet his physical pain was masked by the adrenaline riddling every cell of his body. He felt the first round hit and then pass through the muscle that wraps around the top of the knee. It didn't slow down either his advance or his rate of fire. *No pain.* The second round, however, was more serious. He felt it knick a bone, near his knee, in that same leg. He couldn't tell if it passed through or not. *There it is. Oh, shit, that hurts.* His right leg felt like a log, a heavy, wet log, that he would have to drag behind him, rather than rely on for balance as he maneuvered with the heavy machine gun and its long chain of bullets. He stopped his advance and pulled the trigger. *I can still fire this bitch!* He'd watched

Riley take good care of this weapon. If he'd cleaned it once, he'd cleaned it a thousand times. Now all of that care and cleaning was paying off. Rock's mobility was nearly stopped, but he doubled the length of the bursts he was spewing forth at their enemy. The weapon performed flawlessly, but he knew, now that his mobility had been slowed, he was a sitting duck. He suffered no illusion. His death in the next few seconds was imminent.

By now, nearly all of the enemy's fire had been turned in his direction. He kept waiting for that round that would tear through his gut, pierce his heart or scramble his brain. It never came. Instead, he began to see the red tracers of his platoon mates, heads up now, returning fire, and catching their enemy in a crossfire every bit as deadly as the one that had them pinned down. As quickly as it started, it was over. The gunfire ended as their enemy faded into the dark jungle around them, the rain quickly cooled his machine gun. Now all he heard were the moans of his injured brothers and his lieutenant screaming into the radio that they needed medevac and they needed it now.

0100 hours, 15 August, 1969,
DaNang, South Vietnam
He walked a tightrope between consciousness and unconsciousness as the helicopter flung its way out of the monsoon's dark night sky. He felt it settle onto the landing pad, the heels of the UH-1's skids hitting first and then the entire aircraft lurching forward to a full stop as the pilot settled it on the ground. He saw the medic jump off and heard the engine power down as the pilot rolled the throttle to idle. Immediately, the huge blades rotating above them relented to slower circles. In his peripheral vision he saw two corpsmen push a gurney to the helicopter's side door. A third person walked alongside. All were garbed in

dark, olive drab ponchos with the hoods pulled over their heads as protection against the downpour. He closed his eyes as he felt the stretcher move. The pain from his right leg was excruciating. He almost passed out. As the two corpsmen moved him onto the gurney, he heard the aircraft's medic say to the third person, "He's alive, but he's lost a lot of blood. I think the right leg is a goner."

"OK, I've got him from here."

It was a woman's voice. The stretcher plunked down on the gurney. The pain moved from his leg to his brain and it hurt like hell. He felt a hand touch the back of his right hand where an IV needle had been inserted. When she bent over to see if her new patient was conscious, Rock opened his eyes, reached across with his left hand and grabbed her arm just above the wrist. She let out a yelp. One of the corpsmen at one end of the gurney moved toward her, but she motioned him away. Rock pulled her down toward him, "Don't let them take my leg."

She took her free hand and tried to pull his loose, but he held on. Louder this time, more demanding he said, "Don't let them take my leg."

She laid her free hand on his shoulder. "Relax, Marine. You're in good hands now. You're at the Aid Station in DaNang. You're going to be fine. In about ten minutes you're on your way to the Third Field Hospital in Saigon." She could feel his grip ease up.

He could feel the last bits of strength oozing out of him. Softly he said, pleading now, "Don't let them take my leg."

She bent over and put her head next to his ear. "Save your strength so you can tell the doctors in Saigon." He saw her step away from the gurney, telling the two corpsmen pushing and pulling him, "OK, he's outbound on Eagle 26 at Pad 2. Get him over there ASAP."

One of the corpsmen laid a poncho over him, but it was too little, too late. The monsoon's downpour had already diluted the blood that soaked the fabric of his jungle fatigues. The blood was not only his, but that of about a dozen other more-seriously wounded Marines he had pulled to safety, despite his badly damaged leg, and put on medevac flights ahead of the one that had brought him to this place. As they waited for Eagle 26, Rock drifted in and out. During one of his more lucid moments he wondered about the rest of his platoon and especially about Sluwinski. Worry helped him stay awake. He had to stay awake. He had to be able to tell them in Saigon. He closed his eyes and tried to remember the last time he'd seen Sluwinski. Where was he? Was he hurt? Events of the ambush were so muddled in his memory.

0230 hours, 15 August, 1969,
Eagle 26, on final approach into
Third Field Hospital, Saigon, South Vietnam
The last thing he could remember was the sinking feeling in his stomach, like the feeling when an elevator goes down, as the medevac pilot reduced the power and set up for a steep final approach to the illuminated iron cross that marked the Third Field Hospital's primary helipad. Rock Graham's valiant effort to stay awake had fallen just a minute or two short.

Far-Far-View was still gripped in darkness as he regained consciousness nearly as quickly as he'd lost it. Confused, dazed and hurting, he immediately reached for his right leg. He recalled the sheer relief he had felt when he'd done that same thing years ago after waking up in the Third Field Hospital and realized it was still there. With that reality behind him, he took stock of what had happened. He remembered the lights going out; he remembered being back there; he realized that he had a pounding headache; and then he realized that he'd bled massive amounts of blood on the floor. As he used his hands to push himself up, he could feel and smell the blood. Instinctively he put his hand to his head and felt more of the same. He was still bleeding. In the blackness he struggled to stand and tottered toward the light switch that had plunged him into this mess. Keeping his hand over the gash, he made his way to the bathroom and found a towel and compressed the wound. He felt dizzy and lightheaded. He sat down on the toilet seat and recomposed himself. He needed to get to a doctor and have his wound examined. *There's a hospital in Shelby,* he remembered telling Patti.

At 6:30 a.m. on September 29th, he sat in the Emergency Room at Lakeshore Hospital trying to explain to the ER nurse how it had happened.

After his brief explanation she asked, "When did this happen?"

"I dunno. Best guess is sometime around 9:30 last night."

"Um," she said ominously. She checked his pupils and called for a doctor. Hospital records indicated he was treated for a cut on his head and a mild concussion. Post-Traumatic Stress Disorder never came up, because Rock never mentioned anything that might lead the medical staff to consider it. But as he left the hospital and walked into another beautiful Indian summer day, Rock was considering it, fearing it.

The doctor advised that he shouldn't drive. He had said he would call somebody, but knew it was a lie. Other than a slight headache, he felt fine. There was no double vision or any other symptoms of a concussion the doctor had warned him about. And besides, who was he going to call? He had driven himself there, he could drive himself back to the cottage. He started the Jeep, but before he could put it in gear a memory returned. He felt a surge of adrenaline and he could feel his heart speeding up. For a second he thought he was going back to the jungle, but that wasn't the memory. He recalled waking up his first night at the Third Field Hospital in a cold sweat that soaked his hospital gown and dampened the bed sheets. His leg was anchored in a cast and traction, but he twisted his upper body and flailed his arms around so violently that he knocked over a bedside table that held a water glass and a metal pitcher. The racket woke up the other patients on the ward and a nurse came immediately to his side. His next memory brought a brief smile to his face. As she leaned in with her hands on each of his shoulders and settled him back into the bed, he looked into her face and thought she was beautiful.

"It's OK. You're OK," she said to him in soft tones. At that moment another nurse appeared and handed his nurse a syringe. As she injected it into his IV she said, "There, this will help calm you down. You'll sleep better now."

"No," he recalled practically screaming at her. "I can't sleep. If I sleep, I dream and he's there in the dream."

"Who's in the dream?"

"Riley... Billy Riley."

She had no idea who Billy Riley was except that he was the cause of upset in her patient. The sedative was flowing into him now, but she could see him fighting it. She patted him on the shoulder and said, "OK, let me get something. I'll be right back. OK?"

Rock remembered not wanting her to leave his side, but before he could object, she was gone. When she returned he was still awake, but barely so. She held up a small night light in front of his eyes and then bent over to plug it into the socket next to his hospital bed. When she stood back up, she leaned in close to his ear and whispered, "There, that light will always stay on. Even when you are asleep it will light the way for you. So go to sleep now, Marine. Your work in this war is over. Sleep well."

For the last four decades that night light had stayed by his bed, always lit, and had kept the ghosts of that night in the jungle buried deep in his mind. But last night they had returned and he worried that the light might no longer hold them at bay.

Chapter Eight

Alphabet Soup

October had come and gone since Beth had chosen her wedding gown and, as far as Claire could tell, plans for the near-Christmas wedding were still moving ahead. Beth had two wedding planners, MJ from Brides-to-Be and another one from the country club. Because things seemed to be progressing and because Beth had not brought up again her concerns about marrying Doctor Hathaway, Claire was feeling a little less guilty about not following Natalie's advice to "be honest" with her daughter. She had, of course, told Beth about Natalie Perkins' offer to talk with her. But in the intervening time since then, Beth gave no indication that she had taken Natalie up on her offer. Claire was curious, and tonight she and Beth would be dining together at the Yacht Club. Claire made up her mind to ask, even if it might sound as if she was meddling.

First, however, she had some business to tend to today; some stuff she really didn't like to do. Since Alan's death, these things had fallen to her. To make matters worse, the warm Indian summer had given way to autumn. Today's weather seemed a precursor of the winter to come. On this last day of October, strong winds and heavy rain lashed up and down Michigan's western coast, and Holland had actually had snowflakes. The foul weather matched her mood as she parked her car in the parking garage and descended the steps into the plush offices of her accountants. The stenciling on the door read *DeBoer, Klassen & Formsma,* followed by a bunch of alphabet-soup letters that had no meaning to her except that they represented important credentialing for the only accounting firm Alan and she had ever used. For nearly thirty-five years D K & F-alphabet-soup had handled the corporate accounts of Van Zandt Engineering, America, Van Zandt Engineering, International, and their family's personal finances. Revenue to the accounting firm from all of these accounts was measured in the millions annually. So chicken Caesar salad with freshly grated cheese and imported sparkling water was the least they could do for Claire at these quarterly meetings. For an hour she and the three senior partners were alone in the huge conference room. Conversation was light, cheerful and centered on questions about wives, children, vacation plans and, of course, Beth's upcoming nuptials.

Somewhere around 1:00 p.m. they got down to business as an army of D K & F associates filled the room. Claire always thought it humorous the way the accountants tried to dumb-down the information they chose to give her. They had no idea how savvy she really was, and it was one of the things she hated the most about these meetings.

Both of her parents had been math teachers, so Claire's entire upbringing had been analytically-based. It had paid big dividends as she and Alan opened his business. He was a gifted mechanical engineer, but his first contract to do repairs on six bridges in Oceana County didn't challenge his abilities. Nonetheless, he poured himself into the work and began to create a network of contacts. The Oceana County contract led to other county contracts, which led to state contracts, which led to federal contracts. After the first couple of years, Alan was receiving more Requests for

Proposals than he could complete. It was then that Claire's abilities came into play. She developed a matrix for him to use to determine which proposals had the potential to be most lucrative. Once a proposal cleared that hurdle, she set up another matrix that allowed him to accurately calculate costs for labor, equipment, overhead and profit in a fraction of the time he had been spending. A final matrix made it possible to forecast which proposals held the most potential for future work. All of this allowed Alan to concentrate most of his time on what he loved, the engineering end of the business. Claire had loved those lean years, as she referred to them. She and Alan huddled around the dinner table eating cereal while she plugged numbers into the matrices and Alan worked with his slide rule and developed engineering plans and drawings. When Ingrid was born, he still had time to be home with them in the evenings, when he could dote on his new-born daughter. However, by the time Elizabeth came along, Alan was so busy he and Claire had not had time to consider a name. Alan suggested naming her Elizabeth, which was Claire's middle name. It was Claire who insisted, "OK, but we call her Beth." By this time, Van Zandt Engineering had become so big there was little time for Alan to dote on either of his daughters, much less Claire. The business was soon to expand to other countries, and Claire began to miss him and the simpler times. But she kept that to herself. Alan was in his element and that mattered too.

She was acutely aware that the news from Wall Street thus far in 2008 was nothing but doom and gloom. Projections had the Dow Jones Industrial Average losing half of its value by year's end. However, she had kept abreast of Van Zandt Engineering's balance sheets during the year and concluded that the bridge construction and maintenance businesses, both domestically and internationally, were recession-proof and revenues were up. This would be the thirtieth profitable year for the family-owned businesses. Claire would claim twenty-five percent of these profits as her own even though she had nothing to do with the operation of Van Zandt Engineering, America or Van Zandt Engineering, International. All of this had been carefully put in place by Alan twenty-plus years ago, just after Van Zandt, International, was established. Apparently he had been blessed with perfect vision regarding the profitability of bridge-building and repair. Despite the best consultative efforts of DK&F to get him to invest in life insurance, he fought them off every time, telling them that guaranteeing Claire a percentage of the profits from the company each year would take better care of her than any insurance policy they could possibly set up. Claire's twenty-five percent share of the profits was looking as though it would come in at around twenty-five million dollars this year, which D K & F would happily reinvest for her. To incentivize them to invest wisely, Alan had allowed them to reap a small percentage of any profit created by such reinvestment that was above and beyond their regular management fee. Claire had never meddled with the arrangements Alan had made, though she understood them well. And she thought her lack of meddling was why they felt the necessity to oversimplify with her.

"Claire, the U.S. economy is dropping like a rock," was the opening gambit offered by Arthur DeBoer and accompanied by the bobble-headed nodding of Stuart Klassen and Bart Formsa and their army of accountants. For two or three mind-numbing hours she listened to these people propose intricate schemes to move money to overseas banks and to scrap this investment or that investment in American companies while there was still some value to their stock and, then, reinvest in foreign companies. Claire could almost hear Alan turning over in his grave. She wondered to herself if they would have had the temerity to propose such things to him if he were still alive. Finally at about 4:00 p.m., she had enough. She wanted to thump the table with her fist, but thought better. Instead she turned to the three senior partners who were sitting immediately to her right and simply asked, "How much money do I have left in all of my personal accounts?"

The three men looked apprehensively back and forth at one another. Arthur DeBoer, the eldest of the three partners, began, "Claire, that number is still a substantial amount..."

Claire nodded and asked, "So, Arthur, I'm not about to be put out on the street looking for shelter and a free meal?" Her question spawned nervous laughter among the partners, followed by more nervous laughter from their minions.

"No, Claire. You are still one of the richest women in the Free World," replied DeBoer, "But we are simply trying to propose some ideas..."

Again she wanted to thump the table, but, more politely, she held up her hand, an assertive gesture she had never used before with the guardians of her financial kingdom. "Arthur, do you know what an aristocrat is?" She paused to allow him to squirm in the slimy implications an unconsidered answer might reveal about him or his firm.

"Well, yes, Claire, but I assure you..."

He was dodging. Again Claire raised the assertive hand and asked, "Do you think there is a privileged aristocracy in this country that may have quite possibly caused this recession through its greed?"

"Well, I..."

This time she interrupted him. "Arthur, I make substantial charitable contributions, which you manage. I'm sure I'm not the only client whose contributions to charity are handled by D K & F." She wanted to add the *alphabet soup* here, but didn't, keeping the joke that she and Alan had shared for years confidential. "Tell me, what advice are you offering me? I don't expect you to breach any confidentiality, but I would be interested to know what advice you are offering your other clients regarding charitable contributions during these troubled times."

DeBoer was turning red. Claire wanted to make a strong point with them, but hoped she had not induced a stroke or heart attack. She was relieved when he finally started stumbling with an answer. "Ah, you see Claire, we try and advise persons of wealth like yourself that in times like this..."

That phrase, *persons of wealth,* stuck bitterly in her craw; it smacked of *aristocrat.* She spat it back at him, "So that's what I am: A *person of wealth.* So how much is *this person of wealth* worth?" Claire looked around the table; the tension was palpable. Arthur DeBoer was visibly uncomfortable, and he looked at his army for support that was not forthcoming.

"Has this recession..." She caught some of the staff accountants shaking their heads as if to deny the fact that the country was in a full-blown recession the likes of which it had not seen before. Looking at them instead of the senior partners, she prodded, "Well, that's what this is, isn't it ... I mean that's what they're calling it, right?" The questions were rhetorical, so she didn't wait for an answer. Looking back at DeBoer, she rephrased her question, "Would I be too far off the mark if I said this recession has cut my personal wealth in half?"

Arthur DeBoer put his palms flat on the table and smiled, "Well, no, Claire it's not that bad. You are well diversified..."

"So, let's just suppose then, Arthur, that it was cut in half. Ball park for me how much I'd still be worth." She let him and everyone else in the room squirm for a minute, knowing that they could not produce a definite number given the diversity of her many holdings. When she was satisfied she had completely stumped them, she continued,

"Wouldn't it be around half a billion dollars?" She paused again, briefly, "Give or take fifty million?"

Again DeBoer looked around the room and caught a couple of bobble-heads nodding. "Well, yes, I suppose that is a reasonable estimate of the value..."

"Do you even keep track of the two thousand dollars a month deposited into my checking account from my retirement from the public schools?"

"Um, well, I don't, except for your 1099 at the end of the tax year, but Claire..."

She looked him in the eye with a steeliness that made him look away. "Arthur, I'm sorry. You have been a loyal friend and advisor for a long time, but I want to say some things to you, to all of you," she said as she waved her hand around the table, "About how I want my personal accounts handled going forward. First, there will be no moving of money to off-shore banks. Alan always thought there was something immoral, if not illegal, about hiding money like that. I doubt that you would have ever proposed such a scheme to him, and you all should know that I feel the same way about such shenanigans."

"But Claire..." Bart Formsa began but was immediately interrupted by the more senior DeBoer.

"We understand, Claire," DeBoer said, shooting Formsa a silencing glance.

"Good," Claire continued. "Second, there will be no divesting of investments in U.S. businesses, unless that business becomes morally bankrupt like Enron or WorldCom. I would expect this firm to be able to sniff out that kind of thing and move the investment. If you are wrong and I lose some money because of your cautiousness about things like this, then you will still have my thanks. If you are right and we divest from this kind of a firm before the horrid truth comes out, then I will be quite generous with bonuses. Third, I want you to look at all of my current charitable contributions and notify the recipients that for the upcoming year of 2009 and for each year for as long as I am able, I will double my contribution to them." She paused while everyone seemed to be making notes and then resumed, "Finally, in regards to my charitable contributions, I believe some years ago, Alan and I designated a dozen or so food pantries that we wanted to support. Is that right?"

From the corner of the room one of the staff accountants said, "That's correct, Ms. Van Zandt. You donate a quarter of million dollars a year to each of twelve different food pantries. Would you like me to tell you which ones?"

"No, that's not necessary, but what I would like for you to do is up my donation to each by five hundred thousand dollars starting in 2009 and continuing on each year after that."

"But, Claire..." It was DeBoer this time who got the withering glance followed by a dismissive wave of her hand.

"Arthur, don't fight me on this, especially the point regarding my contributions. If I have to, I will liquidate other investments to afford these contributions. This is important to me, Arthur, and it should be important to everyone that you call a *'person of wealth'*. I have an obscene amount of money at my disposal. More than I could ever possibly spend. I know there are people right here in Holland who have just today lost their homes, half their retirement funds, and who aren't sure where they will eat their next meal. Nothing I have heard indicates that this is going to be over soon or that housing, banking and investing sectors will ever recover to where they were before the bubble broke. So, if people like me, *'people of wealth'* as you call us, don't come down off of our pedestals and do something, then we don't deserve the wealth that God has blessed us with." Claire looked around the room and caught Arthur DeBoer staring uncomfortably into his lap. She hoped he'd gotten the message that while she just might be a *"person of wealth"* then he also just might consider never using that phrase again around her. "Any questions?" She watched the minions folding note-books and laptops. She smiled at Arthur DeBoer. "Good. So when we meet again, I'm expecting to see the increase in contributions across the board and I'd like a separate briefing on each of the twelve food pantries... you know the standard stuff. How much was their annual budget? Were there budget shortfalls? How is the half-million being used? Are there still shortfalls? Where? Anything else you think appropriate for me to know. I don't want to get into their business, I just want to know how I can help." She looked around the room and, seeing no questions, stood up. "As always, it's been a pleasure, Arthur." She shook the hands of all three partners and thanked the others.

Claire was proud of herself for the way she stood up to them and taken control. However, the drive-time news on the car's radio put a damper on whatever good she thought she might have done. There were more details of the Lehman Brothers bankruptcy, the largest corpo-rate bankruptcy in U.S. history. There was news that the President was considering bailing out the Big Three U.S. automakers as well as U.S. banks that were consid-ered *too big to fail*. What bothered her in these reports was that *the little guy* was never mentioned. She wasn't thinking about the small independent banks, or the auto parts suppliers who fed the Big Three. No, she was think-ing smaller still. She was thinking about that *person* she mentioned in her meeting: the *person* who had just lost his job; or the *person* who was just foreclosed on today. *Who's helping that person? Who's helping their family? How did we get into this mess? Who are the geniuses in government and corporate America that were asleep at the switch as people were allowed to borrow more money than they could afford?*

She arrived home from her meeting at about 5:30 p.m. Maria and Jesus were gone for the day, but Maria had left her a note telling her that Flower had eaten. She made herself a vodka and tonic, put on Brahms and sat down to relax at the kitchen table, musing as to whether or not Alan would have been as generous as she had been today. He was a good, kind man, but he was a staunch Republican. The more she thought about the meeting, the more she realized how much she must have sounded like a Kennedy-Democrat today. The thought brought a wry smile to her face.

She was meeting Beth at 6:00 p.m. and it was just a ten minute drive to the Yacht Club. At 5:45 p.m. she stood, reached for her drink glass, and then something very odd happened. She watched her fingers and thumb close around the glass, she thought she felt them clamp down, but when she raised it up, over and away from the table, it slipped out of her hand and shattered into pieces all over the Italian-tiled kitchen floor. She stood for a minute trying to realize what had just happened and chalked it off to the glass being wet and, therefore, slippery. Quickly, she found a broom in the kitchen closet and swept up the mess and wiped the last remnants of vodka and tonic from the floor. Realizing that she was going to be late for her appointment with Beth, she forgot the incident. She quickly patted Flower on the head and headed out the door.

At dinner Beth's conversation centered on the wedding, a sign Claire took to mean that she had reconciled her feelings. However, when Beth didn't mention it, Claire asked, "Did you ever speak to Natalie Perkins?"

There was an awkward moment of silence between them, and finally Beth said, "Yes. We met for lunch last week. Did you know she was retiring?"

"I knew she was considering it."

"Well, she's past that point. She says this is her last year. She's pretty frustrated."

Claire wanted to say *Tell me something I don't know, Beth. Tell me what she said to you about marrying a doctor!* But she didn't. She recalled Natalie's advice to be honest but quickly decided it would serve no purpose or be considered meddling. Beth had apparently made up her mind that she and Dr. Nathan Hathaway were going to be married. She was level-headed; much more so than Ingrid, Claire thought. *If she doesn't feel the need to talk to me about this, then I should not feel the need to meddle.* They finished their meal by sharing a dessert and hugged in the parking lot. Just before going their separate ways, Beth asked, "Mom, can I use Daddy's 'Vette next weekend? Nathan and I are driving to Purdue for the Purdue-MSU game, and I thought it would be fun to take it on a road trip."

"Sure, Sweetie, the garage door code and keys are in the console. Help yourself."

Chapter Nine

Phyllis

For nearly a month now, it was Billy Riley who greeted him every time he closed his eyes. It was Billy Riley who woke him, and he almost always found himself soaked in a cold sweat. *No, man! No, Rock! Don't! I'm goin' home soon.* Every sense would be heightened. He could smell the deadly mix of jungle rot, gunpowder and blood. He could hear the rain pelting down; the sounds of gunfire. He'd jolt awake and bolt up in the bed. He had tried taking Aleve to aid his sleep. It didn't help. He thought about going to a doctor and requesting something strong, a prescription sleep aid perhaps, but then he'd have to explain why he wanted the prescription. No. Going to the doctor might involve talking about something that he just didn't talk about. Instead he would get up, go into the kitchen, make himself a mug of tea, stoke the fire in the fireplace and settle in front of it to read, read anything that he hoped might take his mind off Billy Riley.

What made matters worse, the weather here at the end of October had started to deteriorate. The beach had become his escape, the place he could go to and not have to worry that Billy Riley or any other memories were going to spring themselves on him. But twice in the last week he'd been chased off the beach and back inside the cottage. It was the wind more than the rain. He had planned for bad weather, bringing heavy Carhart overalls and coat with him. The coat had a hood he could pull up over the ear warmer and watch cap he wore. A thick, wool scarf could protect his face. He had thick thermal gloves and good insulated Keene hiking boots that he wore over insulated socks. Yet the western wind, often sustained at forty or fifty miles an hour and coming unchallenged off the vast expanse of Lake Michigan, drove the rain hard at him and soaked him in only a matter of minutes.

Thinking about it, he shivered as he stood in the sunroom and stared out into the 4:30 a.m. blackness of October's last day. He couldn't see it, but he could hear it. Rain, torrents of it, splattering against the window. *Maybe Patti was right.* He tried to suppress the thought. With the exception of the storage locker owner in Silver Lake and the clerk at the convenience store where he bought gas and groceries, he could not recall talking to another human being in the last month. He recalled Madeline Murphy's warning, *This place is pretty desolate in the winter.* He again tried to suppress the thought, but like Patti's warning, it lingered.

By noon, the day had worsened, something he had not thought possible. He had tried the beach when the weather had turned to a half-sleet, half-snow mix, but he'd only walked north for about half a mile when he noticed the left side of his outer wear was stiff with ice. The right side was the same by the time he'd walked back to Far-Far-View. Once inside, he hung his gear to dry and heated soup in the microwave. Now standing in the sunroom with the mug of soup clinched with both hands to take the chill out of his fingers, he looked down at the huge waves being shoved ashore by the storm, and made the decision to get out of here for a while.

Walking to the laundry area, he found the rag rug that had soaked up most of the blood he'd lost the evening he passed out. After four or five washings, the blood stain stubbornly remained. On the reverse side he found what he was looking for. A tag sewn to the rug read:

Evelyn's Everyday Gifts
10 East 8th Street
Holland, Michigan 49423

The driving was miserable. Strong winds and heavy rain marked the entire eighty miles of his trip. He'd gotten wet stopping for gas when the wind blew the rain under the overhead cover at the gas pump. He was just beginning to dry out when he found a parking place along East 8th Street just after passing the address he was looking for. The rain was unrelenting as he grabbed the ruined rag rug off the floor between the Jeep's two front seats and scrambled back toward Evelyn's Everyday Gifts, but the gold stencil on the door window now read *"Home At Last."* Peering in, he shivered as the cold rain pelted his back and ran down the neck of his jacket. He pushed the door open and stepped in, if for no other reason than to escape the elements.

"It's pouring out there," the middle-aged lady behind the cash register offered as he swiped a hand at the rain running down his neck.

"All the way from Shelby to here," he offered.

"Well, you've come a long way. Is there something I can help you find?" She had observed the rolled-up rug in his hand.

"I'm looking to replace this with one just like it, if possible," Rock said as he held up the rug. "The tag on it, says, 'Evelyn's Everyday Gifts'. Obviously it's not Evelyn's place anymore, but I'm hoping you may still stock these rugs."

"We do," she offered with a smile. "Is there something wrong with that one?"

He told a harmless lie. "Nothing wrong with the rug except I spilled an entire bottle of red wine on it and I can't get this stain out. It belongs to a friend and I told her I'd replace it." He pointed to the stain, still quite visible after his attempts to wash it out.

"Well, let's see what we've got in stock. Does it have to be an exact match? I'm not worried about the size, but exact pattern and color may be a challenge. Each one of these is a little different from the next. An Amish lady makes them. No two are exactly the same, you see." She led him to a large pile of rugs in the back of the store, where she offered to help him look. When the bell attached to the inside of the store's door signaled that another customer had entered, Rock told her he could manage, and she left. There were at least two hundred rag rugs spread between two large tables, but it didn't take him long to find one that was similar to the one he'd ruined.

She smiled at him as he approached the counter, "You found one. Oh, good."

He handed her a fifty-dollar bill. She gave him a twenty-dollar bill in change, a receipt, and his rug rolled and tied in the middle with a colorful ribbon, "Home-At-Last" stenciled on it.

"Is there a barber shop close?" he asked.

"Ummm... a barber shop? Not that I know of. There's a salon next door. I know they cut men's hair, I've seen men going in there, and I think they take walk-ins, but they may be a little expensive..." She caught herself. In her effort to be helpful, this wasn't coming out as she had wanted. She didn't mean that he couldn't afford it, nor did she mean to imply that he was some hick from up north.

Rock sensed her uneasiness, so without removing it, he put his hand on his stocking cap and while adjusting it said, "Well, I need a little help up here. It would probably be worth a little extra this time to get it done right." Sensing her relief, he offered a smile and turned to leave. Glancing at his watch, he noted the time; *4:31 p.m.* The storm with its low-hanging clouds and torrential rain would usher in an earlier nightfall than usual this evening, and it was already getting dark. He wasn't crazy about returning to Far-Far-View after dark, but that was now inevitable. Dashing to the Jeep, he dropped off the two rugs and dashed back to the salon. As he opened the door to The Styles of Holland Salon, he made up his mind that if there was any waiting required he would leave and head back home, maybe find a barber shop on his way out of town.

For the last thirty-plus years Rock had his hair cut in a neighborhood barbershop in Flint called Harry's. He often wondered, but never asked, if the name was meant to be a pun or not. If Harry had a last name, Rock never knew. Men were Harry's only customers. The place was full of hunting trophies, sports memorabilia and dirty jokes. A small wall-mounted TV was never tuned to any other channel than ESPN even if it could receive more. And Rock judged Harry to also be a bit of a racist from some of the jokes he told. In all the years Harry had cut his hair, Rock had never seen a person of color in the shop.

The Styles of Holland Salon could not have been more different. The wooden, curved reception desk rose out of the blond wood floor as if it had been carved there. A Nora Jones song was playing softly through a state-or-the-art sound system featuring speakers so small they were almost undetectable. In the corner, in front of the plate glass window fronting 8th Street, was an inviting waiting area with pale pastel leather easy chairs for customers to sink into while waiting. A tea cart with coffee, tea, sparkling water, spring water, fresh fruit, cheese and crackers sat in the corner with a sign reading: *Sorry for your wait, please help yourself.*

From the rear of the shop a woman approached and asked, "May I help you?

He stammered a little as he told her he needed a haircut.

"Sure. You've come to the right place. I'm Phyllis." She extended her hand. He took it and didn't want to let go of its softness.

He stammered again, "Er... Rock... Rock Graham."

"Nice to meet you, Rock Graham. I have a customer in the chair that will take me about fifteen minutes to finish. Can you wait?"

As he sat down in one of the easy chairs with a glass of spring water, a cracker and a piece of cheese, he chuckled at himself and how quickly he'd forgotten his promise that he would not wait. *She is quite attractive, though,* he thought. *Worth it! Harry never looked that good!*

At 5:00 p.m., fifteen minutes longer than she said she'd be, she walked an elderly lady to the door and asked her if she needed help getting to her car. When the woman declined, Phyllis closed the salon's door and turned to Rock, "OK. Sorry that took longer than I expected. She likes to talk... and so do I."

"No problem," Rock said matter-of-factly, noticing as he got up that it was now nearly dark. She waved for him to follow her, and as he did he found himself unable to take his eyes off of her. He noticed the way her long blond hair bounced softly with each step. She wore a very flattering short black dress that delicately accentuated her curves while the black leggings extending to just above her ankle emphasized her long legs. She wore black, patent-leather shoes with tall, stiletto heels. From his vantage point he thought she had one of the most sensuous walks it had ever been his pleasure to observe. She stopped behind one of the chairs and motioned for him to have a seat.

As she placed a cape around him, she looked at his reflection in the mirror and said with a smile, "Well, Rock Graham, the hat is going to have to come off if I'm going to cut your hair."

He laughed uneasily, dreading this part, but reached up and pulled the stocking cap from his head. Phyllis stifled the gasp on the end of her tongue, but Rock could see her expression in the mirror in front of him. Half of his hair was two to three inches long, while the other half was stubble bristling in every direction and approaching half an inch in length. Nearest her and just to the right of his crown was the scar, still red and angry looking, but gone were the stitches and any scab.

"I fell. Cracked my head open. Stitches are all out and it's growing back on the side they shaved, but can you do something with this?" and he stroked the longer hair on the unshaved side of his noggin.

"You poor thing." She put her hands on his shoulders. In the mirror he saw her studying him. She moved from one side to the other, never taking her eyes off his reflection in the mirror. Finally she offered her opinion. "Not much I can do except cut this long side to a more reasonable length to match this side," and she ran her fingers lightly through the stubby bristle. "How come they shaved off so much?"

He didn't like talking about the accident, and he refused to talk about what had caused it, but he answered her question. "The fall knocked me out for a few hours. The blood dried and matted the hair. They couldn't tell how big the gash was, so they had to shave all that," and he waved his hand around in a circle on that side of his head.

"You were alone? Nobody was there to help you?"

He hoped she wouldn't pursue this.

She seemed to sense his uneasiness and repeated, "You poor thing," and patted his shoulders lightly. Backing away from the details of the accident, she looked at the wound and observed, "You're going to have a scar here," pointing to the gash, "But you've got a good head of hair. It'll get long enough to cover it. In a few months you will never know. For now, let me just work a little on this side; it won't take long. You're going to look like a recruit for a while, but, like I said, you've got a good head of hair and it'll all grow back. That sound like a plan to you?" She was smiling at his reflection in the mirror.

Looking at her reflection, he said, "You're the expert. I trust you." As she worked, he noticed that she was not wearing an engagement ring or a wedding band. He found her easy to talk to. He volunteered that he was just visiting Holland and that he actually lived along the lakeshore near Shelby. She volunteered that she'd lived in Holland all of her life. Rock wanted to know more about her, but he was too much of a gentleman to blurt his questions out. She told him at the beginning that this wouldn't take long and the more she worked, the more he wished she'd take her sweet time. As she was finishing up, she leaned into him and brushed her bosom against his shoulder as she removed the cape she'd placed over him. Her perfume was delicate and she felt good to him.

"OK. That's about all I can do today," she said as she spun him around with his back to the mirror and gave him a hand mirror to examine both the front and back of her work.

Rock laughed.

Phyllis did too. "What? I told you. Recruit, right?"

"You did and unfortunately you were correct."

She turned the chair back around so that he was facing the wall of mirrors. With her hands laid delicately on his shoulders, she said, "Well, you're just going to have to come down here from Shelby every now and then to see me and let me keep after this head of hair until we get it back to where we both want it." In the mirror Rock looked at that dazzlingly beautiful smile of hers. Her tone, her words seemed like an invitation, not just a practical matter of hair-trimming. He hoped he wasn't wrong.

At the counter he asked, "How much do I owe you?"

Somewhat sheepishly Phyllis replied, "Five dollars OK with you?"

Rock put his hands on the counter and smiled, "The lady next door recommended your salon but said you 'might be a little expensive'." At Harry's he'd paid nine dollars. "So, Phyllis, c'mon, how much do I owe you?"

"I didn't do that much ..."

"Listen, don't feel sorry for me. The fall was my fault. If I have to pay to get my hair back to some semblance of normal, a good haircut deserves a fair price. So..."

She put her hand on his, innocently or maybe not, he wasn't sure. "Really, Rock. You saw how little time it took. All I did was cut some hair off. I didn't even do your whole head; just the side with the longer hair. You could have done the same thing yourself. Five dollars is fine..." she paused, smiled mischievously at him, and then added, "For this time."

Again he took this as an invitation. He gave her the twenty-dollar bill that the clerk next door had given him in change for the rug he had bought. She gave him a ten and a five as change. He put the ten back on the counter.

"No, that's too much." She pushed it back at him.

He locked eyes with her and slid the five her way. "OK, but no more arguing."

"OK, but you have to come back to see me." She gave him a card with her name and the salon's number on it. *Another invitation,* he thought. As he turned to leave, she said to him, "When you come back, I want to know how you got your name, Rock." She was smiling that smile at him. He wanted right then and there to ask her out, but he quickly thought the better of that kind of impulsiveness. Rock Graham liked women. His life had not been that of a monk. He had dated many and bedded a lot of them, but he had always been the complete gentleman and, in his mind, gentlemen were not impulsive.

Chapter Ten

A New Arrival

If the afternoon trip to Holland had been difficult, the trip back to Far-Far-View was harder. It was either miserably dark on the highway or he was blinded by the glare of other car headlights off the wet road. When he pulled onto the Little Point Sable gravel access road, he slowed to a crawl because the rain had become torrential and he instinctively knew to be on the lookout for washouts that might swallow up one or more of his wheels. As he turned on the upslope of the dune behind the cottage, he could see the glow of the porch light. Though thinking about Phyllis had made a tough trip easier, he was glad to be home safely. However, as the Jeep broke over the crest of the dune his headlights caught the outline of something sitting in front of the cottage door.

As he pulled to a full stop, and the wipers were better able to keep up with the wind-driven rain, he still couldn't distinguish what it was, except that it was some kind of animal. He turned the Jeep off. The wipers stopped and everything was instantly a blur through the windshield. Whatever it was, it wasn't big enough to pose a threat to him, so Rock opened the door, thankful for the courtesy light option that would keep his headlights on for another minute or so. He advanced slowly, even though the rain was soaking him, but the animal didn't move. It just sat there looking at him. Carefully he began to descend the six or seven steps from the parking area down to the front door. He was half way down when he was able to see that it was a dog. "Where did you come from?" he asked as he descended the final step and was now only about eight feet away. "It's OK," he said, extending his hand toward the animal. Rock was no expert on dogs. As a kid he and his sister had begged his mother for one, but there was barely enough money to feed themselves, much less feed a dog. As an adult, long hours of overtime at the plant didn't lend themselves to responsible dog ownership. It was medium size; given his limited knowledge and experience, he couldn't name the breed, but noticed its deep chest and long thin legs. It was mostly white, with a saddle of tan, medium-length hair spreading over the middle of its back. Its ears were neither floppy nor pointed. One ear lay flat along the side of its head, while the other looked like it wanted to be pointy, but half way up lost its desire, causing the wanna-be point to fall back over the bottom half of the ear. He thought the dog looked thin as it sat there on his porch, a shivering, bedraggled mess. He ran his hand down her side and could feel her ribs. "Been a while since you've eaten, hasn't it, girl?" He'd been able to determine her sex as he stroked the underside of her belly. He brought his hand back to her chin and held her face up to the light, and it was then that his heart melted. She whimpered slightly and lifted her left foreleg into the air and the paw drooped as she did that. He surmised that whatever bone and tendon meant to hold it in place had been broken or torn. Her round eyes stared into his; the left one was half blue and half brown, the right one, all brown.

"You're hurt," he said and reached down to put a hand under the injured leg.

She looked down at his hand under her leg, looked back into his eyes and whimpered softly.

"OK," Rock said to her as he took his hand away from her injury. "Can you walk?" The dog gently lowered the paw to the ground, but he noticed she wasn't putting any weight on it. He inserted the key into the lock and swung the cottage's door open. "OK. Let's try it. Go on in," he said gently.

The dog looked at him and stood on three good legs and hobbled into the cottage where it did what any wet dog does when it escapes the source of water causing the dampness. It shook from head to toe as best it could from its three-point stance, which was good enough to throw water everywhere.

"Whoa, there. Hang on." Rock reached around the doorway of the spare bathroom, just to the left inside the cottage's back door, grabbed a towel and bent down to place it over the animal. He began patting at the nape of the neck and worked his way toward the tail. She shook again, but this time less water spattered and she looked up at him as if to ask, "What's next?"

"Come on in and let's have a look at that leg." Guided by the glow of his night light, Rock led the way down the entrance hallway into the kitchen area, where he turned on more lights. He watched her hobble into the room, placing no weight on the injured leg. She sat down in front of him, and he knelt to examine her. She whimpered as he touched the upper leg and again as he took his other hand and touched her paw. "OK, that hurts, doesn't it?" There was no blood, but he did not try to move the forepaw, sure that there was a break or serious sprain at best. He stood up. She stared up at him with those eyes. Gently, he asked, "Where did you come from? How did you find this place? Why me?" She blinked at him as if trying to answer his questions. There were other questions, but he kept them to himself. Questions like, *"What's wrong with your leg? Where's a good vet?"* and, one that bothered him maybe a little more, *"What's Jan going to say about you being here?"*

She'd been very explicit when she pointed out the no-pet clause in his lease agreement. However, he reasoned these questions were not going to be resolved tonight.

He stared back down at her; her eyes locked on him, "Yep, you're right! What does it matter? You're here now. So, how about it? Are you hungry?" He turned and went into the kitchen to find something for her to eat. "Tomorrow morning I'll call Jan and tell her about you. I'm not supposed to have a pet in here, you know, but she's got a dog of her own, so I'm sure she can steer me to a good vet who can take a look at that leg of yours."

He didn't have a single left-over in the refrigerator, so he fixed her a bowl of Cheerios and milk. When he put it down for her, she lay down in front of the bowl. Rock watched as she slowly, painfully, he thought, stretched out the injured leg, but he was wise enough to let her work it out for herself. Slowly and steadily, she ate every morsel of cereal and licked up every drop of milk. While she ate, he built a fire in the fireplace. He took the bloodstained rag rug and spread it out in front of the hearth, not knowing if the residual smell of his blood would keep her away. He didn't need to worry. She seemed to know the rug was for her and she promptly lay down. He sat in an easy chair opposite the fireplace and read for a few minutes before he became tired himself. Putting his book down, he looked at the dog, whose eyes were closed, and watched her rhythmical breathing. When he rose to go to bed, she looked up at him. "It's all right, girl. Go back to sleep." As if she understood his every word, she put her head down on the rug between her two front paws, but watched him walk to his bedroom. He took a shower, donned his pajamas and brushed his teeth. Before turning in he checked on her, and this time she did not wake.

The wind-driven rain pounded against the lakeside window in his bedroom. It had been, weather-wise, the worst day he'd seen on the lake, but as he laid his head on the pillow, it was the first night since his tumble that he wasn't afraid to close his eyes. His thoughts shifted between the woman he had met in Holland and the dog asleep in front of his fireplace. For the moment, Vietnam was a memory too distant to be worth remembering and the deep recession that was killing off his company, his hometown and his country was of less importance than helping his new-found friend. Tomorrow he would find her help. Tomorrow he had some convincing to do. *Don't know what Jan's going to say,* he thought as he fell soundly asleep.

Chapter Eleven

The Little Guy

Flower met her at the door with wagging tail as she arrived home from the Yacht Club. Clair patted her on the head somewhat dismissively, preoccupied with thoughts of Beth. "OK, Flower, go take care of things." The lab padded outside, looking back briefly as Claire closed the door. A bit of a night owl, she normally would not think about turning in at 9:00 p.m., but she was tired and ready to call it a night when she heard the beep from her answering machine. It was Maria, "Ms. Claire can you call me at home when you get this message, no matter what time it is." Maria's urgency alarmed her. Her first thought was that something had happened to Jesus.

After Claire punched her number on speed dial, Maria answered after three rings. "Ms. Claire, thank you for calling me back."

"You're welcome, Maria. I'm sorry it's so late." She knew Maria was usually in bed by this hour. "Is everything all right?"

There was a pause and she thought she heard Maria sob once or twice. "No, Ms. Claire. We have some trouble here," and then there were more sobs, unmistakable this time.

"What is it?"

"It's our oldest son, James, and our daughter, Mary."

Claire's heart began to ache. "What's happened, Maria?"

Composing herself as best she could, she explained, "They have lost their jobs, Ms. Claire, both of them on the same day. I can't believe it! James was downsized and Mary was let go because her school district's enrollment has declined and she has not been a teacher there long enough. She and two others were let go."

Claire's anger began to rise. The *little guy* she had wondered about now had names, faces and a long history with her. Maria and Jesus's kids had grown up with her two girls.

"Jesus and I were wondering, Ms. Claire," Maria paused. Claire wanted to reach through the phone and put her arms around her. "We were wondering if you would allow us..." another pause. "We were wondering if we could take a month or so off. Day care is so expensive and without any income..." her voice trailed off. "Jesus and I thought we might be able to help James and Mary with the children while they try to find work. You know how hard that is right now, Ms. Claire..."

"Maria," Claire interrupted. "You take all the time you need. This will be paid time off, of course."

"No, Ms. Claire, we don't expect you to..."

Claire cut her off. "Nonsense, Maria. I want to help in any way I can. I'm so sorry this has happened to James and Mary. Talk it over with them and then call me and let me know how else I can help."

"Ms. Claire, will you be all right?"

The question made tears well up in Claire's eyes. The Chavez's were not *people of wealth,* yet here was the matriarch of that family worried if Claire would be all right.

"Ms. Claire?"

Claire choked down the lump in her throat, "Oh, yes, Maria. I don't want you to worry about me. I will be just fine." Looking back on this conversation later, Claire was never able to determine what had possessed her to say what she said, but out it came, "In fact, I was considering taking a month or so and going to the other house for a change of scenery."

"Oh, good, Ms. Claire. Florida will be good for you. It's starting to turn so cold here."

"Well actually, I was considering going to the Lake Michigan house for a while." There was a pause while this sank in, but Claire provided the perfect explanation, "I don't want to be too far away with the wedding approaching and everything."

"Oh. Well, yes. I see," said Maria, but Claire sensed from her tone that she didn't. Why would anyone want to go to northern Michigan's lakeshore in the dead of winter, especially when they owned a lovely beachfront home in Florida?

"But Maria, I still want to help. You and Jesus have the number up there, don't you?"

"Yes, Ms. Claire, I have it."

"Then you shouldn't hesitate to call me. I can be back in Holland in less than two hours if you need me."

"Ms. Claire, you do so much for our family..."

"And you do so much for mine, Maria," Claire interrupted. "Try not to worry. James and Mary are two talented people. They will find work."

"Yes, Ms. Claire.

Claire hung up the phone and stood there for a minute, trying to take in this miserable news. She remembered Flower only when she barked at the door. Claire let her in, walked in the kitchen and slumped into a chair at the table. The last of the year's roses were in a vase, their delightful scent long dried up, and beginning to lose their bloom. Claire began to cry and Flower sensed her distress. The dog laid her head in Claire's lap and looked up at her mistress with tail slowly wagging, as if to say, *"Is there something I can do?"*

Claire looked into the dog's eyes and wiped at the tears on her cheeks. "I know. I don't know where the idea came from either, but what do you think?" The big dog wagged her tail more vigorously. Claire took that as a *Yes*. "OK, then Lake Michigan it is."

No longer tired, and with complete disregard for the late hour, Claire made three phone calls. She wasn't surprised when the first two went to voice mail, but in her messages to the Managing Directors of Van Zandt Engineering, America, and Van Zandt Engineering, International, she asked each of them to call her to discuss possible employment opportunities for a computer engineer and a teacher who might possibly work out as a corporate trainer. Even Claire, however, thought she might be reaching too far with Mary. She was an elementary teacher. What did she know about engineering? But Claire was determined to give every option a try.

Her third call was to her caretaker for the house up north. It was almost 10:00 p.m., but there was an answer on the second ring. "Bob, it's Claire Van Zandt."

"Ms. Van Zandt, it's good to hear from you. It's been a long time... what, at least a year."

"Longer than that I suspect, Bob, but Flower and I are planning a trip to the house."

"Oh, that's great, Ms. Van Zandt. It will be good to see you, and I haven't seen Flower since she was just a puppy. Do you know when you will be arriving? I haven't closed it up for the winter just yet, so it won't take much to get things ready for you."

"Thank you. I'm not certain of the date. There are a few loose ends I need to tidy up down here, but I would like to get up there by next weekend, the 8th or 9th of November. Will that work for you?"

"Yes, ma'am. That will work out just fine. I'll get groceries laid in, put some firewood in the bin next to the fireplace and I'll check the furnace to make sure it's ready for the cold nights. You can come on up anytime."

As Claire hung up she drew in a deep breath and let it out. *There, that's done. He's keeping the house open; you've got to go now.* She thought this just might be the nudge that she would need to keep her on track in spite of the resistance she knew she would encounter, especially from Ingrid.

Chapter Twelve

Jan

The morning after Rock's trip to Holland broke clear and cold. Yesterday's storm had moved east and was now battering New England. He let the dog out after she had gone to the door and whimpered. It was hard to watch her hobble on three legs, even harder to watch her maneuver into position to do her business without putting too much stress on the injured leg. When she came back in, he patted her on the head and praised her for her efforts, knowing she could have more easily soiled the carpet in the cottage. They each enjoyed a breakfast of cereal and milk, exhausting Rock's supply. He made a shopping list of things he needed and things he thought the dog would need. It gave him something to do until a respectable hour when he could call Jan. He waited until 8:00 a.m. and then made the call, not without considerable apprehension. Explaining his predicament, he asked her for the name of a good vet. Neither he nor she mentioned the prohibition against pets in his lease agreement. However, once she gave him the name and number for Dr. Meyer, her vet in nearby Fremont, Jan firmly suggested he stop by her house after the dog had received treatment. "We'll need to talk about this, Rock," she'd said to him gravely.

After Rock dropped Jan's name with the vet's receptionist, he was told to bring her in immediately and that the doctor would see the dog. Rock had to help her into the Jeep, but once that was accomplished, she seemed content to sit in the front passenger seat and watch the countryside roll by during the hour-long trip to Fremont. At the vet's office, Rock learned several things. First, the dog was a border collie and, according to the vet, as a breed they are one of the smartest dogs in the world. Second, they are "working dogs." Dr. Meyer told him that they thrive on having something to do on a regular basis. Rock told Dr. Meyer he was retired, and the doctor suggested she might be the perfect companion for him. She would challenge him to get out of the house. "Perhaps you could walk every day. Good for you, good for her. Right?" Their relationship, the good doctor explained, could be "perfectly simpatico."

Rock also learned that she did not have any broken bones. But she did have a severe sprain of muscles and tendons in her left, front leg, which the doctor decided was bad enough to set in a cast running from her paw to nearly her shoulder. The doctor told Rock that she would need to remain quiet for the next couple of weeks as everything healed. "She's a young dog. Healthy. She'll heal quickly and be as good as new, but keeping her quiet will be a challenge especially as she starts to feel better, which will be soon. You'll have your hands full just trying to keep her calmed down."

His final lesson from the vet's office was a financial one. Vets aren't cheap. He wrote a check for $500 and thanked the doctor and the receptionist for getting her in so quickly.

As Rock pulled into Jan's driveway, the dog was in her spot on the passenger side front seat of the Jeep. Turning the car off, Rock looked over at her and suggested, "This is important. We both need to look pitiful; you especially." The dog perked her ears up and cocked her head as if trying to discern his instructions. Rock lifted her down from the

Jeep and the two of them, Rock with his limp and the dog with her cast, hobbled to the door. Jan watched from her living room window. At the door the dog sat at Rock's side and looked up at her, and though she never whimpered a sound, she held the cast leg out in front as if to be sure Jan could see the extent of her injury.

Pleasantries behind them, Rock waded in to the reason he knew Jan wanted to see him, "I know my lease says no pets, but I can't just take her to the pound..."

Jan merely nodded and asked, "What did Dr. Meyer say?"

"She's got a severe sprain. He put her in the cast because he says she will want to be active long before she should be and maybe the cast will help to keep her slowed down. He wants us back in three weeks."

"Have you given her a name yet?" Jan asked.

He hadn't, but he quickly thought that if he had, it might help to soften Jan up. Thinking quickly, he scratched his cheek and said, "Well, I was kinda' thinking of calling her *Flotsam,* because of the way she just washed up on my doorstep during that storm last night."

Jan knelt down and petted the dog. "Any idea where she could have come from?"

He thought she might be melting. He needed an answer that would finish the job, but all of his spur-of-the-moment inventiveness was used up in naming her. "Not really. The vet checked for a microchip. There isn't one, but I think she had a family, a home once, and somehow got separated from them. You know how deserted things are at the lake this time of year. I don't think there's anyone living within five miles of me. I think she has learned to trust people, but somehow lost hers and had trouble finding someone out there at the shore. I have no way of knowing how long she has been roaming around. The vet says she's too thin and that she's probably been on the loose a while. Then when she got hurt, she knew she needed help. Maybe she could smell that there was somebody living at Far-Far-View and she just decided to hold on there until someone came, and she was just hoping that it would be somebody that would help her."

As she continued to stroke the newly-named creature, Jan's sternness surprised him. "Rock, you know that carpet in the living room and the two bedrooms just off the living room is all new, just this fall before you moved in?"

"Look, Jan..."

She stood up, not yet finished making her point; interrupting him, she continued, "I love dogs, but I was mad as hell at those renters this summer. I can't have a dog tearing up the place."

Things were not looking good, but he wasn't about to give up. "Jan, I'll keep a good eye on her. I've only had her for less than a day, but I can tell she's a good dog." He told her about how Flotsam had gone to the door this morning and alerted him that she needed to go outside. He gave Jan just a moment to digest this and then continued, "Listen, I want to stay at the lake, but she came to me for help. The vet says it's her nature to be active and that I'm going to have to temper that for the next three weeks or so while she recovers. I'm not going to give up on her." He paused, not sure what else to say. He didn't think money would solve their dilemma, but he gave it a try. "What if I pay you an extra hundred a month in rent, just to cover your risk?"

Jan looked at the dog and then back at Rock. "I watched the two of you walk up to the door. I know why Flotsam limps, but what happened to your leg, Rock?"

Where the hell did that come from? The question almost angered him. It was his rule not to discuss Vietnam with anyone but Russ and Josh, his nephew. Thirty-six years ago, the only other time his service record had been discussed outside this small group, Russ had leveraged it with the union local to get Rock in the door at GM. Now, as

he stood on Jan's porch, he realized maybe he could leverage it again. And, right now, this was every bit as important to him as his employment at GM had been way back
then. He thought carefully, quickly, and then looked Jan
in the eye as he doled out information he thought might
help. "I got shot in the leg when I was in Vietnam," he said
thumping the thigh of his shorter leg. "Doctors, all except
one, wanted to cut if off. I was lucky the majority didn't
rule. Scar tissue makes one leg a little shorter than the
other. I limp. But at least I've still got both legs."

She'd been right. It had been her theory that the limp
was a product of the war. Ashamed that she'd asked, Jan
averted her eyes from his. "I'm sorry. I... I don't know why
I asked you that. It really isn't any of my business, but now
that I know..." Her voice trailed off and things fell silent.
Rock gave her the time she needed to think. She knelt
back down and took Flotsam's chin. The dog, wagging her
tail just enough to let Jan know she appreciated the attention, let Jan lift her eyes to meet hers. Without taking her
eyes away from Flotsam's, Jan said, "You'll leave if I don't
let you keep her there, won't you?"

Without hesitation he answered, "Yes."

Jan patted her on the head and stood. "She's got a good
home now and that's what matters the most." Jan looked
away and wiped something from her eye. "No need to pay
me more, Rock, but watch her. That new carpet..."

Rock was beaming. "Jan, I guarantee you that we will
take such good care of the place that when you get it back
next Memorial Day you will never know we were there."
He held out his hand and they shook on it. Then he looked
down at the dog, "OK, Flotsam, you're legal now, so let's
go home." Flotsam stood, somewhat wobbly, still getting
used to the cast on her left leg, and walked next to Rock as
they headed back to the Jeep.

They were about half way back to their car when Jan
called to them. She stepped out of the doorway, down off

the front porch and met them as Rock and Flotsam made their way back to her. "I have my brother, Larry, and my sister, Diane, and her husband, John," she paused and then added, "He's a retired Army Colonel and a Vietnam vet like you, up every year for Thanksgiving. Would you and Flotsam like to join us? We're all dog people, well, except for Larry, but he likes dogs. He's a confirmed bachelor and just too stubborn to let his heart go and get one." She smiled at him.

The invitation was unexpected, but he liked her. The only issue was Josh. Rock had been thinking that he would go home to Flint for Thanksgiving and invite Josh to come over from Michigan State for the holiday. "Can I let you know? I have a nephew. He's a student at MSU, and I don't know what his plans are..."

"Then he's invited too. The more the merrier. What do you say?"

Rock thought for a second and said, "Then I say yes. I will confirm with you about Josh. Like I said, I don't know what his plans are."

Chapter Thirteen

The Difference Between Them

Claire glanced at her watch. *10:10 p.m. Maybe I should wait 'til morning.* The handset lay in her lap. She thought for a few more minutes before concluding that procrastination is controversy's handmaiden. She punched Ingrid's number on speed dial before it got any later. The phone rang four times before she heard Ingrid say, "Hello."

Claire had been prepared for the call to drop to voicemail. With surprise evident in her voice she said, "Ingrid?"

"Yes, Mother, is everything OK? You don't usually call this late."

"I know, dear, but something has come up that I think you and Ethan should know about."

"What is it, Mother? Are you all right? Is Beth all right?" Ingrid responded with clear urgency in her voice now.

"Beth and I are fine, dear. It's the Chavez family."

"Who?"

"Jesus and Maria Chavez."

"Oh, what's the trouble?"

Ingrid's *Oh, them* tone immediately infuriated Claire. "James and Mary... you remember them, don't you?" she sniped. She didn't wait for a response and added, "Both of them lost their jobs today!"

In the background she could hear Ingrid, who didn't have her hand clamped tightly enough over the mouthpiece, say, "Go to page 34..."

Claire could hear pages shuffling as she cut into Ingrid, "What are you doing?"

"Ethan and I are preparing for a case I am presenting in court in the morning..."

Claire kept her cool. "Ingrid, these people have worked for our family for almost three decades." When Ingrid didn't respond, Claire stepped it up a notch, "Did you hear what I just said?"

"Something about James and Mary Chavez?"

Claire flared at her, "Ingrid, forget about your damned job for once, get over that sense of entitlement of yours and listen to me. The Chavezes need our help right now. James and Mary are without work. Both of them have families; small children. In this economy there's no telling when they will find work. We need to help them."

It had been years since Claire had spoken to her oldest daughter in genuine rebuke, and it caught Ingrid by surprise. She reacted to Claire's anger with an angry tone of her own, "Well, what can we do about it, Mother?"

Dammit! Claire was fit to be tied. She hung her head. *So high and mighty!* Her instinct was to rage on at her.

She heard Ingrid ask, "Mother? Are you still there?"

The question prompted a thought to hang up and test her oldest daughter. *I wonder if she'd have the conscience to call me back?*

"Mother?" she heard again, fainter still, from the handset that Claire had lowered to her lap.

Claire quickly decided that this was not the time to test her. Her purpose was to help the Chavezes. Biting her tongue, she put the handset up to her ear and said, more calmly now, "Your law firm must use computers. Could you inquire if there would be work for James? He is a computer engineer. Do any of your co-workers or friends need a tutor?" she paused and then sniped again, "Or a nanny?" Claire knew a nanny was doing most of the caring for her grandson. But then she realized that perhaps she'd stumbled onto a real possibility. "Mary is an elementary school teacher. She loves to work with young children. You must have friends that could use a good, reliable person like her." Claire paused to try and think of any other ways the Hoffmans could help, but realized she'd run out of suggestions. "I don't know. Use your imagination, but please..."

"Well, I suppose..."

"Don't *suppose*, Ingrid," Claire was almost snarling at her daughter. "Do it. Take some time and try. As a family, we owe the Chavezes that much."

"OK. OK. We will give you a call if we come up with anything. I really have to get back to work, Mother."

"I have some other news." She could almost see Ingrid rolling her eyes. "I'm going to the other house for a month or so."

"Oh."

"The Lake Michigan house..." Claire paused to let that sink in.

"What?"

"I'm going to spend some time at the Lake Michigan house. I've asked Bob Mumford to have it ready by the 8th of November. I don't think I will go earlier than that."

Now Ingrid's tone became scolding, "Mother, that's next weekend. What in the world are you thinking? Do you have any idea how cold and desolate it will be up there?"

Not any more cold and desolate than your heart, Claire wanted to reply. Instead she said, "Yes, I know, but this recession is wearing on me. I want to go someplace where I can be by myself and think. So Flower and I will head up north."

"But, Mother, it isn't safe for you to be up..."

"Oh, come on, Ingrid, don't be so dramatic. I'll have the Range Rover to come and go as I might need to. If I need something, all I have to do is call Mr. Mumford. I'm perfectly safe."

"What about the wedding? Have you told Beth? She will be livid."

She wanted to lie and say she had, but thought better of the deception. Ingrid, no doubt, would be on the phone to her sister as soon as she hung up from this call. Claire needed to beat her to that punch, "Beth is my next call, and I'd appreciate it if you would give me the opportunity to tell her."

"Mother, it's like you're deserting her."

"Well, I'm sorry you see it that way. I hope Beth won't."

"She will, Mother, even if she won't tell you to your face. You need to rethink this crazy idea."

"It's late and I still need to phone Beth. Please, Ingrid, will you and Ethan try and come up with something for James and Mary. Don't forget about them. This is important to them. It's important to me." Pausing, she waited for Ingrid's answer.

"I'm going to call Beth tonight, later on. I'll give you a chance to tell her, but it's crazy. You can expect to hear again from both of us about this craziness."

Resignation evident in her voice, Claire said, "Good night, Ingrid," then added with a warning tone, "And remember, I want to be the one that tells Beth about this, so check back with me before you say anything to her." She hung up the phone.

The call to Beth was not without some angst; all of it about Claire's retreat to the Lake Michigan house. But Ingrid had been wrong about how her sister would receive both pieces of news.

In regards to Claire going north, Beth's only question was, "What if I need you?"

"Bethie, I wouldn't be doing this if I didn't think you and the wedding planners have everything under control. But all you have to do is call, and I will be here in a couple of hours. I promise. Little Point Sable isn't that far from Grand Rapids. I will come. I promise." Satisfied that her youngest was not feeling deserted, Claire warned, "Ingrid is going to call you. She doesn't understand. You may have to listen to her rant. I'm sorry for that, sweetie."

"It's OK, Mom. I'm used to it." They both laughed at the vision of Beth standing with the phone held a foot from her ear while Ingrid vented her objections to Claire's trip. The comic relief was good for both of them. "Don't forget I'm coming over to borrow the 'Vette for the weekend. Would you like to have dinner someplace on Thursday evening?"

"Terrific," Claire responded. Her two daughters were such opposites. *How does that happen in a family?* Claire knew there was no defining answer. Beth, unlike her older sister, had asked Claire if she wanted to talk about the recession, so Claire told her about the meeting with the accountants.

"Well, I think what you are doing with the Food Banks in Michigan is a really good thing. I feel badly sometimes because business at the gallery hasn't dropped off at all. Yesterday I sold a piece to a client for ten thousand dollars. It was an anniversary present. You know I love art, but..." she paused.

Claire said, "I know."

Pensively, Beth continued, "That money could have helped a lot of people pay their rent, their electric bill, or buy food. Mom, I don't know what more we can do to help, but I know you are working on it, aren't you?"

Finally, someone who understands! "Yes, I am, honey. I'll keep you posted. Love you. Good night."

"Good night, Mom. See you on Thursday."

So different! Claire rubbed Flower's ears and together they headed upstairs and to bed.

Chapter Fourteen

Date Night

The first two weeks of November were gone in a flash. Though memories of Billy Riley and Vietnam had shown up a few nights, for the most part, he had been able to sleep. He credited this to his dog and the weather, which had been decent. He and Flotsam had become inseparable. During long walks on the beach, he taught Flotsam to fetch, come and speak for her treats. She taught him patience right from their first full day together.

After arriving home from the vet, Rock had tested the doctor's theory about walking and took Flotsam down to the beach. She was tentative descending the twenty-five steps to the dune below Far-Far-View. Unsure what to do to help or even if he should try, Rock gave plenty of slack in the leash and patiently waited on the step above as she slowly made her way down. At the bottom of the steps, he made his first mistake. He detached the leash from her collar and Flotsam clumsily bolted directly into the freezing water, thoroughly soaking the plaster cast on her injured left leg. In less than a minute he could see the cast was starting to deteriorate. They had been lucky to catch the vet just as the office was closing. Dr. Meyer reset the leg, replaced the cast and accepted another $200 payment from Rock before suggesting to him that a "nice length of rope might work better than a leash." He explained that border collies like to range, "So she's going to really dislike being on a leash, but if you got a nice long rope..." On the way home, his lesson learned, Rock bought a hundred feet of good rope. Flotsam's walks on the beach would be strictly limited to the amount of rope Rock was willing to dole out to her.

Today, Saturday, November 15th, not quite three weeks from the day he'd found her, Flotsam was to be liberated from the cast, which would, in turn, liberate both of them from the rope. Even at the early hour of 8:00 a.m., Dr. Meyer's office was busy. Flotsam sat in the waiting room watching the other dogs and cats gathered there, content to remain at Rock's feet. It wasn't long before a technician collected her, explaining, "Dr. Meyer wants an X-ray of the leg just to make sure everything is where it's supposed to be."

Apparently she was good to go, because when the vet tech brought Flotsam back, the cast was gone and the dog seemed to be beaming. Rock paid his hundred-dollar bill, anxious to get home. He had an appointment at 3:00 p.m. today in Holland that he was very much looking forward to.

At noon he let Flotsam out in the yard behind Far-Far-View and stepped out the door himself to take in the blue sky and sunshine that, despite its brilliance, was unable to raise the temperature above freezing. Both of them heard the car coming down the road long before they could see it. He caught his first glimpse of the Range Rover as it rolled past his driveway. Through the leafless hardwoods, he observed it turn into the driveway of the house immediately south of him, a magnificent place he'd observed many times as he and Flotsam had walked the beach. He could hear the garage door roll up and then he heard a dog bark. Flotsam alerted immediately to the sound, but one of the things she'd learned quite well over the last few weeks was to obey her master's command to come.

She looked longingly in the direction of the house next door, but turned after a few seconds and returned to him. "Good girl," he rubbed her ears and they went inside, where he offered her a treat. For the rest of the afternoon, Flotsam, uncharacteristically, sat in a chair in the sunroom where she could observe the beach. Normally she would be at his side wherever he was in the house. But she seemed to be watching for something and, whatever it was, she apparently thought her best chance at seeing it was when it came up the beach.

Rock busied himself until 1:00 p.m. getting ready for his trip to Holland, his haircut and whatever else the evening might hold in store for him. Dressed neatly in black slacks, an open-collar dress shirt and sport coat, he stared at his reflection in the bathroom mirror. He ran his hand through his hair and then took a comb and tried to part it, but it lay a bit unruly on both sides. *At least it's growing out.* "Flotsam, come on, girl. Let's go." For the past two weeks all he had had to do was say the word *go* and Flotsam responded with wagging tail and scrambling feet. Today there was nothing. He walked to the door of the sunroom. She was transfixed on the beach to the south, in the direction of the newly occupied house next door. "Flotsam, come on, girl," he repeated, this time patting his leg.

She looked at him and then back to the beach.

"What's this? You don't want to go with me?" he said with special emphasis on the words he thought always thrilled her. He had never left her in the cottage unattended. Quite frankly he was afraid to, knowing what an exception Jan had made to her hard and fast rule about pets. But he was not going to miss this appointment. He walked over and patted her head, "Come on, girl. Let's go. I can't be late." He checked his watch, 1:05 p.m. He'd already put her water, food and dog dish in the Jeep. If she wasn't going to go with him, he'd have to move that back into the house and then feed and water her, all of which would only make him later than he thought he already was.

Flotsam whimpered at him.

"Last chance. You can stay here if you like, but I better not find anything torn up." He walked away to collect his car keys. When he turned around he saw her standing in the doorway to the sunroom, looking at him. When their eyes met, she whimpered again.

"You going or not?"

With an obvious reluctance, she moved toward him.

"OK. Good choice." But as they made their way out of the house and toward the Jeep, her enthusiasm to go was far below what it had always been before. On the hour-and-a-half trip to Holland, instead of occupying her normal seat next to him as co-pilot, she curled herself up in the back of the Jeep. Occasionally Rock would look back or move the rearview mirror to see what she was doing, but she never moved.

His haircut with Phyllis had been carefully arranged for 3:00 p.m., so that he was her last appointment of the day. He hoped that had not changed. When he had called two weeks ago he asked the receptionist if he could speak directly to Phyllis if she wasn't too busy. He had been lucky enough to catch her in between appointments. She remembered him and told him she'd thought of him often and wondered if he would come back as he promised. Rock didn't remember promising but was flattered that she'd remembered him. He had also decided there was no discreet way of knowing if she was married, engaged, or seeing someone except to simply wade into those waters and test them. While he had her on the phone, he asked if she'd allow him to buy her a drink after their appointment. Without hesitation she had said she'd like that.

At 2:55 p.m. he found a parking spot, almost the same one he'd had before, a little past the salon. He pulled a bag from between the seats and took out Flotsam's dog dishes, a baggie containing her food and a bottle of water. It was her habit to express boundless joy at the sight of these things, but this time she did not budge from her curled position on the back seat. Equally as uncharacteristic, she made no move to eat when Rock set the food and water next to her. Concerned, he reached over and stroked her from the top of her head to the base of her tail. "Are you all right, girl?" In response she did not move. It was now 3:00 p.m. and reluctantly Rock closed the car door, clicked the remote lock and headed for the salon with mixed emotions. Part of him was incredibly anxious to see Phyllis again, but another part was concerned about his dog.

"Well, I see we've dispensed with the stocking cap," she said cheerfully as Rock pulled open the salon door and stepped inside. Standing behind the reception counter, he could only see the top part of her, but that was enough. She was, he thought, as stunningly beautiful as he'd remembered.

He smiled at her, "It's growing!"

She clapped her hands together gleefully, "See, I told you it would grow back. So how's the noggin? No side effects from the fall, I hope." As he stopped in front of her on the opposite side of the reception counter, she extended her hand.

He took it, replying, "I'm just fine." Her hand was soft, and he was gentle in how he held it and shook it, not wanting to let go.

She blushed slightly but kept hold of his hand, leading him around the counter saying, "Come on back and let's see what we need to do today." She held his hand all the way back to her station. Her perfume was intoxicating, and for the moment he forgot about Flotsam and whatever was ailing her.

As she began her work, she asked him, "What's new?" He was relieved that she had apparently forgotten about wanting to know the origin of his first name. He told her the story of how he'd come upon Flotsam. Attentively, she "Ohoo'd" and "Ahhh'd" at the appropriate times. Rock asked her if she liked dogs.

"Cats," she replied, not exactly answering his question. "I have two of them. I live in a condo, so cats are just easier," she continued.

Rock told her the story of how Flotsam had melted his landlady's heart, then added, "But I can understand why property owners are reluctant. If you don't take care of them properly..." he paused thoughtfully, "Well, any pet for that matter can make a mess of things real quick."

Phyllis had a different take. "Oh, I don't know. I think cats are pretty maintenance-free. If I go away for a long weekend or go on vacation, I just ask my neighbor to stop in to fill up their food and water dishes and clean the litter box. You couldn't do that with a dog."

You wouldn't do that with a dog, he thought, but didn't pursue it. They were apparently at different places when it came to pets, so he changed the subject. Wanting to make sure he still had a date he said, "I hope you don't think I was too forward asking you out for a drink."

She stopped trimming his hair, put her hands gently on each shoulder and looked at him through his reflection in the mirror. "If I tell you something will you not think I'm too forward?"

"Of course not," he replied.

"I was disappointed you didn't ask me out the first time you were here."

Staring at her in the mirror, he said, "I wanted to, but I didn't know..." he struggled to find the right words... "What your situation was. You know what I mean? I thought about you all the way back home. I almost turned around once, but thought better of it."

She winked at his reflection, "Well, Mr. Shy, I'm glad you didn't forget about me." Returning to her work, she asked him, "So, how long have you lived on Lake Michigan?"

"Not long. I rented the place at the end of September, and I'll go back to Flint on Memorial Day weekend."

"Oh."

He thought he detected some disappointment.

"So what takes you back to Flint? Work?"

"Work and Flint, Phyllis, are two words that do not go together these days. I'm recently retired from GM because they decided to close the damn plant." He could feel his anger rising. "I have a place there."

"A house?"

He explained to her about Patti and Russ and the loft, compressing decades of life into a couple of minutes.

When he was finished, she asked, "What did you do at GM?"

He told her and was surprised at her take on things.

"Well, Rock, you must be doing all right for yourself. It can't be cheap to rent along the lake even if it is the off-season." He wanted to tell her that 'how he was doing' wasn't the point, instead he said, "Yeah, I came out of it OK, but a lot of others didn't."

"Maybe they weren't as careful as you." She stopped her work for a minute and looked at him in the mirror. "You know what I mean? Maybe they didn't manage their money as well or something. I don't know..."

He stared at her in the mirror before he answered because what she was saying was in a large part true, so he decided to agree with her. "Yeah, you're right. When half of your take-home pay is overtime and it's been that way for years and then that rug gets yanked from underneath you, if you haven't planned, it will bite you hard."

Then he switched gears, "Can we talk about something more pleasant?"

"Sure," she said, smiling at his reflection.

"Is there someplace special you'd like to go for drinks and maybe a bite to eat? I mean I'm going to rely on you to tell me where to take you, because you know Holland and I don't." The 'bite to eat' part might have been pushing the edge of the envelope a little bit, but he thought, *what the hell; nothing ventured, nothing gained.*

Before answering him, she put her hands on his shoulders again and asked, "OK, how's it looking?"

Staring at his reflection in the mirror and moving his head from side to side, he said, "Another three weeks and you will never be able to tell I had my head shaved."

"Good" she said, loosening the cape. "Just let me trim your neck up a little bit and we can get out of here."

"Are you done for the day, I hope?"

"Yes. I'm all yours," she smiled at him in the mirror, bent close to his ear and whispered, "I rescheduled two appointments after you called and asked me out." She lifted the cape from him, handed him the mirror and spun him around to face her.

He looked at her and she winked at him. Rock handed the mirror back to her and said, "Then let's go! I've been looking forward to seeing you since I left here the last time. Tell me where you'd like to go."

"OK. Can do. Why don't you wait for me up front, sweetie. I'm going to change out of this smock." As he turned to walk away he noticed her reflection in the mirror. Her back was to him, so she must have thought he couldn't see. In the mirror, he saw her whisper something to another hair dresser at the station next to them and flash her a thumbs-up. Rock had no idea what she had said, but he read the thumbs-up as a sign that Phyllis was looking forward to the evening as much as he was. She was beautiful, and that was always the first ingredient that had ever drawn him to a woman. He wondered briefly where the evening might go and allowed a faint smile to cross his face.

As she approached the reception desk where he was waiting, she was smiling. His eyes struggled to take all of her in. She'd changed from a low pump to stiletto heels. Her black slacks were skin tight, hugging every sensuous curve of her hips and legs. The leopard-print blouse plunged at the neckline revealing just enough cleavage that his eyes couldn't help but land there. He looked at her and simply said, "Wow."

"You like?" She put a hand on one hip and slowly turned around for him.

"You look fantastic."

They argued good-naturedly again over how much Rock owed her. They wound up settling on a five-dollar price for the haircut, as they had last time. Phyllis pocketed the ten dollars Rock slid back to her from the change for the twenty he'd given her.

He helped her on with her coat and, as they headed for the door, Phyllis took his hand in hers. Rock's heart soared.

Chapter Fifteen

Flotsam's Misbehavior

Outside the salon, still holding hands, Rock glanced down the street at the Jeep, remembering Flotsam, but before he could say anything, Phyllis suggested that they walk in the opposite direction to a microbrewery she knew. Rock explained that was fine, but he needed to check on Flotsam first.

"She's with you?" Phyllis asked with surprise.

"Yes, but on the trip down here she wasn't herself. I hope she's not sick. This will just take a minute."

"Uh, yeah. OK. Not a problem."

From half a block away, Rock clicked the automatic door locks and saw the taillights flash. Usually that sound caused Flotsam's head to appear in the window, but not this evening. He opened the passenger side door and the two of them peered in. Flotsam, who was still curled on the back seat, lifted her head, looked at them for a moment and then put her head back down. From what Rock could tell, none of the food or water had been touched. "This just isn't like her," Rock said with real worry.

The two backed out of the car; Rock closed the door and clicked the remote lock. A strong gust of wind pushed Phyllis against him. He caught her, took her arm and wrapped it through his. She snuggled close to him.

Over drinks she asked the question he'd been hoping she'd forgotten about. "So how did you come by the name Rock? Is that your given name?"

"No, but it's what everyone calls me." Phyllis smiled at him. He continued, "A Gunnery Sergeant in Vietnam gave it to me. He thought I was 'steady as a rock.' A couple of the guys heard him say that and it has stuck with me ever since."

"You were in Vietnam?" she asked, sounding somewhat incredulous.

Rock laughed, "Yeah. Hope that doesn't make me too old." He figured Phyllis was between forty-five and fifty. While more than ten years difference in age is a lot between a couple, he didn't think he was too old for her. Unless, of course, he had miscalculated her age and she was younger than he surmised, a likelihood that he thought possible given her great body.

"I mean," she continued laughing at the awkwardness of her earlier response, "I was only about ten or so when that was over, but I remember seeing it on TV almost every night. It must have been horrible."

Rock did some quick math, figured he had her age pegged about right and then answered, "It was and then some."

"Is that how you got the..." she had started to ask this, not thinking how awkward it might be, so she cut the question off.

"The limp?" Rock completed the question.

She nodded.

"Yes."

His brief answer spoke volumes to her, so she let a silence fall between them, unsure where to go from here.

Rescuing her, avoiding memories that still haunted him and changing the subject, he said, "So you've always lived in Holland?"

"Yes, born and raised here. I've traveled a little in the states, but never abroad. When my daughter graduated from high school, I thought we would get to travel then, but it didn't happen. Sometimes things have a way of just never working out."

"We? You mean you and your daughter?"

She shook her head. "No," and she paused before adding, "I've been married twice, Rock. My first husband is my daughter's biological father. He bailed on us when she was three."

"That must have been tough."

"Well it was, for a while, but I remarried when she was six." My second husband ran his own construction company. Two years ago I caught him in an affair with a woman twenty years younger than him. He broke my heart..." He thought for a moment she was going to cry. Then her fragility swept away, she looked at Rock and said, "But I got a good settlement out of the jackass, and he's out of my life for good, forever."

There was no mistaking the vindictive bent to her tone. Rock asked, "So how old is your daughter?"

"Twenty-one. Janelle is a cosmetologist now, like me. In fact, her station is the one next to mine at the salon. I should have introduced you, but the customer she was with is a bit finicky. Likes to think that Janelle is completely devoted to her when she's in her chair, if you know what I mean," Phyllis said, her tone somewhat mocking, "But you might still get to meet her. She may join us if her seven o'clock appointment doesn't show up."

Rock was surprised at this, but not necessarily disappointed, depending on how Phyllis answered his next question. "Do the two of you live together?"

"Oh, heaven's no, Rock. That would be a recipe for disaster. She has her own life to live. All I can do is hope she doesn't make some of the same mistakes I made."

He probed further, "Is she seeing anybody?"

"Yes." She hesitated, but then decided to disclose, "He's in the Marine Corps. He's in Iraq," Phyllis paused and then added, a tone of disgust in her voice, "On his second tour of duty there."

"I was in the Marine Corps," he said with that certain sense of pride characteristic of all Marines, past and present.

Almost dismissively, Phyllis replied, "Well, you at least had the good sense to get out. He's told Janelle that he plans to make a career of it. I've told her that's no life for her, following him all over the face of the earth. Besides, she's too young to commit to any one man. That was the mistake I made with my first husband. I married that idiot when I was eighteen. I told myself I was not going to make that kind of mistake again and then look at what I did. Sometimes, Rock, I think marriage is the worst institution there is. I try to live my life without regret, but if I had it to do all over again, I don't think I'd ever get married."

It was a bit of a rant, Rock thought. He wasn't offended by her observations on marriage, but he was slightly offended at her opinion concerning Marines. However, Phyllis was not the first divorcée Rock had ever dated, nor was she the first divorcée he'd dated who was also a mother. As he quickly evaluated what he'd just heard, he had to give Phyllis kudos for at least being forthright and honest with him. He recalled one woman from the plant he'd dated for two months before she had told him she had two young children. When he'd asked her why she had not told him earlier about them, she answered she was afraid they would scare him off. He'd stopped seeing her after that, not because the kids had scared him off, but her deception had.

Phyllis asked him, "How about you? Ever married?"

"Once, but it didn't work out."

The detail was insufficient for Phyllis. "Was it long term?"

The term "long term" sounded a little too "legal" to Rock, so he replied, "I don't know. I guess it depends on what you mean by 'long term'."

Phyllis responded, "Well, ten years or longer. I mean that was the term my lawyer used to get my settlement."

Rock filed that bit of information away and said, "No, not that long; only about a year." The memory of opening the bedroom door and finding his wife in bed with a co-worker still hurt him, but he'd learned to cope. "It was a long time ago. I don't even know where she is now for sure. Last I heard it was Florida. We didn't have any children, nothing left in common, so we just parted ways."

Phyllis's cell phone buzzed, and she looked to see who it was. "It's Janelle. I should take this."

Rock nodded.

Phyllis took the call and hung up after saying, "I'm sorry. I wish you could have met him." She explained that her daughter's appointment had indeed arrived on time and wanted a full array of services, all of which were going to run well past 9 p.m..

Both of them had finished their drinks, so Rock said, "Is there someplace special you'd like to go for dinner?"

Phyllis thought for a minute and suggested an Italian place down the street. Outside, she took his arm and snuggled close. There was little doubt that the attraction was mutual, but the chilly air reminded him of Flotsam. He estimated they were about four blocks away and, at the risk of spoiling the moment, he told Phyllis he wanted to walk back and check on his dog. There was a blanket on the back seat beside her. He thought she was smart enough that if she really got cold she could curl up in it. So arm-in-arm they returned to the Jeep, only to find Flotsam still curled where they'd left her almost two hours earlier, her food and water untouched. Rock opened the door and asked her if she was all right. She raised her head, looked at him and then returned to her curl. He shrugged his shoulders and told Phyllis, "This is so unlike her. I can't imagine what's wrong. She was fine this morning."

"I'm sorry," she purred.

Before he closed the door he took the blanket and placed it over Flotsam. With that done and satisfied he could do no more, he turned to Phyllis and said, "Well, let's go have dinner. Would you like to drive or walk?"

She pulled him close to her and said, "Let's walk, if you promise to stay close and keep me warm."

"Done," he said, hiding his concern over his dog.

The restaurant was crowded and they did not have a reservation, so they waited thirty minutes at the bar and drank wine. Each enjoyed a superb pasta dinner with salad and more wine. Before the waiter arrived with the dessert menu, Phyllis took Rock's hand in hers, leaned into him conspiratorially and said, "Before he comes and offers you dessert, I made some chocolate chip cookies for us and I have a fresh bottle of Bailey's Irish Cream that goes great with coffee. Why don't we go to my place?"

This was not his first rodeo. He had bedded women on the first date before. In fact, Mary Ann, his ex, had been one such woman. He'd often thought that he should, perhaps, show more caution, more restraint, and things might work out better in the long run. But he'd never followed his own advice when it came to women, nor the advice of Patti. She had always told him, "Slow down, don't move too fast, instead get to know her a little more before you bang her, you big stud."

As Phyllis squeezed his hand, he thought that he would probably not heed that advice tonight either. "I'd love to."

Rock paid the bill and they walked to the Jeep. Flotsam did not move as Rock opened the door for Phyllis and she settled into the passenger seat. "Tell me where to go."

"It's not far. I walk to work unless the weather is really foul." She directed him to a beautiful brick condo development just off the center part of Holland's downtown business district. He pulled into the driveway in front of her garage door, shut the car off and looked around at Flotsam. "You haven't been out of the car all day. Do you need to go?" He looked over at Phyllis, "Would that be OK? She's quick and I've got plastic bags to clean up if she..."

"Yeah, sure. I'll go on in and put on the coffee." At this point she leaned over and kissed him on the cheek, which prompted Flotsam to lift her head and look at her. "Just come on in when you're finished. I'd invite her in too, but, you know, my cats just wouldn't..."

He interrupted, "That's fine, Phyllis. I'm not sure how Flotsam would react to cats, either. Those introductions will have to wait for another time." He got out and went around to open her car door. Phyllis went in as Rock took a minute to exercise Flotsam. "Come on, girl. You must have to at least pee."

Nothing.

"You're going to make me come back out here and check on you every fifteen minutes, aren't you?" Again, the dog lay still, curled in her spot. He closed the door, tapped the lock button on the remote and headed for the condo's front door.

As soon as she heard the locks engage, Flotsam jumped from her spot on the back seat to her spot on the front passenger's seat and began to bark as loudly and frenetically as Rock had ever heard her. It was after 9:00 p.m., and the racket she was setting up in this quiet street of condominiums sounded like Michigan Stadium on a football Saturday. He hustled back to the Jeep, opened the door and said, "OK, I thought so, come on let's go."

The dog did not move. For the first time since he'd found her, he was losing patience. "You are going to come out here and take care of business, one way or the other." He reached down between the two front seats, grabbed her leash and attached it to her collar. He pulled, she resisted at first, then seemed to think better of it, and jumped down to the ground. "Now, cut out the foolishness and get down to business."

The patch of grass in front of Phyllis's condo was small, measuring maybe fifteen feet wide and twenty feet deep, and that included a well-cultivated bed of shrubs lining the walkway to the front door. Frozen blades of thick grass crackled under their feet and their footprints, illuminated by the condo's front porch light, were visible in the heavy frost that already covered the ground. Flotsam seemed intent on smelling every blade of grass as she worked her way back and forth across the patch. "Flotsam, let's not make a career of this."

The dog looked over her shoulder at him and put her nose back down to the grass. Finally, after what seemed an eternity and more coaxing than he'd ever done, she squatted and peed. As she returned her nose to the grass for more smell-grazing, Rock tugged her lead and said, "Oh, no you don't. You're done. Let's go. Back in the Jeep."

She did not struggle. She knew the collar and leash were her master as much as was Rock, but she did not hurry, either. At the Jeep he had to coax her to get in. Again he closed the door and clicked the locks. Again, before he had taken two steps toward the condo, she began her racket, so loud, so constant, that the Jeep's windows did little except to amplify the sound before it echoed off the brick façade of the condo. He let her go this time, thinking that she would quickly settle down. But as he closed the door behind him, Phyllis was there asking him if something was wrong.

The closed door muffled her barking somewhat, but the pair could still hear her. "I don't know what's wrong with her. I've never seen..." he smiled at her, "Or heard her like this." Flotsam gave no indication she would relent.

Weakly, Phyllis smiled back at him but said, "Rock, I'm sorry, but the neighbors..."

"I know." He had not removed his coat so he stepped back out into the cold and returned to the Jeep. "Flotsam," he said with an angry edge to his voice he'd never used with her before, "What the hell is the matter with you?" Her barking had stopped as soon as she'd seen him coming back to her. She stood on the front passenger seat and looked at him, her ears cocked forward and her eyes glaring an intensity characteristic of her breed. "You've got to settle down." He sat down on the driver's seat and stared into those plaintive eyes that had captured his heart. His wrath diminished somewhat, he reached across and rubbed her ears, "C'mon, girl. Don't ruin this for me." His touch seemed to settle her, so he lingered for a minute or two, rubbing her ears and stroking her neck. "There, that's better. I'm sorry you have to stay out here, but there are cats in there and they don't like you, and I'm pretty sure you won't like them. I'll come out and check on you every now and then. Now go back there and eat your dinner and settle down."

He got out, ritually locked the car, and this time got all the way to the front door before the racket began anew. He threw his hands up in disgust, knowing his plans for a big evening were now officially over. He opened the door and his jaw dropped. Phyllis stood under a light in the hallway in a black negligée, open in the front to reveal a red brassiere, red panties and black hose running up her magnificent legs and held in place by garters. She was holding a tray of cookies and a steaming mug of Bailey's and coffee.

He could feel himself becoming erect, but the racket from outside was officially announcing the end of anything else to come. He shrugged his shoulders and whispered, barely audible above the din, "I am so sorry, but..."

She set the tray and the coffee down on a table in the hallway, came to him and kissed him deeply. He would have been lost in her fragrance and her body if it hadn't been for the infernal racket coming from his damned dog. "Do me two favors," she said as she laid her head next to his ear.

"Anything."

"First, come back soon. Second, leave her at home."

He laughed, kissed her again and then said, "You got it."

As he walked to his car, he could see condos that had before been dark were now lit, and he could see parting curtains and blinds as neighbors were disturbed. They were in all likelihood angry, for which he could not blame them. He knew only too well whom to blame. However, by the time he was halfway to the Jeep, Flotsam had gone quiet, a silence that carried over for quite some time except for a couple of minutes as she ate her food and drank some water as they drove. Once that was done, she took her usual position in the front passenger seat, peering out of the windshield into the late night's darkness as if nothing had happened.

Finally at some point near Muskegon, Rock's anger spilled out of him. He looked over at her and angrily asked, "Do you know how badly you showed your ass tonight?"

Flotsam glanced over at him and then returned to her co-pilot's vigil.

"Dammit Flotsam!" he roared. He turned his eyes from the road and gave her a long, angry look.

The dog, never wavering from her duties, stared ahead into the darkness. They drove on. "You hear me. I know you do. I know you know how angry I am at you right now." He saw her blink a couple of times, but her head and eyes remained straight ahead.

You idiot! He turned his anger on himself, where it would get a response. *You're talking to her like she can understand you. She's a dog, stupid.* Frustration kept its grip on him and he, in turn, held a death's grip on the steering wheel. When they pulled up the dune behind Far-Far-View, Rock shut the Jeep off and got out, followed immediately by Flotsam. At the edge of the porch light's illumination, she proceeded to empty both her bladder and her bowels while Rock collected her food and water dishes from the backseat. She waited at his side while he fumbled with his keys trying to find the right one. Once inside, she went directly to her stained rug in front of the fireplace and lay down. Rock said nothing to her as he went about his bedtime preparations, but before turning in he decided to have the last word. Striding into the living room, he looked down at her and said, "This isn't the last you're going to hear about this."

Flotsam awoke at the sound of his voice and looked up at him. As he spoke, she leaned her ears forward, fixed those intense eyes on him and turned her head from side to side quizzically, as if she was really trying to understand him, but couldn't.

What the hell! You don't understand. You're just a dog.

Chapter Sixteen

An Apparition

Events conspired to keep Claire from departing for the lake house until November 15th. Some of the delay was her own indecision which, on several occasions, had led her to almost cancel the trip. That would have been just fine with Ingrid, who continued to hound her. Then there was the hope that she had actually helped James and Mary find work. Just yesterday that optimism had been dashed. Last night, she'd decided it was time to move forward, retreat to the lake house and think things through.

She had just started to load the Range Rover with her and Flower's things when the Chavezes pulled in the driveway behind her. Maria was in the passenger seat with a panicked look on her face. Jesus, who was actually shorter than Maria, sat a full head higher than her behind the wheel of the Ford F-150 truck. He was beaming and waved at Claire as he pushed the gear selector into park and turned off the clanking diesel engine. As Maria stepped down, Claire heard her mutter something that sounded like a Hail Mary. As she stepped up to give each of them a hug, she was able to see the pillows on the driver's seat that gave Jesus his heads-up advantage. She suppressed a chuckle, keeping it inside her, as she watched him retrieve a carry-tray of three hot beverages from the truck before closing the driver's side door. "Good morning, Ms. Claire," he said sweetly to her.

"Good morning. I didn't expect to see you two this morning."

Maria offered, "We just wanted to stop by and thank you for what you did for James and Mary."

"But I..."

Jesus interrupted, "Ms. Claire, why don't you and Maria go inside, and I will finish loading the car for you." He took one of the beverages from the carry-tray and said, "I bought you a Mexican Starbucks. Go inside and relax while I do this." He handed Maria the carry-tray with the other two beverages and Maria led her inside the house.

Over her shoulder Claire said, "Thank you, Jesus." Once inside, she asked Maria, "What is a Mexican Starbucks?"

Maria chuckled, "It's what he calls a mix of gas station cappuccino and gas station coffee. This one is half hot chocolate and half coffee. If you don't like it, it's OK, Ms. Claire."

Claire chuckled and tried the drink. "It's actually quite good. I might not buy Starbucks again." They both laughed.

"Ms. Claire, James and Mary are really appreciative of what you tried to do for them. We all want you to know that."

"I'm just sorry it didn't work out, Maria. I should have thought about their family situations more carefully." Van Zandt Engineering, International, had offered James a job troubleshooting their computer networks, but a requirement of the job would be to travel internationally as much as twenty days out of every thirty. Mary had been offered a position as a full-time nanny with an affluent client of Ethan Hoffman's, but that job entailed daily travel into Grand Rapids and frequent weekend work. Both James and Mary had spouses and small children of their own. Both had declined because they could not be away from their families as much as these positions would require.

"No, Ms. Claire, please don't blame yourself. What you did was wonderful. They discussed it with Jesus and me. It was not an easy decision for either of them. We assured them that we understood and that we were sure you would understand, too. You, do understand, don't you, Ms. Claire?"

Claire nodded. She could feel the tears welling up. "Yes, Maria, I understand." There was a long pause in their conversation, and then Claire continued, "I want you to tell them both that I think they made the right decision, the courageous decision. Family is important, the most important thing, and I'm proud of them for keeping their families first."

Before Maria could respond, Jesus stepped into the kitchen and announced that he'd finished loading the car, including Flower, who was raring to go.

Maria reached across the table and took Claire's hand in hers, "Ms. Claire, I know Mr. Mumford is there if you need anything, but if you should need us, you know all you have to do is call and we will be there. Please be careful. It's going to get cold and snowy, and that house is so big."

She patted Maria's hand and said, "Flower and I will be fine, but it's kind of you to offer. Thanks, Maria. Jesus, thanks for loading the car. Flower and I need to get going."

The drive from Holland to Shelby usually took about an hour and a half at the speed limit. Once she was through Grand Haven, Claire set the cruise control at sixty-five, just below the seventy-mile-an-hour limit, content to enjoy the blue sky and sunshine, even if the temperature was hovering around freezing. Flower sat for a while on the passenger seat, but somewhere around Muskegon lay down and took a siesta until Claire turned at the farm stand on to the gravel road leading into Little Point Sable. Stretching, the dog looked out the window, and when Claire turned at the Stone Church onto the two-track road that led to the lake house, Flower began an excited whimper. "You have to go potty, girl? Hang on, we're almost there." Claire was certain that was the difficulty. Flower had not been here in over a year and a half. She had just been a puppy then. She couldn't possibly know where she was. For Claire, the distraction of the dog was welcome. For the past half hour she'd been dreading going into the house that was filled with so many memories.

She had never been up here much in the winter months, and as she approached Glenn Road she was struck by the solitude that had closed in around her. Traffic on US 31 north of Muskegon had been light. On Shelby Road between US 31 and the farm stand, she had seen one or two other vehicles. Since turning onto the gravel road at the farm stand and the two-track at the stone church, she had seen no other signs of life except a car parked at the top of the dune behind the house next to hers.

At about noon, as she pulled into her driveway, she hit the remote and the garage door rolled up. "OK, girl, ready or not, we're here." Flower looked at her, cocked her head from side to side, acknowledging that she knew Claire was talking to her. When Claire opened the car door, the lab jumped down and bounded on to the driveway. Claire was surprised when Flower stopped a few feet outside the garage, turned toward the house north of them, lifted her big head up and barked excitedly as if to announce, "OK, I'm here. Where are you?" Claire gave her a few minutes, but the dog never moved from her spot in the driveway and continued to look toward the neighboring house. Finally Claire called her, and Flower followed her into the house.

Bob Mumford had laid in basic necessities and made sure the heat and the hot water were ready upon their arrival. Still, the house had been closed up for the better part of two years and had a stale smell. Claire knew the remedy lay in the refreshing winds that rolled off Lake Michigan. As her first act of settling in, she opened the thick, heavy, lined curtains that covered a wall of windows facing Lake

Michigan. The sudden light into the dark house made both Flower and her blink. Despite the fact that the heat was on, Claire looked at Flower and said, "What do you say, girl? Let's open this slider and get some air in here." The slider opened onto a stone-walled patio, the only break in the wall giving way to a few steps that led to the dunes. Flower went out on the patio and again stared northward toward the neighboring house. "Hey you, come on back in here. We've got to get unloaded and settled in. Maybe after that we can go down to the beach." Obediently, though reluctantly, the big dog wandered back in and followed Claire to the garage, where she began unloading.

They spent the next couple of hours getting settled. With all the curtains opened and the sun moving more and more westward, the inside of the house brightened and the stale air cleared. It was late afternoon before she and Flower ambled down the steps to the beach, where Claire followed Flower's lead as she headed north past the neighboring house. Flower kept her attention focused on that house until they were well past it, as if expecting to see something or someone there. After about twenty minutes of walking, Claire decided that she was not dressed for the wind chill, which made it colder than she had thought it would be. As they turned and headed toward home, Flower returned her focus to the house just north of theirs. By the time they were walking up the patio steps to their house, the big dog seemed to be almost dejected.

Back inside, Claire fixed herself a cup of hot chocolate and settled into a deeply padded rocking chair next to the lakeside windows at one end of the great room. In her hand was a book she'd selected from the large library that she and Alan had collected. That library had gotten a lot of use in the summers during the years the girls were growing up. She sat down and began to read from Charles Dickens' *Tale of Two Cities*:

It was the best of times, it was the worst of times, it was the age of wisdom, it was the age of foolishness, it was the epoch of belief, it was the epoch of incredulity, it was the season of Light, it was the Season of Darkness, it was the season of Hope, it was the winter of Despair...

It was about 5:30 p.m. when she awoke with a start, as the book fell from her lap onto the floor. It woke Flower, who had been asleep on the floor beside her. The sun was low in the western sky and deepening shades of yellow, orange and red were flooding into the darkening house as night descended. Claire bent down to pick up the book and was about to stroke Flower on the head, when she looked in the direction of the floor-to-ceiling stone fireplace at the opposite end of the great room. She saw Alan kneeling in front of the raised hearth; she watched him strike a match and reach for the handle that would turn on the gas. Her heart was racing as she saw him turn his head toward her and smile that warm, gentle smile of his that always said to her how much he loved her. Then Flower nuzzled her hand and broke the spell. Sitting up now, the big dog could only watch as Claire covered her face with her hands and cried.

Chapter Seventeen

The Introduction

Despite not getting home until 1:00 a.m. after his ill-fated evening with Phyllis, Rock awoke at his usual time, 7:00 a.m. He had slept soundly, and since his fall he was always thankful for a peaceful night's sleep. He also had a roaring hard-on after dreaming of Phyllis and her filmy negligée, an erotic reminder that he was still mad as hell at his dog.

From Flotsam's spot on her rug in front of the fireplace, she could hear him stirring in the bathroom. She lifted her head, but did not get up, already sensitive to a change in their routine. Normally, when Rock got up he would come to her and playfully rub her head and ears before heading to the bathroom. Now, when he came into the kitchen, he did not acknowledge her; another change to the routine. He fixed her food and set it on the floor in its usual spot without a word; more change. She let it sit for a moment as if she was expecting him to say something. When he didn't, she got up, ate and headed for the back door. He followed her, opened the door and let her out. But Rock did not stay at the door as he usually did as she went about her morning duties. This morning he kept her waiting while he fixed his tea and a bowl of cereal and popped two slices of bread in the toaster. When she woofed, he ambled to the door and wordlessly let her in, then returned to his breakfast in the sunroom. Rock knew how sensitive she was, and these subtle changes to their rhythm clearly signaled his displeasure with her. From his seat at the table, he gave her a hard stare.

She raised her head and turned it from side to side.

Seeing he had her attention, Rock said, "Don't play like you don't know what you did," his voice stern. "You've never acted like that. So why did you pick last night to show your ass? You were an embarrassment," he wagged his finger at her.

Her head twisted from side to side.

"I should have been waking up with Phyllis this morning instead of sitting here angry at you. You would have been just fine in the car. There was a blanket in there and it wasn't that cold last night. What the hell got into you?" He wasn't screaming; he knew better than to do that. Early on in their first few days together, Rock had accidentally dropped a metal mixing dish on the kitchen's tile floor. Flotsam ran to the bedroom and hid under the bed for hours. Loud things frightened the bejesus out of her, but there was no mistaking the anger in his voice.

"So here's the deal. The next time I go to Holland, your ass is staying here and, if you make a single mess, there will be hell to pay." Flotsam, who still had not moved, simply laid her head down between her front paws without taking her eyes off of him. "Listen to me. I'm talking to you like you can understand any of this." He shook his head.

After cleaning up from breakfast, he shaved, dressed, and settled into an easy chair in the sunroom with *The Collective Works of Thomas Paine*, which he was still trying to comprehend. By 9:00 a.m. on Sunday, November 16th, *Paine* had proven to be an effective soporific. He was sound asleep when Flotsam erupted in a fusillade of barks and frantic running between the windows of the sunroom and the back door.

Her behavior did little to endear her to him. "Flotsam," he ordered, "Stop it!" She did not listen. He got up, went to the windows and saw a woman and a dog on the beach below, both of them looking up at him. He wasn't sure if the woman could hear, but it appeared her dog could hear Flotsam. It was barking, straining against its leash and looking up at him.

Flotsam was frenetic. Cranking up his voice a bit, Rock sternly told her, "Flotsam, settle down." She jumped into a chair to gain a better vantage point, leaning forward on her forepaws and straining her back legs forward. Every muscle from head to tail was taut, and she shook as she fixed that intense stare of hers on the woman and the dog. She was so close to the window that every time she barked a circle of vapor formed on the inside. Her tail was furiously wagging in wide, fast strokes. When she wasn't barking, she was pitifully whimpering. "What the hell is the matter with you?" She swiveled her head around at him for a second and returned her attention to the two figures on the beach. Rock looked at his watch, 10:05 a.m. He'd been asleep about an hour. He checked the thermometer mounted outside one of the sliders off the sunroom. Though the sky was dark and threatening, the temperature was about thirty-three degrees. He checked the dune grass, long dried to a light tan by the killing frosts that had come with October's lengthening nights. The grass's lack of movement told him the lake's winds were down. It would be a good day for at least their morning walk, but not now. The way she was acting, and with that other dog on the beach, Rock figured she'd go down and make a fool out of herself. Flotsam quieted as the pair made their way north up the beach, but did not move from the chair as she continued to watch them.

At about 10:30 a.m. Rock looked out the window. Flotsam still sat in the chair, looking up the beach in the direction of the woman and the dog. They were now out of sight.

"OK, let's go for our walk, girl." The suggestion elicited a high-pitched squeal of delight. Flotsam bounded off the chair and scrambled for the cottage's back door. "All right. Just a minute. Let me get my gear on." While Rock donned his overalls and jacket, Flotsam sat by the back door, shaking, whimpering and padding her two front feet up and down in eager anticipation of their walk. Rock was used to this eagerness of hers. She couldn't wait to get to work. It was her habit, just as Dr. Meyer had suggested. However, he was not prepared for what was about to happen as he opened the back door and Flotsam hurtled past him toward the steps and the beach below, completely ignoring his repeated commands to "Stop!" "Wait!" "Come!" By the time he was at the top of the steps, she was already on the beach, apparently in hot pursuit of the woman and the dog. His anger at Flotsam returned with a vengeance. He vowed that when he caught her she was going on a leash, not the rope, and all walks for now and well into the future would be with her directly at his side, whether she liked to range or not.

By the time Rock reached the beach and looked north, Flotsam was a good quarter of mile ahead of him. Since the cast had come off he had been amazed not only at her speed, but her endurance. Beyond Flotsam, he could see the woman frantically trying to control her dog, which she had apparently unleashed. A chilly gust of wind made his eyes water, so he couldn't see clearly, but it appeared the other dog was running directly toward Flotsam. Within only a couple of seconds they collided, and Rock hoped he could get to Flotsam before the larger dog could do any significant damage to her. With his limp, he had never enjoyed running, nor did he look good doing it. He thought he must look like the hunchback Quasimodo, but this was no time to be self-conscious. His dog might be getting ripped to shreds. However, as he closed the distance between him and the two canines, he realized that they were frolicking together, rather than fighting. "Flotsam, come here!" He was close enough now that he could hear the woman, who like him had been jogging toward the dogs, calling, "Flower, come here!"

Their play had carried them into chest-deep water by now, and, as he approached, Rock commanded, "Flotsam, get over here to me!" He clapped his hands and patted them against both legs. Both dogs stopped their play and looked at him, but as quickly as they'd stopped, they began again. Rock threw his hands up in the air, and seeing neither dog trying to hurt the other, he altered his course, deciding he would talk with the woman.

"I'm sorry," he sputtered as he approached Claire. "I don't know what's gotten into her. We go for walks all the time, and I never have a problem with her coming when I call. Today she just bolted as soon as I opened the door." He turned to look at the two who were oblivious to the humans in their lives, fully engulfed in their own fun. When he turned back to her, he said with a chuckle that admitted both relief and frustration, "They do look like they are having fun. It's just that I don't like for her to disobey when I call her back to me."

Claire was watching the two run, jump and splash, "It's OK. I'm not sure how they can stand to be in that water. It must be close to freezing." She was bundled in a down jacket with the hood pulled up over her head. Around her neck hung a scarf that Rock thought was probably more fashionable than it was warm. At one point it likely had been pulled across her mouth, nose and cheeks to provide protection against the cold, but it was now pulled down so it hung around her neck. His first impression was that she was about his age, with a sparkling smile and quite attractive.

"I know," he said. "Yesterday was the first day she was allowed down here off of the leash. She's had a cast on her left front leg for the last three weeks, and yesterday the doctor removed it. The first place she headed for was the water." He extended his gloved hand, "I'm Ro--Geoff Graham," he said, wondering why he didn't want her to know his nickname.

"Claire Van Zandt," she replied, extending her gloved hand. "That's Flower, over there," she added, pointing to the Labrador.

"That's Flotsam," Rock said, pointing to his dog. "I've never seen her around other dogs, but she and Flower sure seem to have hit it off. She watched you walk past the house on the beach. She wanted to come down and see you then. I thought you were long gone, but I guess I was wrong, huh?" he said, laughing and pointing at the two, who were running up the beach past them now.

"I think they have senses we don't have," Claire said, laughing as well.

There was an awkward moment of silence between them, and finally Rock asked tentatively, "So have you and Flower ever seen Flotsam before?"

He could tell almost immediately that she found his question odd, but after a brief hesitation she answered, "No. Why do you ask?"

"Well, look at them. They are like long-lost friends."

"That they are."

"I found her... no, make that *she found me* about three weeks ago. I came home to find her sitting on my back door step. One of her front legs was pretty messed up. She was soaking wet, full of burrs and generally down on her luck. The way she took to Flower, I thought..."

"You thought that I might know who her owners were."

He hung his head. "Yes, and you have no idea how thankful I am that you have never seen my dog before. She has, as they say, touched my heartstrings, and the thought of having to give her up to someone else, no matter how good of a home she might be going back to, just tears me apart," he said, forgetting for the moment, his anger at Flotsam from the night before.

Claire responded, "They do have a way of getting to you." She tugged at the scarf to pull it up around her face as a gust of wind ruffled past them.

"We might be warmer if we walked. The lighthouse is this way," Rock said pointing north, "But you probably already know that, don't you?"

"About a mile and a half if memory serves me correctly." She glanced down at the jacket she was wearing, "Although I don't know if I'm quite dressed for that long of a walk, but we can start out and if I get too cold, I can just turn back." They had gone about a hundred yards when Claire stopped, pointed and said, "Uh, oh, better get ready, here they come." Flotsam, the speedier of the two, stopped very near them. Flower was only a second or two behind. Flotsam waited on her arrival, and when Flower had caught up, the two dogs looked at each other.

"Flotsam, don't you dare..."

"Flower, don't... "

The pair paid no attention to these commands and executed a perfectly synchronized head-to-tail shake with a fury that sent water and sand flying all over their owners.

Claire extended her arms and put her hands up, "No, Flower..."

Rock tried to sound scolding, "Flotsam, no! Go over there and twist," but the laugh at the end gave him away. They brushed the sand and the water off and resumed their walk up the beach. Rock turned to Claire and said, "I had to find a word different than *shake* when I want her to shake off the water and sand. One of the first tricks I taught her was to shake hands. So yesterday, after she got her cast off, I let her go in the water and when she came over to me, I told her to *shake*. She did exactly as I'd trained her. She sat down right then and there on the beach and held out her paw to shake hands with me. She is so damn smart."

Claire laughed and said to him, "Geoff, she really is a pretty dog. I think she's lucky to have found you."

"Yeah, thanks, but I'm the lucky one," again forgetting how angry he'd been at her. "I mean, she is such great company." They walked quietly together for a minute or so and Rock asked, "So, how old is Flower?"

"Two. I've had her since she was just a puppy. My daughters convinced me that I needed someone after my husband..." now Claire paused, surprised that she was being so forthcoming with this stranger. It was an awkward silence for both of them, because Rock thought he knew what she was going to say. Claire finished, "After my husband died."

"I'm sorry," Rock said.

They walked on a few more steps in silence, Flower on one side of Claire and Flotsam next to Rock.

"I haven't been up here very much since he's passed. It's been three years now and my daughters were right. Flower has made life easier. She is a great companion." The Labrador heard her name and looked up at Claire as they continued down the beach. Claire patted her on the head. "So do you live up here the year around, Geoff?"

It was weird to have someone call him by his given name. Even his mother and sister had taken to calling him Rock after Russ had told them what he'd done to earn the nickname. "Uh, no. I'm just renting for the winter. I'm renting Jan's place just north of yours."

The name Jan meant nothing to her. She knew that the Little Point Sable Association was a tight-knit community, but she had virtually unplugged from it since Alan died. She was curious, however, about one thing, "Has anyone given you a lot of grief about renting up here in the winter?"

Rock chuckled and replied, "Oh, yeah. People think I'm nuts!"

She laughed, "Me, too." Then she thought how that might sound to him. "Oh, no. I didn't mean..."

He let her wiggle a little bit, knowing what she meant.

"I meant that I have gotten a lot of grief, too, for coming up here in the winter."

"Oh, so you don't think I'm nuts?"

She smiled at him. "Maybe we're both crazy."

Rock liked her easiness. "So how long will you be staying?" he asked and then added, "And remember your answer may be used to calculate exactly how crazy you are!" When Claire didn't answer right away, he was afraid he might have carried the joke a little too far. "I'm sorry, I didn't mean to..."

Claire then quickly responded, "Uh, no Geoff. It's OK. Actually that's a good question; one I think even my daughters would like an answer to, but the fact is, I'm not sure."

They walked a while in silence, focusing their attention on the two dogs, each of whom had found a piece of driftwood that they were carrying down the beach. Rock estimated they were less than half way to the lighthouse at Little Sable Point when Claire suddenly gasped for a breath and grabbed his arm.

"Whoa, now! Hang on. Are you all right?"

Still holding his arm, she gasped again for air. That seemed to help, as did a third gasp. A moment passed, and she said rather weakly to him, "I'm sorry about this..."

"No problem. What can I do to help?"

"If you could help me over to that log." She pointed to a driftwood log on the beach nearer the dunes, "I'll be fine in just a minute."

He guided her to the log. The two dogs followed them. Claire sat down and Flower moved in immediately in front of her and put her head on Claire's lap.

"She's worried about you, Claire," Rock said, "And so am I. What happened?"

Now that someone else had seen, she could no longer continue to pooh-pooh these incidents. The shortness of breath was gone, almost as fast as it had come on her, but these episodes were apparently going to continue. In her head she tried to count, *was it two or three times now?* "I'm not sure," she told him. "They just come out of nowhere and as quick as they come, they seem to go."

"Have you seen a doctor?"

The way he asked the question, not judging her, just concerned, touched her, so she felt she could be honest. "No. My youngest daughter is getting married in December, and we've been busy planning things. I just haven't had the time..."

"Does she know about these episodes?" It just seemed like the logical question to ask.

"Heavens, no. She wouldn't have let me come up here if she had any idea. And my oldest daughter... well, let's just say she would have had me locked up in a hospital ward with the key around her neck if she knew."

"So, who does know besides you and me?"

She looked at him with a smile and winked. "That's it."

Flotsam had positioned herself next to Flower as if she was sensing some distress from her new-found canine friend. Rock looked at her and said to the two dogs, "Everything's all right, girls." He pointed to a bank of clouds to the west and said, "Weather's coming in. We'd better get you back home. Temps are going to drop like a rock this afternoon."

Claire posed no argument. Rock helped her up. "How are you feeling?"

"Fine. I'll be fine."

The walk back down the beach to Claire's house was filled with mostly small talk about the area. The dogs stayed close to their owners. Rock and Flotsam walked Claire and Flower to their door.

"I'm sorry you had to cut your walk short on my account."

"Not a problem. It has been a pleasure meeting you and Flower." He extended his hand, but this time he pulled his glove off. She reciprocated with her ungloved hand. He held on to her hand as he said, "I really think you should see your doctor, Claire. It would make Flower, Flotsam and me feel a lot better."

"Oh, now you are not playing fair," she said, mocking indignity at his invoking their pets' opinions on the matter.

"Well, whatever it takes to make you make that call," he said, smiling at her.

"Do you and Flotsam walk every day?"

"Every morning and every afternoon unless the weather is just too bad. Haven't had a lot of those days, but as winter gets closer, I'm sure we'll get chased off the beach more and more often."

"Well, perhaps Flower and I will see you and Flotsam again?"

"It's a date!" he said, and she could see him turning red.

Over her shoulder, as she stepped inside, she smiled at him and said somewhat coyly, "Yes, it is. See you again, soon."

Once inside the house with the door closed, she pressed her back against it, put her head in her hands and chided herself for such school-girl flirting. But it felt good in a way she had not felt in a long, long time.

Rock and Flotsam took the road the short distance back to their house, and as they walked, he looked down at Flotsam. "It's a date... can you believe I said that to her?" They walked on. "She's nice, isn't she?" The dog looked up at him and then focused her attention back down the road. "So did you and Flower have this introduction planned?" Flotsam didn't look up this time. "Not going to answer me, are you?" They kept walking. Once inside the cottage, Flotsam lay down on her rug and went to sleep. Rock tried to read a little more of Thomas Paine's wisdom, but his mind was distracted by the two beautiful women he'd just met since moving to the lakeshore. *This place,* he thought, *just might not be as lonely in the winter as everybody makes it out to be.*

Chapter Eighteen

Earl Grey

Claire sat at the dining room table with a fresh cup of coffee in one hand. Flower lay on the floor beside her. Unlike her first night at the lakeshore, she had slept well last night and was feeling alternately happy and sad this morning. On the one hand, she was looking forward to seeing the man whom she had met on the beach yesterday. It was comforting to know she had a neighbor so close and that she wasn't completely alone out here. On the other, those kinds of thoughts made her feel guilty. Her first night here, after seeing Alan's apparition in front of the fireplace, she'd gone from room to room hoping to catch another glimpse of him. It scared her to think that she might, yet she could not stop her search until she had looked into every room. She took a sip of coffee, looked down at Flower by her side. The two dogs seemed to enjoy each other's company. That thought seemed to assuage her guilt, so she gave herself permission to look forward to seeing Geoff again, whenever that might be, sooner rather than later, she hoped.

Rock had not talked to Russ or Patti since finding Flotsam, which was a long time for them to go without talking to one another. But he hadn't wanted to bother them while they were busy settling into their winter stay in Florida. Now, he was curious to know how it was going. He grabbed the landline and punched in Russ's cell phone number. He was surprised when Patti answered. "Patti, it's Rock."

"Hey, Rock, we were wondering if you were ever going to call," she said, somewhat scolding, but then her tone relented, "How are you?"

"Fine, Patti. Is Russ around?"

She chuckled, "That ol' boy is in seventh heaven down here. So much so that he went off fishin' this morning and left his cell phone on the kitchen table. I'm fished out, so you caught me just before I headed out the door for the pool. Everything OK up there in polar bear land?"

"Yeah, I just wanted to tell him that I met somebody." He knew that would pique her a little bit. While she didn't exactly interfere in his private life, in all the years they'd been friends Patti had never held back giving her opinion of the women in his life. Her opinions were never good, and that especially included his ex. He could imagine her getting ready for her next put down.

"Really? Who?"

"Well, she's got a face that would melt your heart. When she looks at me with those eyes, I would do anything for her."

"Oh, my God, Rock, you sound like a middle-school boy in love for the first time. C'mon now. Get a grip."

Talking to Patti was so different than talking to Russ. *Good ol' Practical Patti,* he thought as he chuckled to himself. Russ would have asked what she looked like, long hair, short hair, what color, how old she was and things like that. Patti, on the other hand, he was sure, simply wanted to reach through the phone and slap some sense into the silly sap on the other end.

"She's really smart. You can't believe all the tricks she can do." This was fun; he could see Patti cringing on the other end of the line. "And her hair is just beautiful, mostly white, with a brown saddle and a few hints of black here and there." He could barely contain himself. "We've been together for three weeks, almost a month, and after she got over the broken leg..."

"Wait a minute, Rock, you son of a ..." leaving the obscenity hanging, she demanded, "What are you talking about?"

Rock chuckled, unable to contain himself any longer.

Patti knew she'd been had. "Dammit, Rock, very funny. So what are we talking about here?"

He answered with overacted innocence, "Well, my dog, of course. What did you think I was talking about?

"Are you serious? You got a dog?" Patti sounded almost relieved.

"Yep," and he proceeded to tell her the story of finding Flotsam and convincing Jan to allow him to keep her.

"Well, sounds like the two of you were meant to be. She'll be great company for you, but it means we won't see you in Florida. We have a no-pets clause in our lease agreement and our landlady wouldn't be as cooperative as yours."

"So have you started to look around for a place?"

"Not yet. He'll get tired of fishin' so much, and I'll get him to take me around. I've eyeballed a couple of places I like, but you know how he is. What are your plans for Thanksgiving?"

"Josh, Flotsam and I are going to Jan Fremeyer's."

"Wow! The dog, too! Jan really is a sweetie, isn't she?"

"You could say that, yes." He looked out the sunroom window to see the sun break brilliantly through the clouds. "Well, it's about time for us to go for our morning walk. Tell Russ about Flotsam, will you?"

"You bet." Patti chuckled, "Have you solved the world economic crisis yet?"

"Not yet, but I've been reading Thomas Paine."

"Who?"

"Remember your high school history? He wrote *Common Sense*. He talks about the failures of aristocrats to recognize how important the contributions of the common man were to their existence. I kind of think we might be getting into a similar situation now in the twenty-first century."

"Oh, well, OK, Rock, you keep working on that and let me know what you come up with." Rock chuckled to himself, knowing that Patti had no idea who Thomas Paine was or what he'd written about or when he'd written it. "You stay in touch. Russ and I miss you."

"OK, Patti. Talk to you later."

It was mid-morning. The sun was still out, and a check of the thermometer showed that the day had warmed up to twenty-five degrees. The dune grass indicated there was a wind, but it didn't seem to be too severe. Flotsam was well behaved until they hit the beach, when she pinned her ears back and set out on a beeline due south until she reached the path in the dunes that led to the steps going up to Claire's patio. All of Rock's commands to return to him fell on deaf ears. By the time he caught up to her, Claire had the patio slider open, and both dogs were inside the house nuzzling each other. Rock stood at the open door and said, "Claire, I'm so sorry. It seems all I do is apologize to you for my ill-mannered dog." He shot a mean glare at Flotsam, who was totally absorbed in Flower.

"It's OK, Geoff. Please come in out of the cold. Truth is, Flower has been sitting by the slider this morning scanning the beach. I think she's been looking for Flotsam. As soon as she saw her, she started barking and scratching at the glass. How is it down there this morning?"

"Not bad. Wind chill is probably about twenty degrees. If you've got some warm winter clothes, it's actually OK. As for them," he pointed to the two dogs, "They've got their love to keep them warm." They both laughed.

"Well, then, would you mind if Flower and I joined you and Flotsam on your walk?" Claire asked, surprising herself with her boldness.

He bowed and swept his arm toward the slider and said in his most chivalrous tone, "The pleasure would be all ours, my lady."

Claire laughed, smiled at him as their eyes locked together, and said, "Well, now, whoever said *'Chivalry is dead'* has never met you, my lord."

The comfortable ease between them from the day before was still there. He liked it, and he thought Claire felt it as well. While Claire got her winter wear on, he took in his surroundings. The massive floor-to-ceiling stone fireplace with its rough-hewn log mantle first caught his eye. He could tell it was real stone, not the fake stuff that you could buy at Home Depot. He believed the wood was right out of the woods that surrounded the property. There were built-in bookshelves lining the walls of the great room. It reminded him of his own loft in Flint except on a much grander scale. As he stepped in to look at a few of the titles, he could see down the steps that he thought led to the rear entrance foyer. On a raised platform just next to the door and standing in front of a plate glass window that had to be at least fifteen feet tall and six feet wide, was a bronze statue of a frog standing on its hind legs. The bronze was finished in a beautiful, dark-green patina, the perfect color, he thought, for a giant frog that he estimated was at least ten feet tall. He stepped closer. From his new vantage point he could see that the frog was smiling. Its legs were crossed right leg over left, with the left foot flat on the ground and the right leg poised on the toe of the right foot. In one hand the frog held a cane, and in the other it was doffing a top hat to all those who came to the door.

Claire came into the room and saw him looking at the statue.

He saw her out of the corner of his eye. "Now that," he exclaimed as he pointed at the statue, "Is a real conversation piece! There's got to be a story behind that."

"There is," she replied as she pointed to the dogs, who were standing in front of the slider, both padding their two front paws up and down, "But let's get them out to run off some of their energy, and I'll tell you about it as we walk."

On the beach the two dogs were into a world of their own as the group headed south down the beach. "When the girls were young, very young, like Ingrid was nine and Beth was five, Alan bought this property." Before continuing, she paused as one does when poignant memories come flooding back, "Alan was truly gifted and could design anything. Most of his work was on bridges, but he designed and built that house," she pointed over her shoulder. After another pause she continued, "Anyway, the first summer we were up here both girls were scared to death of the tree toads that seemed to be everywhere. Alan tried and tried to make them understand that they were harmless, but that first year everything we tried only seemed to make them more scared. At the beginning of the second summer, we started out with Alan capturing a tree toad and putting it in this aquarium we had. He named it 'Tommy,' 'Tommy-the-Tree-Toad' was its full name, mind you." Rock looked at her. There were tears in her eyes and, though it was cold, he was pretty sure it wasn't the cold causing them. "At first, Alan was Tommy's caregiver. Even I wasn't very fond of having that creature in the house. The girls wouldn't have anything to do with him, but as the summer wore on, that toad started to develop a personality of its own. Ingrid was the first to pick him up. She was ten and by far the more adventurous of the two. Beth idolized her, though, and as Ingrid became more at ease with Tommy, so did Beth. Anyway, long story short, before that summer was over, this place was called The Frog Farm, and the girls would spend hours trying to catch them and let them go. Alan wanted them to love nature, and this was their beginning lesson, I think."

They walked for a while in silence, surrounded by the desolate signs of winter's approach. Rock asked, "What happened to Tommy?"

Claire laughed, "That frog lived for five years in that aquarium and came back to The Frog Farm every summer with us. When he died the girls were devastated. Oh, they had other pets; dogs, gerbils, a guinea pig once. They lamented all of their deaths, but they really took Tommy's demise hardest. So Alan did a drawing and then commissioned a sculptor to make the statue. He didn't tell any of us about it. We came up to The Frog Farm the summer after Tommy died and there he was, greeting us in that foyer window. He's been there ever since. Isn't he grand?" she asked, as she wiped a tear from her eye. Again its cause, the wind or the memories, he couldn't be positive, but the story even gave him a lump in his throat.

Rock looked over at her and said, "Alan sounds like a great husband and father. I'm sure you miss him a lot."

She nodded, "I do. So much, in fact, I've avoided this place for the last three years. We, I mean the girls and I, don't even call it The Frog Farm anymore. We just call it the lake house. Why do we do that, Geoff, when we had so many good memories of The Frog Farm?"

It was a question he was not prepared for, and he didn't really think Claire expected him to answer. Instead he asked Claire, "So what brought you up here now, in the face of winter?"

They walked in silence for what seemed like a long time to Rock. So long, in fact, that he said to her, "Don't answer that, Claire, if it makes you uncomfortable."

She liked his sensitivity. "No, it's OK. It's a good question, and one I think I'm figuring out the answer to as I go. But let's start with my disappointment right now in the system." It was the way that she emphasized *the system* that caught his attention. She continued, "I had been struggling with the hardships that this recession is having

143

on people, but it became very real for me when some very good friends of our family lost their jobs. These are really good people, and I really wanted to help, but they are still out of work, and I don't know what I can do to help them or to help others who are struggling with the same issues." Rock let her think for a minute, sensing that she wasn't quite finished. She told him about the Chavezes.

As he listened to Claire he began to form an image of who she was, where she'd come from and the kind of life she'd lived. He realized that she came from a place that was about as diametrically opposed to where he had come from as anyone could imagine. She was wealthy; exactly how wealthy, he did not ponder. Yet here she was, at the lakeshore, struggling with the same kind of questions that had brought him here. He assumed her prosperity was considerably more than his, but the irony was not lost on him. Prosperity in the face of widening poverty was the very reason that had brought each of them to this place.

Claire was cold. Her winter gear, though considerably more fashionable than his Carhartts, was not designed for the frozen edge of nowhere. They turned around at his insistence. "I'd like to do this again with you and Flower, but if you get sick, then..."

Claire liked the sweet way he put things. She wanted to know more about him, and on the walk back to her house she put the question to him, "So what about you, Geoff? Where are you from? What did you do?"

He told her about his years at GM, about Russ and Patti, about Josh, and finally he told her about his anger and frustration with the company, the government and the impending demise of his hometown. Claire asked questions periodically, Rock provided easy answers. The one question she wanted to ask was about his limp, but she didn't. She figured there would be a time and a place, that he might even volunteer the information. But it was not her place, at this point, to either let him know she'd noticed, or that it mattered. To her, it did not.

Back on the patio, she invited him and Flotsam in. "Would you care for a cup of coffee?"

He averted his eyes. "I can't drink it." But he really didn't want to leave her and go home either. Boldly, but tempered with a certain uneasiness, he asked, "Do you have tea?"

While the dogs settled themselves comfortably in front of the fireplace, Claire went to the kitchen, opened a cabinet door and said, "All I have is Earl Grey tea, will that be OK?"

He chuckled at the coincidence.

Chapter Nineteen

The Trap

He had enjoyed his time with Claire and, after their walk on the beach with the dogs, had stayed for tea longer than he imagined he would. Their conversation had ranged from books they were currently reading, to the stark economic times, to her daughters and to his recent forced retirement. On the matter of his retirement, he tried to emphasize the positive. No plans for future walks were discussed, but Rock knew they would be seeing each other again soon if for no other reason than their dogs would see to it.

Arriving back at Far-Far-View near 1:00 p.m., he heard the distinctive beep of the cottage's answering machine. He pushed the speaker button first and then the play button. "Rock, this is Phyllis. It's about noon. Call me when you can. I have a favor to ask. Just call the salon. I'm here late every day this week except Friday, which I'm keeping open until I hear from you." Flotsam, who'd been standing beside him, disappeared at the sound of her voice. Looking around, he found her on her rug in front of the fireplace, staring at him. "What? I have the feeling you don't like her." Flotsam raised her head, perked her ears forward and twisted her head from side to side. Rock thought for a minute she was agreeing with him, but then reminded himself he was talking to a dog. He took out his wallet and fished around for Phyllis' business card.

"Styles of Holland, this is Phyllis. How may I help you?"

"Phyllis, it's Rock. I can't believe I got you this easily."

"It must be karma, hon," she said sweetly. "How are you?"

"Well, we made it back home and the dog is still alive, so I guess I'm OK. I'm really sorry about the other..."

She interrupted, "Listen, hon, it's OK. It took me some time to climb down off the ceiling, if you know what I mean," her voice had a sexy edge to it, and he knew perfectly what she meant, "But I settled down. How about you?"

"Well, I sure don't want another evening to end like that one did." They both laughed. "You said you needed a favor. What can I do?"

"Well," the sexy edge still there, "I was kind of hoping you could come back to Holland on Friday night. I'd love to see you again and..." she paused. Rock sensed the other shoe was about to drop. "... and I'd like you to have a talk with Janelle."

"Phyllis, I'd love to come to Holland and to meet your daughter." Despite his surging testosterone, there was a little warning buzzer going off in his brain that told him some caution might be required here. He asked, "Is everything OK?"

There was a pause. "Well, to be honest, things could be better. Janelle and I had a big argument over this Marine she says she's in love with."

He quickly realized he was being put directly in the middle between a mother, whom he sexually longed for, and her daughter, whom he'd never met. It was, to say the least, a position he did not care for.

"I'd like for you to have a talk with her about what it's like being a Marine."

"Phyllis, I don't know. It's not the same for everyone..."

"I know, hon," her voice now almost pleading, "But I don't have anyone else I can turn to, and I'm hoping you can just share some of your experience with her."

Rock still didn't like it.

"Please, Rock. I think you can really help her think things through."

It was his turn to pause now and frame his answer, not wanting to set up any unreal expectations, "OK, I'll be happy to talk to her, but, Phyllis, she's an adult and neither of us can really..."

That he would do it is all she wanted to hear. "Great. So why don't you meet me at the condo about 6:00 p.m. on Friday and we'll go from there."

He could not forget, of course, the last time he'd been at the condo. Rock pictured Phyllis in that negligée. "I'll be there at six."

Every day since their dogs had introduced them to one another, he and Claire spent time together, most of it walking on the beach, but also at her house having tea as a warm-up after their walks. He had come to look forward to both the walks and the talks. He was sleeping well at night, and the nightmares that had plagued him just after his fall had let up, not completely, but considerably. He gave most of the credit for this to Claire and Flotsam. When he was with Claire, Vietnam never came to mind. When they were apart, he had Flotsam, and, of course, the night light.

Thursday, during their morning walk, Claire invited him to dinner that evening. She was making a meatloaf, her specialty she had told him, and he was expected at six. He'd made a special trip into Pentwater, to a wine shop he'd been told about, where he'd selected a quality cabernet sauvignon. Claire had told him that she had a soft spot for dry, red wines. After dinner he'd helped with the dishes. The dogs lay quietly in front of the fireplace, each contentedly chewing on a rawhide bone that Rock had thoughtfully brought along with him. When they'd finished cleaning up, Claire offered, "I have a really nice port here. Would you like a glass?"

Rock nodded, "That sounds wonderful, the perfect conclusion to a fantastic meal." He wasn't just saying that, either. He'd had two pieces of the meatloaf along with a small second helping of the garlic mashed potatoes she had fixed. The gravy she had made from the drippings was poured on top of everything. He'd relished every bite.

She poured the wine and brought it to him as he sat on the leather sofa facing the fireplace. She sat in a leather armchair just to his right. Each took a sip of the sweet after-dinner wine. "This was Alan's favorite..." She cut herself off quickly and averted her eyes from him. "I... I'm sorry," she said, "I don't know why I said that."

He let things go quiet for just a minute. The log in the fireplace crackled loudly and a red spark splashed against the screen. The noise alerted Flotsam and Flower, who stopped chewing long enough to determine that it was nothing, and then they went back to their rawhide bones. "It's OK, Claire. He was your husband. You loved him. You should never have to apologize for that."

A tear trickled down her cheek. She looked at him and nodded. His heart ached for her. He could not imagine what it was like to love someone so much that three years after his death something so simple as a glass of wine could trigger tears.

"I have a favor to ask."

Something in the way he said that alerted her, but she said, "Sure, anything, Geoff."

"Well, don't be so sure of anything," he said, and then added, "Would you mind watching Flotsam tomorrow evening for me? I have an errand to run in Holland and I'm a little afraid to leave her alone in the cottage. I mean I've never done that, and I don't think she'd tear up anything, but..." He was searching for words.

"Don't be silly. Of course I'll look after her. Flower will be thrilled to have her here. Will you be overnight?"

It bothered him, but the truth of the matter was he hoped that would be the case. After an awkward pause, finally he said, "Would it be too much to ask if you could keep her overnight, just in case I get hung up?"

Inside Claire felt something crush her heart. *He doesn't have an errand, he has a date.* She knew it. "Oh... no... no... of course not," she sputtered, not looking him in the eye. "Take your time. We'll be here when you get back."

For the next thirty minutes or so, the talk between them, that had always been lively and easy, dried up to near nothing. It was somewhere right around 9:00 p.m., Rock thanked her for dinner, awkwardly shook her hand, and then he and Flotsam headed home walking down the road behind their houses.

As she closed the door behind her, Claire leaned back against it and let a tear trickle down her cheek.

On that short walk to Far-Far-View, he reviewed what he had expected to happen that evening. It hadn't been sex. He hadn't even thought that they might part with a good night kiss. But it hadn't been this either, although he had had pangs of conscience about asking Claire to dog sit while he ran off to... *to do what? To bang Phyllis.* He had to admit to himself that he'd nearly forgotten that he was also expected to talk to Janelle about the Marine Corps, and likely that was to entail a discussion of Vietnam. He didn't talk a lot about the Marine Corps, but wasn't ashamed to admit serving. He never talked about Vietnam, something he'd just as soon forget altogether. *How did you get yourself into this mess? What did you expect to happen tonight? Errand! She saw right through that lie!*

He did not sleep well that night. The ghosts of Vietnam left him alone. It was the woman in Holland and the woman in the house next door that kept him awake.

Friday morning Flotsam spotted Flower on the beach about 9:00 a.m. and put up a racket. It was a beautiful day, but Rock continued to feel guilty. He probably would not have gone down to the beach if Claire had not seen him in the window as he looked to see why Flotsam was barking. *What the hell! You are going to have to see her at some point today when you drop your dog off.* On the way down to the water he'd tried to think how he could start the morning conversation with her. As it turned out, he'd worried needlessly.

"Good morning," Claire said, without a hint of the disappointment in her voice he'd detected the night before. "Isn't it a beautiful day?" They walked a little over half way to the Little Point Sable Light House and back. While Claire was chipper, he felt like he was struggling, yet their hour together had flown by.

As they reached the beach below Far-Far-View, Claire asked, "Will you and Flotsam walk this afternoon before you leave for Holland?"

"Well, I hadn't thought about..."

She interrupted him, "I don't know what time you have to be there, but, if possible, I'd like to walk them again this afternoon. That way we will all sleep like babies tonight."

They met at two in the afternoon, walked an hour, south, down the beach this time, after which Claire took Flotsam from him. Claire told him to be safe. He thanked her. She led the two dogs up the dune and onto the patio, where Flotsam stood watching Rock walk up the beach toward their house. Her ears drooped pitifully and her tail, which normally arched gracefully skyward, was tucked soundly between her legs.

"It's OK, girl," Claire said to her. "He'll be back." Once inside, Claire hung up her coat and scarf and returned to the great room to find Flotsam standing by the slider staring up the beach in the direction of her house. Flower was next to her. She walked over to the two of them, bent down and, while stroking both of them, said to Flotsam, "It's OK, girl. He's been a bachelor for a long time. He has his ways. We can't change that. If he's seeing someone in Holland, so be it. He's good to all of us," she said looking back and forth between the two dogs. "We shouldn't complicate things more than that."

As Rock walked the short distance down the beach to Far-Far-View, he didn't look back. Inside he felt as if he was betraying her, the *her* being both Flotsam and Claire.

He took his time driving to Holland, stopping along the way for gas, coffee and flowers. He made the final purchase as he recalled Phyllis standing in the hallway holding spiked coffee and cookies in a see-through negligée. She intrigued him and testosterone is an efficient salve for the labored male conscience.

Arriving early, he circled around the city for fifteen or twenty minutes before pulling into the condo's driveway at precisely 6 p.m. Phyllis met him at the door, this time fully clothed, but dazzlingly so. Dressed in a sleek, black dress that plunged in the right places and rose perfectly in all the others, she kissed him on the cheek as he stepped in the door. Her shoes were black patent-leather, with deep red accents and tall, stiletto-heels that accentuated her long legs and perfect figure. A simple silver necklace and pendant dangled tantalizingly above just the right amount of exposed cleavage, and her delicately fragrant perfume reminded him of a distant spring day. He gave her the flowers. She took his chin in her hand and pulled his lips to hers. She was, he thought, an exciting woman. He knew, though, that Janelle would be meeting them. But even as this disappointing thought interrupted his rising anticipation, Phyllis promised him that there would be more to come after dinner.

Five minutes after his arrival they were off to a local restaurant. On the way, he'd tried to ask some questions about Janelle and her relationship with her Marine, but Phyllis was either evasive or non-committal. Not knowing what to expect made him uneasy as they arrived at *The Chalet,* a small bistro specializing in French cuisine that Phyllis had raved about as a way to avoid answering his questions.

"Rock, I'd like you to meet my daughter, Janelle." She was taller than her mother, trim like her, but her style of dress was more conservative than Phyllis and Rock thought that a bit unusual. After introductions and during dinner, their conversation took a casual direction. He learned that Janelle had always been close to her mother; had been a good student, good enough to have gone to college, but had pooh-poohed that idea, opting instead for a career in beauty. As Rock listened to her, he could tell that she enjoyed her work as a stylist and that Janelle considered herself an artist more than a cosmetologist.

It was when coffee was served at the end of the meal that the Marine Corps came up. There was nothing subtle about the transition as Phyllis plunged right in. "Janelle, Rock was in the Marine Corps."

The comment was met with a stiffening of Rock's shoulder muscles and a rather perfunctory "Oh," from Janelle. After a long pause, during which Phyllis was staring at Rock and Rock and Janelle were considering what they should say next, Janelle smiled at him and said, "Thanks for your service, Rock."

Rock sensed a wariness on Janelle's part, as when a wild animal can sense when it is about to be trapped. "It was my pleasure," Rock said, as he looked at Janelle smiling, trying to put her back at ease.

Phyllis, who had set this trap, was not going to let either of them escape that easily. She started with Rock. "My pleasure?" There was a sharp tone of disbelief and disgust in her voice. "Are you sure about that, Rock?"

And there it was. Phyllis's agenda for him laid out clearly. Immediately he hated that he had allowed himself to be put in this position. On the trip to Holland earlier he'd gone over possible scenarios of how the evening might play out. This had been one of them, but he'd managed to push it out of his mind by letting thoughts of Phyllis creep in. The hackles on the back of his neck stood up, his shoulders tightened more, and he felt a knot in his stomach. He didn't like being used like this and he glared at her.

Undaunted, Phyllis glared back and said, "It was the Marine Corps that saddled you with that limp wasn't it?" She spat out the words *Marine Corps* with a bitterness that caught both him and Janelle by surprise.

"Mother," Janelle said, half scolding, half pleading.

Phyllis turned to her daughter and through clinched jaws advised, "Janelle, you need to listen to what this man has to say. He's been there. He'll tell you what it's like to get shot up and left with a permanent disability all for some concept of God and Country." Again she spat out *God and Country* as if they were concepts to be despised. Then she turned to Rock and said, "Tell her. Tell her what that's like."

Rock's anger was rising. He looked directly at Phyllis. "If you expect me to..."

From the other side of the table Janelle interrupted him. "Mother, I can't believe you are doing this."

"Doing what? Listen to what he has to say."

Rock had had it with her. He put his napkin down on the table and asked Phyllis, "Exactly what is it that you think I have to say?"

"Tell her how that happened," pointing to his leg. "Tell her what it's like to lose something for the rest of your life and get nothing back for your sacrifice. Tell her what war is really like." She had no idea of the difficulty of what she was asking him to do and when he didn't respond, she turned to Janelle. "Darling, I don't want to see you throw your life away."

Janelle glared at her mother, "I can't believe you would do this." She glanced at Rock and said, "Excuse me." Then she got up and headed for the ladies' room. Phyllis, who didn't bother to excuse herself at all, slammed her napkin down on the table and followed Janelle, leaving him sitting alone as the people at the two nearby tables stared at him, occasionally whispering to each other. He fought the urge to get up and leave. Instead, he asked the waiter to bring him a glass of their best port. He was sipping it when Janelle returned to the table, her eyes swollen and red.

"I'm so sorry she roped you into this. My mother can be quite manipulative. She's gone, you know."

He didn't, but was neither disappointed nor surprised. "But how will she get..."

"Home?" Janelle interrupted.

"Yes. Should I..."

"Chase after her?" Rock could sense Janelle's frustration with her mother. "You can do what you want, but you should know that that is exactly what she expects you to do, what she wants you to do, and if you do it, then she has you where she wants you."

"How will she get home?"

"She called a taxi after I refused to talk to her. It's on its way. If you want my advice, let the taxi take her home. You didn't do what she wanted you to do, and when you don't do that, she will try to hurt you." And with that a gusher of tears began. Rock grabbed a clean napkin from an unused place-setting next to him and handed it to her. The couple from the other table stared at them until Rock gave them a withering look.

Janelle saw him do that and said, "I'm sorry, but..."

"It's OK. It's none of their business anyway." He let her cry for a minute, until she regained control and began blotting her eyes.

"So tell me about this Marine of yours, Janelle."

Over coffee for her and a second glass of port for him, Janelle told him about Corporal James Axelrod. They'd attended high school together; he was two years younger than she. He'd been home on leave when they'd met at a mutual friend's wedding. She was a member of the bridal party. He was there in his uniform. He was a "west coast" Marine even though he'd gone through basic training at Paris Island, South Carolina. After a tour in Afghanistan, he'd been a weapons instructor at Camp Pendleton, but had volunteered for a tour of duty in Iraq because, and Janelle quoted him here, *"I don't feel right being stateside when other Marines are in harm's way."* His current tour of duty in Iraq would be over in the next couple of months, and he was looking for another assignment in the San Diego area. It was her intention to join him there. In her eyes he was a true American hero with two Purple Hearts, a Bronze Star with V device, and a promotion to sergeant expected sometime in the next six months. He intended to make a career out of the Marines, and it was her intention to be beside him every step of the way. She concluded with, "Mother doesn't understand any of this. Absolutely refuses to try. But I'll bet you understand, don't you, Rock?"

As she was talking, Rock reflected. He did understand everything that she'd told him. He patted his injured left leg. "It happened in Vietnam. I guess your mother thinks I should be bitter about this, but I'm neither bitter nor proud. The night I got this, a lot of Marines died. I was lucky." He hung his head.

"Rock, you don't have to..."

"I know, but I want you to know. In the years since Vietnam I've come to believe that it was a wrong-minded war. I happen to believe that the war in Afghanistan has gotten way out of hand and the war in Iraq is as simple-minded as Vietnam ever was. But I will never fault the intelligence or the integrity of those who have served or are serving in these places. That guy of yours, Corporal Axelrod, he sounds like a helluva Marine, and I can't think of a better compliment to pay a young man or young woman these days. When you write to him, you tell him this ol' Marine thanks him for his service, all of it, the good, the bad and the ugly. You tell him that you love him and that you can't wait to see him..." Rock paused because his mind was slipping back to Riley and his machine gun, "And you remind him that in these last days of his tour he needs to be especially safe and come home to you. When he gets home, be patient and mindful of what he's been through. It stays with you for a long, long time. Believe me, I know what the hell I'm talking about."

Janelle reached across the table and took his hand in hers. "Thank you. I'm just going to have to stand up to her, and she's just going to have to understand or..." she paused for a long time, "Or else."

"I take your Mom for a survivor. She'll adjust, especially when she sees you happy. Tell her I just couldn't tell you something just because she wanted to hear it. Tell her I told you the truth."

"I will." Janelle paused for a long moment. He knew she had something else to say. "Rock, you are a good man. It hurts me to say this, but you might want to stay away from my mother. It's like things have to be her way or it's the highway. I honestly believe that is why both of her marriages ended the way they did."

Rock simply nodded, fully aware that things between him and Phyllis were over. If there was regret, it was that he'd let his male ego lead him into Phyllis's trap. Janelle offered to cover the bill. Rock replied, "No way. This is on me."

She stood and kissed him gently on the cheek, gathered her coat and left the restaurant. Rock paid the bill and headed back to Far-Far-View, hoping to arrive in time to collect Flotsam before Claire turned in. On the trip home he thought, chuckling to himself, *well, at least Flotsam will be happy the way this evening turned out!*

It was nearly 11:00 p.m. and, as he approached Far-Far-View, he thought it might be too late to disturb Claire and retrieve his dog. Driving down the narrow passageway that was Glenn Road, however, he could see lights still on at Claire's. He pulled into her driveway and saw in the beam of the motion light a car he didn't recognize. Apparently Claire had company. He thought perhaps he should just go home and collect Flotsam in the morning, but then decided he should get his dog and let Claire enjoy her company, whoever it was. He got out, leaving the Jeep running with its lights on, fearing that the floodlight would cut out leaving him in the pitch black of the moonless, overcast, lakeshore night. He rang the doorbell and heard the scramble of dogs' feet and, then, their whimpering inside the door. A light came on, deftly backlighting Tommy the Tree Frog, and Rock could see him through the glass panel smiling down on him in greeting.

"Geoff, I didn't expect you back this evening."

He smiled at her, but noted she looked rather tired and drained. He hoped she had not had another attack. "I finished early. I saw your light on and thought I'd relieve you of your burden tonight rather than in the morning. I see you have company, so I'll just get her and let you get back to them."

Claire stepped back and said, "Well, come in out of the cold while I get her collar and leash." Rock stepped inside, and Claire disappeared for a minute, returning with Flotsam's things.

In the better light of the foyer, Rock again noticed the red, swollen eyes and knew for sure she'd been crying. "Claire, is everything all right?"

She dabbed at a newly formed tear. "It's Beth. She's here and she needs me."

He sensed his intrusion. Thanking her, he turned, opened the door to leave and as he did Flotsam and Flower both ran out. As he opened the car door for Flotsam to get in, Claire called Flower to her. When he backed the car around to leave, he saw her waving goodbye to him. He waved back, but couldn't help but wonder what had her so upset.

Chapter Twenty

The Break Up

Rock awoke Saturday morning, well rested, no night-mares, with a clear conscience. Some of his past breakups had bothered him for varying lengths of time. This was not one of those. He and Flotsam ate breakfast, and afterward he sat down to read while she moved to the chair he'd positioned for her so that she could see out the sunroom's windows. By 10:00 a.m. she was getting antsy and he was hoping to see Claire.

It was a fair day by near-winter standards at the lake-shore. There was not much sunshine, but the tempera-ture was just above freezing and there was only a light breeze. He owed Flotsam a walk, and she was not going to forgive the debt. He got on his gear, opened the door, and off she went, around the corner, down the steps, over the dune, southbound towards Claire's. By the time he reached the beach, the wind out of the southwest was car-rying her bark to him. He knew she was on Claire's patio. He was about half way up the beach to Claire's when the barking stopped. Stepping onto the patio, he realized why. Flotsam was inside. Through the glass slider he could see Claire motioning for him to come in.

Pulling her boots on, Claire said, "Geoff, I'll be ready in just a minute. Flower has been pacing for the last hour looking for Flotsam." Claire motioned toward a young woman sitting near the fireplace, "I'd like you to meet my daughter, Beth. Beth, this is our neighbor, Geoff Graham."

She was attractive, he thought, like her mother, even without the benefit of makeup. She had high cheek bones, pouty lips and long, dark blonde hair that was haphazardly piled up and held in place by a big hair clip. A bathrobe that was much too large hung on her. Rock thought it had probably belonged to her father.

Forcing a smile, she walked over to him, extended her hand, and said, "Nice to meet you, Mr. Graham."

Now that she was closer, he could see the red rims around her blue eyes. "It's nice to meet you, Beth," Rock said, taking her hand.

Claire, ready now with her hat, coat, gloves and boots on, walked over to Rock. "Well, shall we? They certainly are ready," she said, pointing to the two dogs standing in front of the slider and gazing out on the beach below, their tails wagging in perfect unison.

"We shall," replied Rock. He pulled the slider open just as a gust of wind came up the dune and poured into the great room.

Claire looked over at Beth, "We'll be back in an hour or so, honey. See you then." Beth forced another smile and nodded.

The dogs were down the beach in a shot. Rock waited until he and Claire were well away from the house before he asked, "Is everything all right?"

Claire sighed and shrugged, "Well, the wedding is off. She broke it off with him last night and then headed directly up here."

"I'm sorry," he said, thinking how inadequate those two words sounded.

"Well, it may not be such a bad thing. I don't think Beth has been happy about things for the last couple of months."

"I don't mean to pry, Claire, but may I ask what happened?"

"It's a series of events, Geoff, but I think it's gotten worse for her over the past couple of weeks. They went to a football game at Purdue, but he flew back early to perform surgery. She had to drive back alone. Then yesterday, they were going to apparently spend a quiet evening at home and he called telling her he had to go to Detroit to perform four operations over the weekend. He expected her to go with him, but Beth just isn't like that. I know she has given this a lot of thought. She's looked at me and my marriage and said, *I want better.'* I can't blame her."

Claire's last disclosure surprised him. Usually he had good instincts and knew when to keep his mouth shut, but they failed him this time and he blurted out, "But I thought that you and Alan..." He caught himself just short.

Claire finished his thought, "That Alan and I had the perfect marriage?" She phrased it as a question.

So he answered, "Yes."

The dogs had come back to them, so Claire bent down to nuzzle Flower, and Rock did the same with Flotsam. Then the dogs were off again.

"Don't get me wrong, Geoff. Alan and I were a great team, and I loved him with all of my heart. I took care of the kids and the house. I worked in the public schools. He built his business."

"Bridges, right?"

Claire stopped and looked out across the blue green lake, "He was a brilliant engineer who could build anything he wanted, but chose to specialize in bridges. He built a worldwide business in the matter of just a couple of decades. But the price we paid for all of that success was that he was away a lot."

Rock could relate. During his time at GM, he'd averaged about sixty hours a week, and there were periods of time when he'd exceeded that. It was the long hours, he'd long known, that were the biggest single reason his marriage had ended in divorce and was a significant reason why he'd never found anyone else after that. He looked over at Claire. She had tears in her eyes, and he was sure this time they weren't from the cold and wind.

Claire pointed back over her shoulder, "This place, this house..." She removed a glove and took a Kleenex from her pocket. Dabbing at her eyes, she continued, "He designed it while he was working in Brazil. He was gone for most of six months. When he came home in June of that year, we watched it being built. We rented a place just up the road from here. I'll show it to you when we get there. That was a fantastic summer, because we had him all summer long, the girls and I, I mean. He taught them to sail, swam with them, built sand castles," and she chuckled, "As only an engineer can build sand castles. When the girls collapsed into their beds at night, he and I would walk on the beach and talk about our plans."

She dabbed at her tears again and sniffled. Rock stepped just a little closer to her. They walked on south along the beach, the dogs playing with one another just ahead of them.

"There was never another summer like that one. We finished the house, but he never spent a complete summer here like he did that summer when we built the place. The girls and I loved spending our summers up here, but Alan would come and go as his work dictated. The girls and I would wait for him to come back, and we learned to enjoy him while we could, but we always knew he'd have to leave again. The job was always the priority. Then, three years ago, he died, quite suddenly. All of our plans were just that, plans, without a single one of them ever having the chance of becoming a memory."

They walked in silence for about five minutes, when Claire pointed to an old log cabin that sat high on a bluff above them, "There, that's the house we rented the summer we built ours."

Looking at the intricate network of stairs that led from the log cabin to the beach, Rock commented, "That wasn't an easy trip to the beach."

She chuckled, "No, it wasn't. If you forgot to bring something down, in most cases, you went without it. The girls complained loud and long about climbing all those stairs that summer. That was one of the things we liked best about our house, there's not a lot of steps between the house and the beach." Claire fell silent for a long time.

Rock stayed by her side, but left her alone with her thoughts. When Claire suddenly stopped, he turned to her.

Claire looked at him and said, "So Beth is remembering how much her father was gone. Her fiancé is a lot like Alan, driven by his work. Beth doesn't want to spend her life waiting for him, like we waited for Alan."

Rock thought it best just to let her talk. He could sense that she was in as much turmoil as Beth, but after giving her a few minutes, he asked her, "Do you think she will really cancel the wedding?"

"Yes, Geoff, I do."

When they arrived back at Claire's, she slid open the door from the patio and both dogs went charging in. Claire and Rock could hear Beth on the phone. She was sobbing. Rock touched Claire's arm and whispered, "I'm going to head home. Unless the weather changes drastically, I will probably walk again this afternoon. Would you and Flower care to join us?"

Appreciatively, Claire nodded, "I'd like that very much, Geoff."

Almost as if he'd predicted it, the weather that afternoon turned for the worse. Windswept rain and sleet pounded the lakeshore. Rock called Claire to sadly acknowledge that a walk was out of the question. He was going to run into Shelby for some groceries and asked if she needed him to pick up anything. She didn't, but thanked him and then added, "Geoff, I enjoyed our walk this morning. Call me tomorrow."

"Me, too, Claire. I'll give you a call."

As the afternoon passed, Claire and Beth were on his mind. Though he'd not heard anything specific at the open slider, he surmised that Beth was probably talking to her fiancé, and that nothing had changed. Flotsam lay stretched on her rug in front of the fireplace, asleep, and, as he watched her, an idea came to him. After stoking the fire and adding a couple of logs to it, he looked up Jan's telephone number and punched it into the wall phone.

"Jan, it's Rock Graham."

"Yes, Rock. How are you and Flotsam doing? Is it as nasty at the shore as it is here in Fremont?"

"It's terrible here; wind, rain and sleet. The pup and I are housebound this afternoon. Jan, I know this is presumptuous, but I was wondering if you could take on any more diners at Thanksgiving?"

"Well, I suppose. How many more are we talking about?" Jan assumed it might be a college buddy or two of Rock's nephew, Josh.

"Two. Have you met your neighbors to the south, the Van Zandts?"

Jan had not. They had owned Far-Far-View for only the last three years and though they had never met their neighbors, they knew the house belonged to the Van Zandt family of Holland. "Well, no, actually. They haven't been to the lakeshore very much since Mr. Van Zandt passed away. Is she there now?" Jan asked.

"She is," and he laughed. "Our dogs introduced us. Her younger daughter, Beth, is also here with her." He proceeded to tell her how he and Claire had met and that they had been walking together almost every day for the last week. He excluded any details about Beth's current troubles. "I haven't asked them yet, of course. I wanted to check with you first, but I was thinking it might be nice if they could join Josh and me for Thanksgiving dinner with you. I know that this is…"

Jan interrupted him, "No, Rock. It's OK. We'd love for you to invite them. Do you know who they are?"

The question puzzled him. *Of course I know who they are! They're your neighbors at the lake!* Instead he said, "What do you mean?"

"Madeline serves on the Board of Directors of our local food bank. The Van Zandt family just made a $500,000 donation to them for food relief this winter. Word is they've done that with every food bank in the state. I'm not exactly sure how many that is, but I'll bet there are a dozen or more agencies like ours, and each one of them got $500,000 from the Van Zandts. Having them for Thanksgiving dinner seems like the least we can do to thank them for their generosity."

Rock truly respected Claire for her strength of character in handling the current family crisis with Beth. Now he admired her for her generosity, but his quick math stunned him. He thought Claire was well off, but he had never dreamed she was so well off that she could give away $6 million.

After a long pause in their conversation, Jan pulled him back into it, "Rock?"

"Yes, Jan. I'm here. Claire and her daughter seem like very down-to-earth people," he said, as if trying to convince himself that he could actually know people with that kind of money.

"I'm sure they are. Their hearts sure seem to be in the right place. Get back to me and let me know what they say."

He was still struggling with the new information Jan had given him about Claire Van Zandt. "Uh…oh…sure, Jan. I'll talk to Claire tomorrow. I'll let you know."

She had not impressed him as wealthy; well off, yes, but not wealthy. He was just a retired GM plant worker and here he'd been rubbing elbows with someone who just donated $6 million, maybe more, a number he could not get his head around. He felt humbled; maybe even humiliated. Still, he liked the woman next door. *She's rich. So what? That doesn't mean you can't walk your dog with her.* He looked out the window at the rain/snow mix that was falling harder now and realized that, if not for the bad weather, they'd be together right now walking on the beach. He hoped the weather cooperated tomorrow. He needed to ask Claire if she and Beth had plans for Thanksgiving dinner. He hoped the answer was "No."

Chapter Twenty-One

Fun People

That evening the phone rang as he was finishing his dinner. Rock didn't bother to check the caller ID and was pleasantly surprised to hear Claire's voice. "Geoff, sorry to bother you."

"Claire, you aren't bothering me. What's up?" He was hoping it might be an invitation to come over for dessert or to walk in the morning.

"I wanted you to know that Beth and I are going to drive down to Holland tomorrow morning and I probably won't be back until Monday morning."

A wave of disappointment overtook him, but he did a good of job of disguising it, "Is everything OK?"

"As good as can be expected, I suppose, but I don't want Beth driving down alone."

He didn't want to ask her about Thanksgiving over the phone, but this news did raise the question of whether or not Beth was likely to be back before Thursday. "Will Beth be coming back soon?" he asked.

"She says she's coming back up Monday evening. I hope she does."

"Me, too," Rock agreed. "I think she needs you nearby, but I'm glad you are planning on coming back. Maybe we can walk the dogs on Monday after you get back up here."

"Flower would like that, Geoff," she said and then quickly added, "And so would I. I'll call when we get back. I promise."

Her voice had an edge of eager anticipation to it, and he liked that. "Flotsam and I will wait for your call. Be safe."

Sunday dragged by for both him and Flotsam. The weather was nasty. He couldn't settle into a comfortable reading pattern because his thoughts kept returning to Claire. He fiddled around with the television, but the weather seemed to be disrupting everything he tried to watch. It was, he thought, the longest day he had spent at the lakeshore. He called Jan and explained he wouldn't have an answer for her on Thanksgiving until tomorrow or Tuesday. She told him she appreciated his call, that there were no worries. Plenty of food was planned, and two more mouths to feed would not change that.

Monday, November 24th, 2008, broke dazzlingly clear. But as he stood in the sunroom looking out at the vast expanse of Lake Michigan's blue-green surface, he first noticed the rolling white caps. Then he checked the dune grass and saw it was pressed down so far the ends of the long seed pods were almost touching the sandy surface of the dune. The outside thermometer registered twenty-five degrees. Intuitively he reasoned that if it was twenty-five degrees and there was a twenty-five mile per hour wind blowing, a reasonable estimate he thought, it would feel about zero on the beach. Any beach walk today would be unbearably cold.

Claire called just before 10:00 a.m.. "Good to hear your voice," he said. "How was the trip up?" As he stood with the phone to his ear, he checked the white caps and the dune grass again. No change.

"Windy!" she exclaimed. "It's pretty chilly out there, Geoff."

"The blue sky and bright sun can fool you," he said. "I'm guessing it's zero or below on the beach with that wind blowing. We could walk the road. Not as pretty as the beach, but the dune will sure cut the wind."

"Flower is standing at the slider. She's looking for Flotsam. Let's give it a try," she said.

"We'll be there in a few minutes," Rock said. "We'll take the road over so I'll come in by Tommy the Tree Toad."

"OK. The door is unlocked. I'll start getting ready."

Glenn Road through Little Point Sable is barely more than a two-track cut in the valley between two very high morainal dunes left there by retreating glaciers as the Ice Age ended and the earth warmed enough to support life. In the summer the road was like a green tunnel. This time of year, leaf-bare hardwoods soared skyward on either side of Claire and Rock like slender fingers reaching into the blue sky. As the sun rose higher and higher and the dunes protected them from the harsh wind, it wasn't too uncomfortable. As for their canines, they were completely oblivious to the cold, lost in their companionship.

"So how's Beth?" he inquired, as they reached a high spot in the road where the vista, unblocked by neither dunes nor trees, spread out over the vast blue-green of Lake Michigan to the distant horizon.

Claire bundled herself against a blast of cold air before answering, "It's very hard for her, but she's not backing down. She's canceling everything today; wedding gown, bridesmaids, the country club. It will be a long day for her, but she said she'd be back up here tonight sometime. She spent last night with me in Holland. She doesn't want to go back to her condo for a while until the locks are all changed. Her co-worker at the gallery told her Nathan has been coming by. Beth thinks that means he's probably haunting the condo in Grand Rapids as well. I don't know, maybe he's even staying there. He has a key, at least for the moment. She won't take his calls. I've had to ask him to stop calling up here; she just won't talk to him. Her sister is making it still tougher, telling her that she should reconsider. She thinks Nathan is perfect for Beth. Truth is, Nathan might be perfect for Ingrid, but he's not the right guy for Beth."

Rock had heard both Beth and Claire mention Ingrid, but he didn't know her. Otherwise his question might have sounded obtuse, "But I thought Ingrid was married."

Claire laughed. The humor was lost on Rock, and Claire noticed his blank expression. "Oh, I'm sorry, Geoff. That was rude of me. I'm not laughing at you. Ingrid is married. But if you knew her, you'd understand. She and Beth's Nathan have similar personalities, I think, and both of them are driven by their work more than anything else."

They walked along in silence for a while as Rock tried to draw a mental picture of Ingrid.

Claire confirmed what he was already thinking, "She's completely different from Beth. It's hard to believe that they came from the same family, but if you had known Alan, you would see him in Ingrid. That's exactly why..." her voice trailed off, and then she picked back up, "That's why Ingrid is so adamant Beth is making a mistake and Beth is so sure she's doing the right thing in breaking off her engagement."

They were going down a sad path for Claire, so Rock thought it time to change the subject, "Have you made any plans for Thanksgiving dinner?"

Claire looked at him, sadness building in her eyes, "No. Ingrid has invited us to her house, but we won't go. First of all, she's also invited the partners in their law firm and their wives." She paused, then laughed again, "You'd have to look far and wide to find a stuffier bunch."

Rock chuckled, "Not a fun group, huh?" Again, he could draw a picture. At GM he'd called them "Suits." They were the executives he'd see occasionally trooping through the production facilities. He likened them to the ancient

Greek gods that descended every now and then unto the earth. Once there, because they could not understand how mere mortals lived, their presence only created turmoil and chaos.

"To say the least. Then there is Ingrid, who would use the holiday to hound Beth face-to-face. It's been bad enough over the phone, believe me."

"Claire, I don't mean to be presumptuous, but may I ask you something?"

She looked over at him, surprised at the way he'd phrased the question, "Certainly, Geoff."

"I was wondering if you and Beth would like to join my nephew, Josh, and me for Thanksgiving dinner at my landlady's home in Fremont?"

"Oh, Geoff..."

He was prepared for an immediate no, so he gently interrupted, "Before you say no, let me just say that I think it would be a bad idea for you and Beth to hole yourselves up for the day." He paused, fearing that perhaps now he had presumed too much. *Who am I to tell her what is and what isn't a "bad idea"?* However, when Claire didn't respond, he continued, "I've always thought that Thanksgiving, Christmas and New Years were three days when people should be close to people that they care about." He looked over at her.

Claire locked eyes with him. "That's sweet, Geoff."

Her tenderness melted his heart. Smiling he said, "Jan Fremeyer and Madeline Murphy, my landlady and her friend, are really good people. Josh is like my son. He needs a break from school. He's biting his nails over getting into veterinarian school at MSU."

"I'd like to meet him," she said.

"Then you'll come with us?" he asked, hopefulness obvious in his voice.

"Let me talk to Beth, Geoff. As much as I'd like to go, I can't leave her on that day. You understand?"

"I do, Claire. I certainly do. But when you talk to her, tell her we are the *'fun people'*." They both laughed.

Chapter Twenty-Two

Everyone Else Calls Me Rock

On the Wednesday morning before Thanksgiving, Rock, looking ahead to the next day's festivities, finally realized he needed to clear something up with Claire and Beth. So that morning, as they walked down the beach, Rock picked up a stick and threw it. In a flurry of flying paws and sand, the two dogs took off after the stick. Then he stopped and turned to her, "Claire, I should tell you that Jan and Madeline call me *Rock*. I'm *Uncle Rock* to Josh."

Quizzically and with some incredulity she asked, "Really? Why?"

She didn't seem miffed, for which he was glad. After all, even though in his mind it had been a deception, it was only a small one. "Uh, well, it's a nickname." He knew that bit of information was lacking in sufficient detail, so he added, "Actually, everyone pretty much knows me as Rock. I don't know why, when we first met, I didn't introduce myself as Rock. It somehow just seemed better if you knew me as Geoff. I can't really explain it."

"Do you mind if I ask how you came by the nickname?"

And there it was; time to talk about what he'd been trying to forget for forty years. It was one of life's ironies, a name he heard himself called dozens of times every day that was a constant reminder of what he didn't want to recall. He avoided details except to say that, "A Platoon

Sergeant said that I was steady as a rock. Couple of guys heard it. It's stuck with me ever since."

Claire had no idea what a Platoon Sergeant was, but she was curious. "Well you must have done something that made him think you were steady as a rock. What was it?"

"You don't really want to know."

Claire looked over at him, but he was staring out into the lake. Claire's training as a counselor quickly told her she'd touched a nerve. "OK, Geoff... uh... I mean, Rock," she said smiling at him, "So what time do we leave in the morning for Fremont, and are you sure it's all right that Flower comes along? I mean, four dogs and all those people. I hope Jan and Madeline know what they are letting themselves in for."

Beth's agreement to go had been reluctant, but she knew her mother liked their neighbor.

Rock wiped away a trickle from his eye and smiled back at her. "About eleven a.m., I think, will give us plenty of time," he paused, then added, "And thanks, Claire."

She only nodded.

That afternoon Rock drove to East Lansing to pick up his nephew after his last class before the Thanksgiving break. "Plans have changed a little bit since we last talked, Josh."

"What's up?"

"We have some neighbors at the lake, and they are going to Thanksgiving dinner with us tomorrow. Claire Van Zandt and her daughter, Beth, will be joining us."

"OK. Sorry Uncle Rock. It's been hectic this semester. Tell me again who's going to be there."

Rock went through the list, giving Josh just a few details on how he'd come to know each of them and then added, "Flotsam and Flower will be going as well. Jan invited them."

"I'm anxious to meet Flotsam..." Josh paused for a second and then added, "I'm anxious to meet everyone, Uncle Rock, I didn't mean that..."

Rock laughed, "I know what you meant, Josh."

"You know border collies are supposed to be the smartest breed of dog there is."

Proudly, Rock declared, "Well, it's good that you know that, because Flotsam won't disappoint you. I swear one day she is going to talk to me."

"What kind of dog is Flower?" Josh asked.

"Yellow lab. She really has a sweet disposition, and she and Flotsam can't seem to spend too much time together. It's fun to watch them play. Claire and I might not as well even be anywhere around. They only need us to occasionally throw a stick or ball for them."

"Sounds like you and Claire get along."

Rock looked over at his nephew and smiled, "Yes, we do."

"Tell me about Beth."

Rock thought for a moment. "She's about twenty-five or twenty-six. She's pretty..." His voice trailed off as if he had more to say but was searching for a way to say it.

"And?" Josh looked over at his uncle.

"Well, there is probably something that you should know, just so you don't say something that may accidentally upset her."

"What's that?"

"She just broke off her engagement and cancelled the wedding."

"Oh. That's tough. Do you know what happened?"

Rock went through the few details he knew and then added, "I didn't think either of them should spend the holiday alone, so I finagled an invitation to Thanksgiving dinner with us."

Josh wanted to talk about vet school, so Rock obligingly listened and asked appropriate questions at appropriate times. Eventually Josh noticed his uncle's polite interest only and turned the conversation back to Claire. He could not recall his uncle ever sharing information about the women in his life, except Josh's Aunt Patti. Josh loved his uncle like a father and often wondered why he had never found someone he might share his life with. "So you and Claire...he paused smiling at his uncle, You're an item?"

Rock blushed.

"I think that's great, Uncle Rock."

Chapter Twenty-Three

Thanksgiving, 2008

It was snowing Thanksgiving Day as they loaded into the Range Rover. Claire was in the front passenger's seat, Josh and Beth were in the back seat. The two dogs shared the rear cargo area, preoccupied with rawhide bones that Rock had given to each. Rock settled into the driver's seat and needed a quick lesson from Claire.

"It's all keyless, Rock," she said. "Put the fob in that slot," she pointed to it, "And then push the start button." She again pointed. The V-8 engine roared to life. He had never been impressed with imports, but as he eased the Evoque out of Little Point Sable, he had to admit that she was built for tough road conditions. He couldn't wait to get her out on US 31 and open her up a little, despite the snow that was coming down harder now.

"Do you know where you are going, or would you like me to set up the navigation system?" Claire asked.

He looked at the panel on the center dashboard and could see a color map that he realized was of the Oceana County area where they were located. *Impressive stuff,* he thought, but he replied, "No. I know how to get there." He was actually enjoying the drive. By the time they reached US 31, the dogs had finished their rawhides and were pushing their noses between Beth and Josh. Flotsam acted as if she was going to jump over the seat. Rock told her to lie down, and she did.

"Flower, lie down," Claire commanded, but the big lab stood there. Rock saw in the mirror Josh looking over at Beth just as she looked at him. Both chuckled.

"Mom, she's ignoring you."

"Flower, lie down," Claire again commanded, but again the big dog paid no attention.

Looking at her reflection in the rearview mirror, calmly Rock repeated, "Flower, lay down," at which point the big dog lowered herself first onto her rear haunches and then settled over her front legs. Everyone in the car except Rock roared in laughter. Rock looked at Claire and then at Beth and Josh through the rearview mirror and merely said, "What?" The ice in the back seat, it seemed, was broken.

While Beth and Josh began an easy getting-to-know-you conversation, Claire asked Rock how he'd come to meet Jan. All she knew was that she was the owner of Far-Far-View and that Rock was her renter. Her heart softened when he told her how she'd relented on the no pets clause of his lease. "Nice lady, then."

Rock nodded in agreement and smiled at her, "Yeah, I'd say so."

Just outside of Fremont, Rock turned the Range Rover into Jan's driveway. Claire, almost imperceptibly, said, "Oh, my." In front of them stood an old, beautifully renovated farmhouse. A long but straight driveway led them past a pond on their right. Frozen on its edges with snow accumulating on the thin layer of ice, the pond bubbled at its center. "Is it an artesian spring?" Claire asked.

No one answered, too busy taking in the beauty of the setting like something out of Currier and Ives. A narrow channel about twenty-five yards long drained the pond's overflow into a creek that switched back and forth in tight curves along the east side of the house. An arched footbridge crossed over it. Bridges had been Alan's life and thus a major part of Claire's. She noticed the careful detail of the arch's construction and for the briefest of moments was reminded of him.

Beth leaned forward from the back seat between Rock and Claire and pointed, "Look at the widow's walk." The brick, two-story farmhouse was framed in beautifully sculpted wood soffits of a kind produced by carpenter-artisans of a century past. These had been painted white, but their grooves and edges were painted red to match the brick. A widow's walk sat atop the apex of the sharply angled roof, and through its old-time ripply window glass they could see the blurred form of a Christmas tree, lit and trimmed in red, white and silver bows.

Claire turned to Rock, "It's like a Norman Rockwell painting!"

Rock rang the doorbell. Immediately he could hear two dogs barking on the other side of the door. Their arrival at Jan Fremeyer's home could only be described as madcap. Jan's dog, a two-year old lab-shepherd mix, and Madeline Murphy's dog, an older but nonetheless enthusiastic collie-chow mix, met Flower and Flotsam at the door. The chaos began. Nothing was broken on their romp through the house, simply by luck. It did not take the adults long to figure out that the canine party needed to be carried out into the fenced back yard, where the four dogs romped and cavorted in the snow.

Rock made introductions, as did Jan.

The farmhouse's foyer and adjoining hallway were painted a subtle tan to compliment the dark grain of the wide-planked walnut floor. In front of them a staircase ascended to the second floor, its railing and balustrades made of a fine-grained maple hardwood. On the walls of the foyer and the hall were framed serigraphs, pastoral scenes mostly depicting the slower pace of life in rural America, perhaps a hundred or more years ago. Pointing to one of them, Claire asked, "Is this..."

Jan was smiling at her. "This house? It is."

"How unique," Claire said. By now Beth, the art history student, had joined her mother.

Jan continued, "The original owner commissioned it. The story goes he had a hundred copies made to give as Christmas presents to family and friends the year he'd finished building the house in 1870." She pointed to one corner of the picture, "This is number one of one hundred."

"It's beautiful," Beth said. "Are there more of the copies surviving?"

"If there are, I haven't seen any of them. Some of the family is still in the area. In fact, some of them still farm the land around the house. I bought this place from the original owner's great grandson almost ten years ago. It was a real mess. Hadn't been lived in for about twenty years. Anyway, when I bought it, the great grandson gave me this serigraph. He said he thought it should stay with the house now that someone was going to be living in it again."

"You have done such a lovely job of restoring everything," Claire told her. Beth nodded in agreement.

"Well, thanks. A lot of people think I'm nuts. I've put a lot of money into this place, but I don't regret a cent of it. This old house deserves to look the way it does," she said. "Most people don't think of a house as having a soul. Most of them don't. It's what you put into them, and I'm not just talking about money here, if you know what I mean. This place touched my soul when I first saw it. Now it's a part of me, just like I'm a part of it."

As they moved into the dining room where the table looked like something out of *House Beautiful,* the smells of roast turkey tantalized their noses. Claire told her, "Jan, everything is so festive, and the smell, well, it makes my mouth water."

"Dinner will be ready in about an hour," Jan announced. After that, gravitational pulls affecting each gender differently took over. Claire moved toward the kitchen. Rock gravitated to the living room where, John, Jan's brother-in-law, and Larry, Jan's youngest brother, were watching the hapless Detroit Lions getting thumped by the Tennessee Titans. The Lions hadn't won a game all year, and it didn't look like this week was going to change that.

Standing next to a tray of appetizers Jan had brought into the room John said to Rock, "Jan tells me you have a vintage Corvette."

"I do," Rock smiled and added, "1972 Stingray."

"Great year. That model, the C2 or C3... I never can keep those model years clear in my mind."

"It's a C3," Rock clarified. "They made some changes to the basic body style, but the C3 went from 1968 to 1982 before they made the leap to the C4."

"That long? Well, that design was a beauty. I wanted to buy one that year, 1972, I mean." He paused as if remembering, "It's the year I came home from Vietnam, but it just didn't work out. In fact, it didn't work out for the next thirty-six years." They both laughed. Then John said, "I finally bought a nice '02 convertible this year. I just put it away for the winter a couple of weeks ago, and from the looks of the weather today, I was in the nick of time."

Rock told him about Green Girl's storage situation in Silver Lake. He added, "They're great cars to drive, but not in weather like this."

Knowingly, John nodded. They each munched on an appetizer and then, easily, casually, John pointed to Rock's leg and said, "Jan told me you were wounded in Nam. Thanks for your service and welcome home." John extended his hand.

Rock took it, nodded and simply said, "Thanks, Colonel. You, too."

Larry lamented something about the Titans scoring every time they got their hands on the ball and the Lions going three-and-out every time. Rock and John joined him in front of the TV. Vietnam was not mentioned again.

In the kitchen Madeline got Claire to the side, but before she could say what she wanted to say, Claire said, "Everything looks and smells wonderful, Madeline."

"Thanks. We're so glad you could come today."

Claire asked, "So you and Jan are best friends?"

"The best. I live just across the street," she said, as she pointed out the window. Claire looked, but could barely make out the shape of a house. The kitchen's windows were steamy from the heat of things cooking. "Jan and I taught for years in the Fremont schools. She was an art teacher, but I'll bet you could have guessed that. I taught math. We both retired at the same time. Now, I do the practical stuff like helping her with the lakeshore cottage, especially in the summer when she rents it week-to-week. We take a lot of meals together since we are both single. I do most of the cooking. It just makes our lives more fun," Madeline said, smiling. "But what I wanted to tell you, Claire, is that I'm the Board Chair of the Fremont Area Food Bank. We're one of the ones that you've donated to for a lot of years, but I really want to thank you for upping that donation this year. We were experiencing bare shelves, something we've never had to deal with before, and I don't know what we would have done without that extra money. A lot of people would be going hungry if it weren't for you."

Claire averted her eyes, but smiled. It had been years ago that she and Alan had agreed to support a dozen West Michigan Food Banks, and she had to admit she had lost track of which food banks they decided to support. It was good to hear. She looked up and said to Madeline, "I'm glad to know that the money is doing some good."

Josh, standing next to his uncle in the living room, noticed Beth drift into a sunroom at the back of the house that overlooked the back yard. While the other men groaned at another touchdown drive by the Titans, Josh walked through the kitchen and into the sunroom. Together he and Beth laughed at the four dogs romping in the snow that was coming down in huge, wet flakes and accumulating quickly.

Tentatively, Josh began, "My uncle told me about your break up. It must be hard."

She thought it was brash of him to bring this up, but, after Flower's ice-breaker, she had found Josh easy to talk to. "It is and, yet again, it isn't." She paused. Josh kept quiet. "He and I simply weren't right for one another. He wanted me to be something I was not. I wanted more from him than he could give."

"Better to find these things out now rather than later."

Beth merely nodded.

Josh sensed Beth had shared as much about the breakup as she was ready to share, so he shifted the subject. "It's nice to be together for Thanksgiving like this. I've never been to a Thanksgiving dinner with so many people. When my mom was alive, it was Uncle Rock, me and her. After she passed, it was just my Uncle Rock, my Uncle Russ and Aunt Patti." Beth nodded again, but didn't say anything, the reference to Josh's deceased mother creating a certain awkwardness. Josh added, "Russ and Patti really aren't blood relatives, but I feel like they are. I've known them for as long as I've known Uncle Rock. Uncle Rock and Uncle Russ were in Vietnam together."

"Is that what happened to his leg?" She realized after she'd asked it, how crass the question must have sounded. Apologetically, she added, "I'm sorry, I didn't mean to..."

"No. It's OK. He doesn't like to talk about it. Neither of them do, but Uncle Russ told me once what happened. If you listen to my Uncle Russ tell the story, Uncle Rock should have gotten the Medal of Honor."

"I... I don't know much about the military."

184

"Neither do I, but he did get the Navy Cross." Josh recognized a puzzled look on her face, then added, "It's given for courage in combat. Only the Medal of Honor is higher."

She'd seen some Medal of Honor presentations covered by the nightly news, so Josh's comment intrigued her. "What did he do?... to earn the medal, I mean."

Josh paused for a long time, struggling between loyalty to what he knew was his uncle's wishes for Vietnam to remain a very private thing and his own desire to continue talking to her.

"Maybe I shouldn't have asked..."

"No, it's OK, Beth. It's just that I know he wouldn't like me talking about it." He looked at her and began, "His platoon got pinned down in an ambush..." For ten minutes he talked, and Beth listened, sometimes just shaking her head. He concluded with a detail that Rock didn't know Josh knew about, a detail that his Uncle Russ had warned, *Don't let him know that I told you about this.* "He sleeps with a night light on. He hasn't been in the dark since it happened. It seems he woke up that first night in the hospital in Saigon after dreaming that he was back in the jungle. A nurse came up with the idea. He's never turned it off."

"He has PTSD, then."

"Back then no one knew what that was, but, yeah, he does. He's read about it. He knows he has it, I think, and he knows the nurse only treated his symptoms, not the disorder, but the light has worked for him all of these years, so he doesn't want to tinker with something that he feels isn't broken."

"He must have terrible memories."

They were still alone on the back porch. The dogs continued to romp in the snow that had covered the ground. Feeling a little guilty about his disclosures, Josh took a risk and placed both of his hands on her shoulders. She didn't recoil in the slightest. "Beth, my Uncle Rock is a very private man about this stuff. I probably shouldn't have said as much as I have, but I trust you."

"But you hardly know me, Josh."

"Yeah, I know. But yesterday, when we were driving, all my uncle could talk about was your mother. He's really quite fond of her. So, I've told you."

"I've heard people with PTSD can suddenly become..." She paused, not knowing quite how to ask the question, but still intent on asking it. "There's no easy way to ask this, but I have to. Could he become violent?"

His arms and hands now drooping at his sides, Josh hung his head. He feared he'd scared her. "Beth..." Now he had to compose his thoughts carefully. "My uncle is more like my father. I know him well. He did some terrible things once in his life because his life and the lives of others depended on him doing those terrible things. But you must believe me now when I tell you, he doesn't have a violent bone in his body."

Beth looked up at him and smiled. "I'm sorry, Josh. I had to ask, but now that you've told me, I believe you."

It was 6 p.m. as Rock stood looking out the big living room window overlooking the pond. The snow, which had relented for the last few hours, had begun coming down again, heavy. He felt Claire step next to him. "Penny for your thoughts," she said.

"I'm glad you and Beth came with us today."

"Me, too. Thanks for inviting us. That was an amazing meal."

"They must have been working on it since the beginning of the week." He patted his stomach, "I honestly couldn't eat another bite." Claire grabbed his hand and stepped closer to him. He liked her closeness. Smiling at her, he pointed out the window, "This stuff's coming down again. I wonder how much is on the ground at the lake?"

"You think we should get on the road?" she asked.

"Yeah, that might be best. By the way, Josh and Beth seem to be getting along well, don't you think?"

"Yes, I do. This entire day has been just the diversion she needed to get her mind off Nathan."

Chapter Twenty-Four

The Kiss

The rest of Thanksgiving weekend passed much too quickly for all of them. Claire, Rock, Beth and Josh went out for breakfast on Friday and Saturday mornings and came home to long walks on the beach in nearly windless conditions under brilliant sunshine. The temps were chilly, but above average for the end of November.

Friday evening they had enjoyed turkey with all the trimmings thanks to Jan sending them home with generous portions of leftovers. Afterward everyone played a hotly contested game of Scrabble in front of the fireplace that Beth eventually won after challenging Josh's word *zozque,* which he said was Ethiopian for *mosque.* Laughter filled the great room as he capitulated with exaggerated disbelief that they wouldn't trust him on this.

Saturday evening, Claire made her famous meatloaf, and as Rock and Claire were cleaning up in the kitchen, Josh found Beth staring out the slider into the last light of day. Quietly he walked up behind her. Clearing his throat so as not to startle her, he said, "You, OK?" Her pensiveness reminded him of how he had found her on the sun porch at Jan's.

Without turning, but looking at his reflection in the slider, she smiled and nodded. "Yes, just fine." They both stood staring out at the ever-darkening lake in front of them, savoring their waning hours at the lakeshore. Then Beth said, "It's beautiful here, isn't it?"

Josh smiled, "I had no idea. When Uncle Rock told me he was spending the winter over here, I thought he was crazy. I mean, who comes here in the winter?"

"Right!" she replied. "Only crazy people." They both chuckled.

From the kitchen, Claire asked, "Anyone for euchre?"

Without answering, they studied one another's reflection in the slider. After a long moment, Beth shook her head and asked, "Would you like to take a walk on the beach?"

"I'd like that."

Sunday morning opened brilliantly clear, but cold. There was a light wind out of the southwest. The plan was that Rock and Josh were to head toward Michigan State about mid-morning. Beth would be leaving for Grand Rapids about the same time.

At 9:00 a.m. the phone rang at Far-Far-View. Rock answered.

"Rock, it's Beth. I'm glad I caught you before you left. Mom and I were wondering if you, Josh and Flotsam would like to take a walk on the beach with us. It's so beautiful out this morning."

Rock looked into the sunroom and saw Flotsam lying in her chair surveying the beach below. Josh was in the shower. He surmised neither of them would object. He certainly didn't. "Sure, Beth. How about 10:00 a.m.?"

"Perfect."

"OK. We'll come to you guys. See you then."

Noon found them settling down at the kitchen table at Claire's while she warmed some soup for all. At 12:30 p.m. Rock glanced at his watch and said, "What time did you want to get back to school?"

Kidding, Josh said, "Do I have to?"

After everyone's chuckle died, Beth said, "Josh, I could take you back to East Lansing." Her offer surprised all of them.

Rock said, "Beth, you don't have to..."

Claire felt her heart skip a beat.

Beth looked at Rock, "I don't mind at all."

Rock looked over at his nephew, expecting support, and when he didn't get it realized that this whole thing had probably been set up the night before.

Josh looked at Beth, "That's really nice of you."

Beth smiled at him and said, "I know." He laughed. She did, too. Rock gave a smile of concession. Claire beamed.

With Josh and Beth gone, Rock and Claire took a brisk late afternoon walk on the beach. It was very cold, so they were walking less than thirty minutes when Claire suggested they return to her house. "I can make some chili."

"How many alarms?" Rock asked and smiled at her.

"How many do you want?" she replied coyly.

They ate in front of the fireplace and talked. "I think Beth likes Josh," Claire observed.

"They did seem to hit it off this weekend, didn't they?" Rock said. "I mean, I like the beach as well as the next guy, but it was cold last night and they were gone for what, almost two hours? Who can stand to be out in weather like that?" He shook his head and laughed.

"He's a very nice young man, Rock. You have every right to be proud."

As their conversation meandered, Claire noticed it inevitably returned to the two young people who were so inextricably wound into each of their lives. "Rock, don't take this the wrong way. I'm not trying to play matchmaker, but did you notice the way Beth's spirits perked up this weekend?"

He looked at her and smiled, "I didn't want to be the one to bring it up, but, yes, I did."

Claire waited for a minute and when Rock did not offer more, she chuckled and asked, "So what do you think about that?"

"About what?" he looked at her. She had a pained expression on her face as if to say, *How can you be that obtuse?* "Oh, you mean what do I think about Beth and Josh?" He gave her a wink and chuckled.

"You know perfectly well what I mean."

"I think what will be, will be."

"Very musical," she chided.

"Yeah, I know, right." He knew she was looking for more of a reaction. "You know, Claire, kids today really can just be friends... boys and girls, I mean... and there doesn't really have to be anything to it except friendship."

She thought for a moment and then asked, "Has Josh ever had a serious girl friend?"

Nodding, Rock answered, "His senior year in high school. It was the year his mother died. There was this girl, Melanie... Melanie Smith. She and Josh saw a lot of each other."

When Rock didn't offer more information, Claire asked, "What happened to them?"

Rock laughed and said, "Life." He paused and then continued, "Josh went to MSU. She went to Mott Community College. They grew apart. I think they're still friends, but they've each gone their separate ways."

"How old is Josh?" Claire asked.

"Just turned twenty-two. Beth?"

"Twenty-seven."

"Not that much difference in years, but the gap gets wider when you consider where each of them is in their life," Rock said. "An awful lot can happen to the two of them, Claire. I'm betting on Josh to get admitted to vet school at MSU. That's at least four more years of school for him. Beth... well... I don't know much about art, but she does, and I suspect she's got a pretty good business head on her shoulders, like her mother," he grinned at Claire, "And with that gallery of hers, my bet is she's going to take the art world by storm. That is what I meant when I said, 'What will be, will be'."

Claire gave a sigh, "I know you're right, but it is so good to see someone raise her spirits so. She needs to get back to work, because she is good at what she does. She's told me about something that she's working on with a lot of other collaborators in Grand Rapids. They are going to call it *Art Prize*. It sounds like it could be something that could really put Grand Rapids on the map of the art world."

It was just after 8 p.m. when Rock glanced at his watch. Both dogs were asleep in front of the blazing fire. "Claire, Flotsam and I had better get going. It's been a wonderful day, a wonderful weekend," he said as he stood up. Both dogs awoke at the movement.

"Yes, it was wonderful, Rock. You don't have to go," she said with a tone of disappointment.

The words were music to him, but there was something he had to do, "Claire, I have two very good friends. Someday I hope you can meet the Sluwinskis. We all go back a long way, and Russ and I go back even further. Since my sister died, four years ago, Josh and I have spent Thanksgiving with them. They are in Florida this year. I have to give them a call."

Claire thought of the Chavezes. "I understand. There are some folks I must call, too." Smiling, she added, "We raised our kids together. Someday you'll meet them. Their names are Jesus and Maria Chavez."

"I look forward to it, Claire," and with that he thumped his thigh, "Come on, Flotsam. Let's go home." Both dogs stood and in near-perfect unison performed downward facing dog stretches. Claire and he laughed at them.

At the door Rock suggested, "Let's walk in the morning, even if it's on the road."

"I'd love to," and then came the big surprise of the weekend. Claire closed the distance between them, placed her
hand alongside his face, and kissed him delicately, letting
it linger, full of warmth and softness.

He put his arms around her and pulled her against him.
When the kiss ended, he nuzzled close to her ear and said,
"I'm so glad you're here, Claire."

On the short walk home he took his flashlight from his
pocket while still in the glow of the garage lights. Flotsam
was not on her leash, but stayed just ahead of him, well
within the length of the flashlight's beam. "You know how
much I appreciate you and Flower introducing us, don't
you?"

The dog turned her head as if to answer, *You are welcome. Now just follow me and I'll get us home.*

Chapter Twenty-Five

Telling Friends

As the door closed behind her, Claire leaned against it and smiled. If she should have felt guilty about the kiss, she didn't. Maybe it wasn't supposed to feel that good to be held by another man besides Alan, but it did. She was smiling as she called Maria Chavez.

"Ms. Claire, did you have a good Thanksgiving?"

With unmistakable enthusiasm, Claire replied, "Wonderful, Maria, just wonderful."

"Did you go with the man next door?"

"Beth and I went to Fremont. We met his nephew, his landlady, some of her family and her friend. It was so much fun. I can't remember a better Thanksgiving in a long time, and I have you to thank."

"Me? No, I don't think so, Ms. Claire."

"Do you remember when we talked last, Maria?"

"Yes," Maria responded.

"Do you remember telling me to enjoy this time with Beth, even though she is struggling so? You said to let myself go, enjoy my time with my daughter, enjoy my Thanksgiving because that is what Alan would have wanted me to do. Remember telling me that, Maria?" It was rhetorical, and Claire did not wait for an answer, "Well that is just what I did, and I had an absolutely marvelous time." She paused and then quickly added, "And so did Beth."

"I'm so glad, Ms. Claire."

"How were your holidays? Any news about work for James and Mary?"

"We were all together on Thanksgiving. All four children." Claire loved that Maria still referred to her adult off-spring as children. "All the grandchildren were here. Jesus is still recovering." They both chuckled. "James is working at Best Buy. He's selling computers. He's good at it because he knows so much about them, but it isn't what he wants to do. Mary is substitute teaching. She works almost every day, but I know she doesn't like it. She isn't in any one place long enough to connect with the children. They are both still looking, but the times are very tough, Ms. Claire."

"I know, Maria. Can I do anything to help?" It sounded like such a hollow offer to Claire, but she felt it had to be made.

"Ms. Claire, none of us know what we would do without you and your family. You do so much for us that you don't even know about."

It was impossible for either woman to know, but both were starting to cry.

Rock had not wanted to let go of her, but he knew he needed to measure his steps very carefully with Claire. Her kiss had surprised him. His taking her into his arms had not. He'd wanted to do that for quite some time now. He was euphoric as he got back to Far-Far-View. He felt almost compelled to call Russ and Patti.

"Patti? What's the deal? Russ doesn't answer his cell phone anymore?"

She laughed. "He's asleep, Rock. I heard the phone ring, saw it was you on caller ID and thought I'd better answer.

How was your holiday? Did you escape the frozen jaws of hell?"

If you only knew, he thought. "It was great! Yours?"

"Russ took me out. Can you believe that? Can you believe I let him do that?"

For Patti, cooking Thanksgiving dinner was a tradition, but apparently not this year. "Wow! No I can't," he responded. "Thanksgiving dinner out is a huge change for you. Speaking of changes, have you started looking at real estate down there?"

"No, but we have come to a couple of conclusions."

"Well, that's progress."

"First off, we aren't going to move down here permanently. Yeah, I like the sun and, yeah, Russ likes the fishing, but, my God, Rock, this place is full of nothin' but old people. Russ and I aren't there yet."

"You're serious?"

"As a damned heart attack," she responded. "Plus, we aren't far enough south. It's been downright cold here this last week. Nothin' like what *you* put up with, but, hell, we come down here to get away from the cold and soak up the sunshine and to do that we are going to have to go down around Fort Myers. So, ol' Russ and I are going to take a little trip to south Florida here in the next couple of weeks, and I'll do some serious real estate shopping then. In the meantime, we're coming home to Flint in April, so we'll be there when you get back from Antarctica. What about your Thanksgiving? Did you and Flotsam eat turkey?"

He told her about going to Jan's for Thanksgiving and then quickly added, "Patti, I met somebody."

Patti shot back, "Rock, I fell for that line the last time. It ain't gonna work twice."

"No, I'm serious. She's my neighbor up here. Our dogs introduced us, if you can believe that. She, her daughter and Josh and I went to Jan's for Thanksgiving. I really enjoy her company and..." He was talking fast, like he had to get everything out quickly or he'd explode.

Patti had rarely heard him like this. "Rock, you are serious, aren't you?"

"As a heart attack." They both chuckled

"Wait, I got to get Russ up and let you tell him..."

He interrupted her, "No, Patti, don't do that." Laughing he said, "He'll just want to know if we've done it yet or how was she in the sack."

Patti's timing was perfect. She let him wait for it. "So have you and how was it?"

She let him hang there for just the perfect amount of time and then she blurted, "Gotcha, Rock!"

Chapter Twenty-Six

Some Nerve

The week after Thanksgiving, the first week of December, weather-wise, was a gift that neither of them expected. They walked morning and afternoon, six or more miles a day, up and down the beach at Little Point Sable. Sometimes they were hand-in-hand, others one or both of them was busy throwing a ball or a stick for the dogs to chase. The temperatures were so mild that on occasion they would throw the object into the lake and shiver as both dogs, completely unaware that the water was near freezing, charged into the gentle waves racing after it. It was during the morning walk on Thursday when Claire asked, "Rock, will you have Christmas dinner with Beth and me?"

The fact is he'd been toying with the idea of having everyone over to Far-Far-View. "Claire, I..."

She held up a hand smiling at him, "Wait. Before you answer, I should tell you that Jan and Madeline have already accepted, and Beth is going to pick up Josh at MSU and bring him up here for the holidays."

Claire's plans were further along than any he had made. "Well, I..."

Again, she held up her hand, stopping him, "Did you know they are going to see one another this weekend in East Lansing?"

"What?" The news stunned him.

"Beth told me last night on the phone that Josh called and asked if she could come over and go to a basketball game with him at the Breslin Center. He apparently has a female friend who has an extra bedroom in her apartment. I haven't heard Beth this excited in a long time."

"He hasn't said a word to me."

"Uh, well, yes," she had an impish look on her face. "Beth explained that, too. Josh didn't want to talk to you about this over the phone. He just didn't think that would be right. But he plans to talk to you at Christmas when he sees you. So how about it? Christmas dinner at my house?"

He looked at her, smiled, shrugged his shoulders and said emphatically, "Sounds like fun. I'd love to."

Claire picked up a stick and threw it. The dogs went charging down the beach. As they retrieved the stick, Flower holding one end, Flotsam locked on to the other, it struck Rock there was someone missing from the guest list. He knew why she had not been around at Thanksgiving, but Christmas was still a month away and it was... well, it was Christmas. In Rock's mind anyway, the biggest holiday of the year. "What about Ingrid and her family?"

Claire averted her eyes and could feel her face becoming flushed. She should have realized that he would be perceptive enough to ask this question. She should have had an answer, but in her exuberance she wasn't very prepared. She simply said, "She's not coming." There was a pause, and she knew Rock was looking for more detail. "I invited them, but she started up again about Beth's break up and apparently Beth had mentioned something to her about Josh, so she's been nagging Beth and me both about that. Ingrid doesn't approve." She spat out the words like they were sour milk.

"Oh, I see." He thought, *and that has to include me, too.*

It was quiet for a while as they walked. They stopped only briefly for Rock to pick up the stick that the dogs had dropped at his feet. Bending over, he picked it up and flung it down the beach. As the dogs took off after it, he turned to her and said, "Claire, I don't want to make trouble between..."

She cut him off. "Rock, believe me, you aren't the one making trouble. That would be Ingrid. I suppose it's one of the qualities that make her such a good attorney, but Beth and I are not her clients. We are her family. Her stubbornness and inability to see things in any other way than her way can sure make her hard to live with." They walked on some more, and then Claire added, "Please don't feel that any of this stuff with Ingrid should keep you from spending Christmas Day with me, because it shouldn't. I don't want it to."

"I wish she'd come. Maybe if she could see how charming Josh and I can be..." They both laughed. Rock put his arm around her and said, "I'd love to spend Christmas with you." Claire looked up at him and smiled as they continued arm in arm down the beach.

Their walk on Friday morning had been exhilarating, five miles, a light breeze out of the west, bright sunshine and an unseasonable high of fifty degrees. When they arrived back at Claire's, the dogs ran ahead of them, up the stairs, and across the patio to the slider, where they stood waiting to be let in. Rock and Claire trailed them, holding hands. Claire offered, "How about I warm some soup for lunch?"

"Sounds great," and Rock pulled the slider open. The two dogs entered and immediately stopped in their tracks. The hair on both of their backs went up, and Flotsam issued a low growl. Flower stood staring. Transitioning from the bright sunshine to the relatively flat light of the interior of the house, it took Claire a moment to see what had frozen them so. "Ingrid," she said, "What a surprise," her tone indicating it wasn't necessarily a pleasant one.

Rock, right behind her said, "Flotsam, stop that!" She pinned her ears back, but stopped growling, never taking her intense eyes off of the intruder.

"Hello, Mother," Ingrid said, her voice dripping with insincerity as she shot Rock a glance.

"Uh, we weren't expecting you," Claire said weakly.

"That's obvious," Ingrid said icily.

"Is everything all right?"

"I don't know, Mother. Why don't you tell me?" She shot another look at Rock that would have withered a lesser man.

Claire, trying to retain her composure, introduced him. Rock greeted her with an extended hand. He was half expecting her to refuse it, but she didn't. Instead she offered him a cold fish, nothing more. "Nice to meet you, Ingrid." He could tell she could not wait to pull her hand away, so Rock could not let go quickly enough. Awkwardly, he turned to Claire, "Uh, well, Flotsam and I had better get home. Shall we try and walk this afternoon around 2:00 p.m.?"

"Rock, you don't…"

Ingrid piped in, "Mother there's some things I'd like to talk to you about, and I don't have much time."

It was Claire's turn now to give someone an angry look, and it splattered all over Ingrid who stood staring at her mother.

"Claire, it's all right. We should go. Call me if you'd like to walk this afternoon." With that, Rock tapped his thigh, Flotsam came to him, and the two of them left through the slider.

Claire watched them make their way across the patio and down the steps to the dune and then turned to Ingrid angrily. "You embarrass me."

Ingrid gave no ground. Unapologetically, she explained why she had made the trip and none of it was good for Claire, Beth, or Josh. And, now, after she had observed the two of them holding hands, most of all, Rock.

Flotsam was asleep in front of the fireplace, and Rock was in the sunroom reading in his favorite easy chair, when there was a knock on the back door. Flotsam awoke and went ahead of Rock, who hoped it was Claire surprising him. It was not.

"Ingrid," he said through the storm door, surprise evident in his voice. He fumbled with the handle and pushed the door open, "Uh, uh, come in. Is everything all right?"

She stepped into the entrance hallway of Far-Far-View. Everything about her, Rock thought, was meant to intimidate. She was tall, perhaps five feet, ten inches, and she stood stiffly erect. Her blue eyes, which under different circumstances might be considered beautiful, felt stone-cold to him. She wasn't wearing much makeup, but what she did have on was perfectly applied to emphasize high cheek bones and pouty lips. It might be considered attractive, but today, he thought, she was trying to achieve an air of superiority. The black leather coat that hung to below her knees was pulled tight around a narrow waist. He was sure the silver accents on it were pure silver. It even smelled expensive. The black leather mid-heel boots gleamed, even in the low light of the entrance hallway, not a scuff mark to be seen. But it was her hair style that was the most intimidating, pulled back against the sides to a tight bun in the back. She appeared gaunt, too severe. She looked like she was about to interrogate a hostile witness. "Mr. Graham, I want you to understand exactly how vulnerable my mother and my sister are right now. I'm sure you know Mother is recently widowed..."

Out of the corner of his eye, he caught Flotsam slithering back to her rug in front of the fireplace. *Chicken!* Then returning to more pressing issues, he thought, *Recently widowed? Are you kidding me! Alan died three years ago.*

"... and my sister has just broken off her engagement the week before Thanksgiving. I don't want to see either of them hurt any more than they already have been. I know that you are fond of my mother and that your nephew, at least that is, I believe, the nature of your relationship with this Josh-person..."

Her haughtiness was so irritating. *Josh-person!*

"... but I just don't think that now is the right time for either of you to be in their lives. You and my mother come from such different backgrounds..."

You over-indulged bitch!

"... that I just don't see it ever working out between the two of you. The same is true of my sister and your nephew..."

Do you have any idea how you sound?

"... so I'd like to suggest that you stop seeing my mother and that you call off this cockamamie plan of yours to keep them up here for Christmas. They both belong in Grand Rapids that day, having Christmas with me and my family."

There was that word again, "cockamamie". Patti had used it. He hadn't liked it then and now disliked it even more coming from her. *Are you crazy? Your mother invited us to Christmas dinner.* He took a deep breath. *Get a grip.*

Rock Graham did not have a college degree. But he could have. At Flint Central High School he had distinguished himself in the classroom and on the football field. He had gotten a partial scholarship to Central Michigan University to play football. His best friend and teammate, Russ Sluwinski, was an All-State nose guard at Flint Central, who was offered a full ride at Central Michigan. There were, however, two problems. Sluwinski hated school and Graham could not afford to pay what his scholarship didn't cover. So, instead, they enlisted in the Marine Corps together. But Rock had forever loved books. Among all of his acquaintances, he was by far the most well-read. His loft was more like a library than an apartment, the walls lined with bookshelves full of books of every variety. At GM he had been one of the first to train on the robotics equipment that would revolutionize both the speed and quality of mass production lines. Their programming required exceptional mathematical ability and logic, both of which seemed to come almost naturally to him. He had excelled at the training and been considered one of the best at programming and troubleshooting these remarkably complex pieces of equipment. If Ingrid thought of him as just an assembly-line worker, putting the same part on the same chassis hour after hour, day after day, then she had seriously underestimated him.

He was dressed in a sweatshirt, jeans with white socks protruding from the legs and lambskin slippers on his feet. It was easy to mistake him for a bumpkin, but in the face of Ingrid's superior attitude, he rubbed his chin, shifted his weight onto his forward foot and began, "Well, Ingrid..." He choked back the instinct to raise his voice. He wanted to explode a bomb of profanity at her, but he held these things in check. He looked her straight in the eye and began, cooly, calmly, "I appreciate your stopping and I appreciate your honesty, but I'd like for you now to appreciate my honesty. I am fond of your mother. I'll not deny that. We are good friends who enjoy one another's company. I don't believe either of us is too old to appreciate a little romance in our lives and, yes, I think we are providing a little of that to one another. I'm terribly sorry that you don't agree. It would be easier for both your mother and me if you did." He paused briefly to let that sink in, but not so long as to let Ingrid think he was finished with her.

"As to your sister and my nephew..." He paused again for a moment, trying to decide if he wanted to make an issue of it. He decided he did. "And, yes, you are correct, this Josh-person," he sneered those words back to her the way she had sneered them to him, "Josh is my nephew. Your sister and my nephew are both of the age that entitles them to do whatever they may want without consulting your mother, me and, least of all, you."

Ingrid stood there. Rock thought that her mouth was slightly agape. It was obvious that she had not anticipated this kind of push back from someone so far below her in the socioeconomic pecking order. As for Rock, any awkwardness had long since passed after she'd pissed him off so badly. When she didn't say anything, he calmly asked. "Is there anything else?" He was proud of himself. Not one swear word.

Ingrid fumed, "You didn't listen to a single..."

"Yes, I did, Ingrid. I listened to every word. The problem is, I just don't agree with you." He half expected her to stomp her feet and throw a hissy fit before leaving, but she didn't.

"Well, we will just see..." and with that hanging in the air, she turned, opened the storm door and left.

As he closed the door behind her, he turned and caught his reflection in a nearby mirror. He was red in the face. This was an ambush! No wonder his pulse was pounding. He walked into the living room and looked at Flotsam on her rug staring up at him. "Well you certainly got out of the way in a big hurry. Don't like her, do you? Kinda' like Phyllis, is she?" He knelt and rubbed her ears as he began to ponder the much larger question, *Should I tell Claire about this?* He didn't have much time to think about it.

At about 2 p.m. the phone rang, "Rock, it's Claire. Want to walk? I need to talk to you."

He was pretty sure he knew what it was about.

Ten minutes later they found themselves following their dogs south down the beach. Claire reached over and took his hand in hers, "If there were any doubts that Beth and I are going to have Christmas here, they can be put to rest after this visit from Ingrid." Rock kept his mouth shut. Still holding his hand, Claire continued, "She is the most contrary, obstinate, know-it-all person I have ever known."

"She does seem to have a lot of self-confidence."

Claire snorted, "It's smugness. You're just being kind to call it self-confidence. She doesn't think you and I have any business seeing one another," she said, leaving out any reason why. Rock thought she was sparing him at least some of the hurt Ingrid had tried to impose on her. "She thinks I'm still grieving for Alan. Can you believe that? All she's doing is trying to make me feel guilty about the way I feel about you."

It would be an understatement to say he didn't like Ingrid. As they walked, Claire continued to berate her daughter's unwanted interference in their lives. He was sure Claire did not know about Ingrid's stop at Far-Far-View. She would have asked about that and wanted to know what Ingrid might have said to him. Rock made the decision there was nothing to be gained by telling Claire of his confrontation with Ingrid. She was already angry with her eldest daughter, so what could be gained by him making her even angrier?

They walked for just over an hour and were climbing the steps to the patio, when Claire became short of breath and reached for him. Rock put an arm around her, held her other arm and helped her up the few remaining steps. He helped her sit down on the stone wall that surrounded the patio. "Another attack?"

She was still gasping for air, but nodded.

He sat down next to her and pulled her close to him. He could feel her gasping ease. When he was sure she was breathing normally again, he looked at her, "I haven't pushed you on this, but have you called your doctor?"

The dogs were huddled around them. He and Claire stood, and the four of them made their way to the slider and stepped in the house. He helped her off with her coat, sat her down in her favorite rocker and tugged her boots off. "I'll get you some water."

"That would be nice. Thanks."

He returned with it and started to say, "Claire..."

She interrupted him, "I know. I need to call my doctor."

"Yes, you do. Is this the only one of these you've had since that day on the beach when we first met?" His worst fears were realized with her answer.

"No."

He asked, "How many more?"

"I don't know. Three or four others. This one may have been the worst. I don't know. It's hard to tell..."

"If you don't call the doctor, I will," he pressed.

"I'll call."

"Now." It wasn't a question. When she hesitated, he said, "If you don't, I will."

She nodded.

"Do you know the number?"

"Hand me my purse."

While she rummaged around looking for her directory, Rock retrieved the telephone remote from its holder and handed it to her. He stood there while she explained to the person on the other end what her symptoms were and requested an appointment for some time next week if possible. "Yes, thanks, that will work. I'll see you then."

After she'd disconnected, Rock took the remote from her and placed it back in its charging cradle. "That wasn't so difficult was it?"

Somewhat sheepishly, she replied, "No."

He smiled at her, "So when are we going to see the doctor?"

"Rock, you don't have to..."

He knelt down next to her and took her hand, "Claire, I am not going to allow you to go alone." He leaned forward and gently kissed her.

Chapter Twenty-Seven

Dear God

Claire's doctor's appointment was 9:30 a.m. on Friday, December 12th, at her family physician's office in Holland. She and Rock decided to make a day of it. Knowing that if they did all that Claire had planned, it would be a long day indeed, Bob Mumford had agreed that he would look in on the dogs.

Claire had managed to scrounge through the few Christmas decorations at the lake house. There were a few nice things, but everything else was junk. None of the lights worked, the tinsel was shabby and the ornaments, with the exception of some that Ingrid and Beth had made as elementary school kids, were tarnished, broken, or out of date. So depending on how long the doctor's appointment lasted, they might shop before lunch. After lunch she had made a hair appointment. She'd asked Rock if that was all right with him. She needed a cut and color and that would take a couple of hours. He assured her it was fine. He would easily find something to occupy his time. He also needed to do some Christmas shopping.

"For Josh? What are you going to get him?" she inquired.

"Yes, and I don't know yet."

Coyly she asked, "Anyone else on your Christmas shopping list?"

"I have to find a little something for my girlfriend."

Claire leaned into him, "You don't have to…"

He put his index finger over her lips, smiled at her and simply said, "Yes, I do."

Claire had already decided what she was going to give him. It was risky, but she had done due diligence. She had talked it over with Josh, who had discussed it with Russ Sluwinski. Josh told Claire that Russ had at first thought it might be a bad idea, but he changed his mind as he and Josh talked. "You know what, Josh," he said to him, "The thing is just lyin' there on one of his bookshelves collecting dust. It deserves better than that and so does your Uncle Rock. Go for it, and if he gets shitty with anyone about it, just call me and I'll settle him down." Last weekend, Josh and Beth had gone into Rock's loft in Flint and gotten it, all of it. Beth had it at the gallery now. All they were lacking was the flag, and Claire was taking care of that.

They arrived at her doctor's appointment barely on time. Rock stayed in the waiting room while Claire was put through her paces. Blood and urine samples were collected. The doctor checked her over, eyes, ears, nose, throat, heart, lungs, reflexes. All the usual stuff, according to the doctor, appeared normal. "These attacks, Claire," the doctor asked, "Are they limited to shortness of breath?"

Claire thought for a moment, "They are the ones that are the most frightening, but now that you ask, there have been a couple of occasions when I've dropped something that I was sure I had a good hold on."

The doctor nodded. "Do you think that these episodes are increasing in frequency or in severity since first coming on you?"

That was difficult for Claire to answer, since she had no basis of comparison. "I wouldn't say so. The first one was in September. Since then I've had four or five others.

There's no warning, and they go away almost as soon as they come on. I'll be honest, they scare me when they occur, especially the ones where I'm short of breath, but they don't seem to last very long at all."

The doctor admitted that for the moment she was stumped. "You told me you are getting a lot of exercise?"

Claire laughed, "More than I have in a long time. I'm living at the lakeshore for a while. My neighbor and I walk our dogs almost every day. It's not a good day if we don't get at least five miles in."

"And the shortness of breath, has it ever occurred while you were walking?"

"Twice."

"But you were able to finish the walk?"

"The first time, yes, but it was one of the shortest ones we've ever taken. The second time it happened was at the end of a five-mile walk."

"So..." she paused trying to give this some quick evaluation, "You don't think it's the walking that causes these episodes."

"No, doctor, I don't. I feel better than I've felt in years."

"Well, don't stop doing what you like. The walking is really great exercise, so, for now, I'm going to encourage you to keep at that. Let me see if the blood and urine workup will tell us anything. In the meantime, try not to worry. I will give you a call on Monday, after I've seen the two lab reports."

It was 11:35 a.m. by the time Claire finished at the doctor's office, so she suggested lunch at Panera. "Beth turned me on to them. They have wonderful salads and they're pretty quick, too."

Claire had been right on both counts. After a delicious salad for her and half a sandwich and a cup of soup for him, they were headed for the Range Rover at about 12:30

p.m., when Claire announced, "We might be a little early. Maybe Phyllis can get me started early and we can have more time to shop for decorations."

Rock heard little of what she had to say after the name *Phyllis. Dear God—don't let this happen!*

"Rock, did you hear me?"

He looked at her, "Uh, yeah, sure. Where are we headed?" he asked, fearing the worst.

"Styles of Holland. It's just downtown on 8th Street. I'll show you." Claire thought he was unusually quiet on the twenty minutes it took them to arrive downtown.

As he pulled into a parking spot near the beauty shop to drop her off, he put the car into park and looked over at her, "Did you say your hairdresser's name was Phyllis?"

She confirmed, "Yes. Phyllis Layton. She's done my hair for years. She and her daughter, Janelle, were going to do our hair for Beth's wedding. I'm sure she'll have something to say about that. Why?"

He didn't answer her question, instead he asked, "Will you mention me?"

She turned and smiled at him, "Of, course. Why wouldn't I?"

He couldn't just let her walk in there. "Uh, well, Claire, do you remember the day I asked you to keep Flotsam for me because I had an appointment in Holland, the day Beth came home and told you about calling off the wedding?"

"Yes, of course I do."

"Well..." he paused dreading what he must tell her.

"What is it Rock?" curiosity evident in her tone.

"Well, that appointment was actually a date," he paused to study her face, "A date with Phyllis." He proceeded to tell her everything that had happened replete with details about their first failed evening together and how Flotsam had sent him home early. He also filled her in on the night she'd walked out on Janelle and him after dinner.

Claire laughed hysterically at his rendition of the night Flotsam had kept them apart. Even Rock chuckled when he saw her getting such a kick out of it. However, the retelling of the night with Janelle prompted a very different response from Claire, "Rock, I'm so sorry. She should not have put you in that position." Claire looked at her watch, "I better get going."

He grasped her hand and, somewhat awkwardly, said, "Sure. I just didn't want you to go in there without telling you. I should have told you..."

"Rock, how could you have known she was my hairdresser? "Yeah, but..."

"But what? The two of you didn't do anything did you? Flotsam saw to that on the first date and Phyllis managed to screw up the second one." She chuckled, leaned over and gave him a kiss. "I should be ready to go by 3:00 p.m. You don't have to come in. I'll look for you right around here." and she got out of the car.

As she expected, Phyllis's opening gambit was an overly-syrupy, "I am so sorry about Beth's wedding. Is she all right? Whatever is she going to do? Her doctor seemed just so perfect for her. Ingrid was in the other day..."

Claire thought, *Oh, boy, I'll bet you got an earful from her.*

"...she told me Beth is already seeing somebody else and..." Phyllis realized that she might be a little too forthcoming.

"And, what, Phyllis?" Claire asked without a second's hesitation.

"...and that you were seeing someone as well. Someone you met at the lakeshore."

"Well, it seems that Ingrid has stolen my thunder."

"Oh, no, Claire. She just said... well, you know... that you were seeing someone. She didn't want to talk about it beyond that, so, you know me, I didn't press her."

What a bunch of bullshit that is! Claire thought.

"So who is he?"

"Ingrid didn't tell you?"

"No. Like I said, she didn't seem to want to discuss it too much, and I didn't want to press."

Claire thought, *Yeah, right!* and then answered, "Well, his name is Geoff and he's a really wonderful man."

"That's so nice, Claire. I'm really glad for you."

You wouldn't be so glad if you knew who I was talking about.

"I recently dated a man from up that way. His name was Rock. He turned out to be a real loser. He was an ex-Marine. I asked him to set Janelle straight about this Marine that she says she's in love with, but..."

Claire had noticed that Janelle's station was empty. "Where is Janelle?"

"Well, that's the thing. I had asked this guy... he's got a bad limp... he got all shot up in Vietnam... anyway, I'd asked him to set her straight on what a crappy job being a Marine is."

Claire wanted to get up and walk out, but she also wanted to hear what other venom this bitch was going to spew.

"Bottom line is he double crossed me. Janelle's gone. She's out in San Diego with that Marine," she pretended to choke on the word.

Claire was civil, but guarded for the remainder of the styling. Phyllis was an excellent stylist, but Claire had reached a conclusion.

As Claire handed Phyllis her credit card, Phyllis asked, "Would you like to schedule something on the 30th or 31st? I'm sure you and Geoff have big plans for New Year's Eve," and she winked at Claire.

Now it was Claire's turn. "No, Phyllis, I won't be scheduling any more appointments with you." She gave that a moment to sink in.

"What? Why? Uh, Ms Van Zandt, what's wrong?"

"It's not what's wrong, Phyllis, it's who is wrong and the answer to that is you."

"I... I... I don't understand."

"Well, then let me set you straight. My Geoff has a nickname. It's Rock."

Claire noticed a glimmer of astonishment in Phyllis's face. "Oh, Claire, I didn't mean..."

"Yes, you did, Phyllis. You tried to use him to manipulate Janelle and it backfired on you. Lucky for me. He dropped me off here, and before I came in he told me everything... and I mean everything. What you expected him to tell Janelle was unfair. Take a look around, Phyllis. You've lost Rock, you've lost Janelle and, now, you've lost me." She signed her credit card receipt, leaving off any gratuity.

"Claire..."

Claire turned and headed for the door. She had just seen Rock and the Range Rover cruise by. Phyllis started to say something else, but Claire held up a dismissive hand and left.

Outside the shop, Claire slid into the car, leaned over and kissed him. Rock pulled into traffic without saying anything, but his curiosity was eating him alive. Yet he was not going to be the one to broach the subject of Phyllis. Finally after a minute or so, Claire said, "So do you want to know what Phyllis said?"

Without looking at her, feigning attention to his driving, he said, "Sure."

"She thinks you double crossed her with Janelle."

Eyes straight ahead, he asked, "What do you think?"

Claire thought for a minute before answering. "Thought you should know, Janelle is in San Diego with her Marine."

Rock looked over at her and smiled.

"As to Phyllis, I'll find another hairdresser."

They shopped on the way home for a couple of hours at Target in Norton Shores, stopped at the Brown Bear in Shelby and downed a couple of huge, sloppy hamburgers that the place was known for along with French fries and onion rings. They washed it all down with a couple of drafts. They arrived back at Claire's a little after 9:00 p.m, tired after their thirteen-hour day.

Flotsam and Flower greeted them at the door and seemed none the worse for wear. They watched as each dog quickly found their spots, took care of their business and returned to them. Once inside, they slipped out of their coats and shoes. Rock headed to the great room to build a fire. Claire went to the kitchen and made them each a cup of tea. Rock had settled into the leather sofa, but before Claire sat down she went over to Flotsam, who was lying next to Flower in front of the fireplace. Kneeling next to her, she took the border collie's face in her hands and tilted it up towards hers. "Flotsam, you are a good girl. You saved your Daddy from a very bad woman, and I thank you very much for that.' She glanced over at Rock, who was laughing.

When he awoke, Rock's arm was around her and her head was on his shoulder. Despite the stiffness he felt in his neck, back and legs, Claire felt good against him. Quickly, however, he became aware that the house was dark and he could begin to feel the panic welling up in him. *Coat pocket, flashlight!* He knew he had to find a light source and quick.

Claire had felt him tense up. She knew what she'd done, or rather failed to do. Beth had confided in her all the details of Rock's experiences in Vietnam and his PTSD. She had meant to leave the lights on under the kitchen cabinets. Their soft light could have filtered around the corner of the wall between the kitchen and the great room and provided the comfort he needed. She'd simply forgotten. Then she caught the outline of the two dogs lying on their sides facing one another in front of the hearth like unmatched book ends. They were illuminated by the faint glow of ash-covered embers on the bottom of the fireplace. "Don't go," she said as she only half-faked a chill. "Stoke the fire and then come back and hold me."

Choking back the panic that was welling up in him, he got up. The dogs watched as he placed a couple of logs on the fire and stoked the embers underneath them until small fingers of flame began to burn against the new logs. Before he finished, both dogs put their heads back down. By the time he returned to her, the sitting area in front of the fireplace was bathed in a warm red-orange glow. His panic practically forgotten, Rock pulled a wool throw over the both of them, put his arm around her, pulled her close and kissed her forehead. She snuggled down against him with her knees tucked under her, and there they slept until daylight lit the house.

Chapter Twenty-Eight

Please God

The weekend was slightly awkward for both of them. Though nothing had happened, both knew that with Rock's overnight stay, something was different, exciting, anticipatory. The problem was that neither of them knew how to talk about it. Rock had decided the evening Claire had first kissed him that he was not going to push her. Then when Ingrid had confronted him, even though she'd thoroughly pissed him off, she was probably right about one thing. Her mother was still grieving Alan's death. When it came time for the two of them to fulfill their love for one another, it would happen when Claire decided it was time, not him. So Saturday morning, they barely spoke as Claire fixed him a mug of tea and made a pot of coffee for herself. Their only saving grace was the season. Claire wanted to spruce up the place for Christmas. "I have an idea," she said as they sat at the kitchen table.

"What's that?"

"I'll make some breakfast and after that let's go cut a Christmas tree. Bob Mumford said we could go on his land just outside of Shelby and find one we liked."

"Do you know where we are going?" he asked.

"Yes, he gave me directions."

"OK," and then he had another question, "Is there a saw around here?"

Claire paused, "I don't know, but if there is one, it would be in the garage somewhere. Why don't you go look while I make breakfast?"

Rock felt odd rummaging around in the garage. This had been Alan's space, he could tell that. There were yard implements and hand tools of every description. He found the saw easily. But even though he felt he was intruding into someone else's space, he couldn't help but keep looking around anyway. A workbench with drawers below and cabinets lining the wall above stretched across the entire back of the garage. When he opened one of the cabinet doors above the workbench, he found a dozen or more pictures of Beth and Ingrid as young girls. A few of them included Claire. He stopped rummaging. It seemed odd to him that Alan was not in any of them. He chose one picture of Claire and the girls, removed the thumb tack that had held it in its hiding spot for who knew how many years and headed back into the house, the picture in one hand, the saw in the other. "I didn't mean to pry," he said to Claire, "But while I was looking for the saw, I found this." He realized he was telling a harmless white lie as he held the picture out.

Claire looked at it, "I remember this. Jesus Chavez took it one summer. Alan was out of the country. I can't remember where. Look how skinny Ingrid is. She was in middle school. Beth was in about the second grade, I think."

"There's more there. I just chose this one. I'm not sure why."

"You'll have to show me. Breakfast is ready. Hungry?"

"Starving."

On their way out to cut the tree, Rock showed Claire the cabinet with the pictures hanging on the inside of the door. Claire studied them for a long time and turned to him, "You know every one of these pictures was taken during summers when Alan wasn't here with us. I didn't know he'd hung them there. What do you suppose that means, Rock?"

He took her hand in his, thought for a moment and said, "I don't know, but maybe it was his way of trying to recapture something he'd lost."

She didn't respond, but kept looking at the pictures. Finally she shut the door, wiped a tear from the corner of her eye and said, "Let's go find our Christmas tree."

On Monday morning, December 15th, they walked on the road because the wind was blowing hard, a precursor of the storm that was forecast to drop six or more inches of heavy wet snow on them before day's end. When they returned home, Claire made lunch, and Rock hung decorations that required ladder climbing and nail pounding. They had just settled down in front of the fireplace to read before their afternoon walk when the phone rang. Claire looked at him, and he could see the worry on her face. Rock asked, "Want me to answer it?"

"No, maybe it's not even her." Claire went to the phone. She looked at Rock and said, "It's her," then she drew a deep breath and answered the phone.

Rock watched Claire and he knew whatever the doctor was saying was causing her distress. He moved into another room, where she could not see him and he put his face in his hands. *Please, God.* When he heard her say goodbye, he returned.

She was standing facing Lake Michigan, her back to him. He walked up behind her and placed his hands gently on each shoulder. "What did the doctor say?"

As she turned to face him, he could see tears welling up. "She wants me to go to the University of Michigan Medical Center after the first of the year for some more tests."

"What does she think is wrong?"

"That's just it, she doesn't know. She wants to rule out muscular dystrophy, multiple sclerosis, and Amyotrophic Lateral Sclerosis. Do you know what that is, Rock?" She didn't give him a chance to answer. "It's Lou Gehrig's Disease. My, God, that's awful. Did you read *Tuesdays with Morrie?*"

He nodded.

"It all scares me, Rock. What a horrid way to die. Every cell of every muscle just slowly dies until the muscle stops working. First you can't walk, then you can't chew your food, swallow water, then you can't breathe and then..." Claire was in tears. "And then you die."

It scared him too, but he didn't dare let her see it. Instead, he put his arms around her and pulled her close, "We will go to Ann Arbor," he said in his gentlest, calmest voice, "But first we'll enjoy Christmas together."

Chapter Twenty-Nine

Christmas, 2008

Christmas morning, 2008, opened bright and beautiful. At Far-Far-View, Rock and Josh began their day with a bowl of cereal as Flotsam settled over her bowl of kibble.

"Uncle Rock, Beth and I have been seeing one another. I didn't want to tell you over the phone."

"I know, Josh. Claire told me."

His nephew nodded, smiling sheepishly and asked, "Is that OK with you?" When his uncle didn't answer right away, Josh thought he might need to clarify, "I mean I don't want to get in the way of you and Mrs. Van Zandt."

Rock truly admired the man his nephew had become. "Listen, Josh, you are not getting in my way. The only advice I might give you is about Beth. You know she broke off her engagement because the guy she was going to marry was all work first and her second." When Josh did not respond, Rock realized that he was probably throwing a wet rag on to what his nephew expected to be good news. But Rock thought it important to keep it real. "When you get into vet school, you will be even busier than you are now."

Josh merely nodded.

"Have you and Beth discussed that?"

Josh replied simply, "We aren't rushing into anything. It's one step at a time."

Rock contemplated what his nephew said for a moment and then replied, "Josh, listen, I'm really happy for the two of you. I just want to..."

Josh smiled at his uncle. "I know, Uncle Rock. You want what's best for me...what's best for Beth. I get it. I do. Thanks."

Trace snow covered the beach and dunes. The temperature was unseasonably warm, with a forecast daytime high of forty-five degrees. Rock and Josh walked over to their neighbors at about 9:00 a.m. Claire and Beth had been up since 6:00 a.m. It was Beth's idea to fix a breakfast for the four of them while Claire started preparing Christmas dinner for the rest of their guests, who weren't expected until about 1:00 p.m. Claire and Rock smiled at each other as Beth greeted Josh with a kiss on the cheek.

Catching their smiles, Beth blushed and announced, "Breakfast is ready. Who wants a mimosa?"

Rock and Josh exchanged glances and then followed Claire and Beth to the kitchen table. Beth had prepared an egg, sausage and cheese casserole with rye toast. Neither Rock nor Josh mentioned that this was their second breakfast of the morning. It was obvious how much work Beth had put into the meal.

Afterwards, Rock with his Earl Gray and everyone else with coffee gathered in the great room to exchange gifts before the guests arrived. Josh had bought Beth a cashmere sweater, which must have cost him a week's pay from his part-time job at MSU's Student Union bookstore. Beth gave him a colorful soft muffler, ear muffs and leather gloves for those long walks between classes at the sprawling East Lansing campus. Rock gave Claire a picture of her with the two dogs. He made it extra special by redoing the frame with driftwood and rocks he had collected along their beach. Claire held it to her chest and told him it was perfect. From Claire, Rock received an invitation to join her for dinner at Ruth's Chris Steakhouse in the Amway Grand Plaza Hotel followed by an evening at the symphony. The American Ballet Company was performing the Nutcracker accompanied by The Grand Rapids Symphony. The date on the tickets was December 29th.

"Wow!" he exclaimed. "I've never been to a live symphony performance."

"Then, my good sir, you have a great surprise in store for you," Claire promised.

Behind the tree, one other rather large package remained. Rock asked, pointing to it, "Whose is that?"

Claire smiled at Beth and Josh and said, "It's for you, from all of us, but we want to wait until tonight, after everyone's gone and it's just the four of us. Then you can open it. OK?"

Rock smiled, "Very mysterious! Very cruel! I have to wait until tonight to find out what's in it."

"That's right, Uncle Rock," Josh asserted as if there was to be no further discussion of the matter, no arguing.

Everyone arrived safely for Christmas dinner. Jan brought several bottles of an expensive Chardonnay and Madeline had made two pies, one pecan, the other pumpkin, along with a quart of vanilla ice cream and a bowl of homemade whipped cream.

Everyone hung around in hopes of a glorious sunset over Lake Michigan, but by 3:00 p.m. that had started to look doubtful, and by 5:00 p.m. it was clear that it wasn't going to happen. A thick layer of dark clouds had covered the lake, the temperature had fallen and a light snow had begun as Jan and Madeline departed for Fremont.

Beth suggested to Josh that they take the dogs for a walk on the beach. Flotsam and Flower, both hearing the magic word, *walk,* hurled themselves toward the slider. Flower was barking and Flotsam keening a shrill whine, both of them padding their front paws up and down in front of the plate glass door.

As Rock and Claire watched the four of them descend the stairs toward the beach, Claire put her arms around him and said, "So, what do you think?"

Rock looked at her and smiled, "I think Ingrid missed a great Christmas Day."

Claire nodded but then pointed to the group on the beach, "That's true, but I was talking about those two."

"We talked. He likes her, I know that. I cautioned him about what he has ahead of him. He's smart, but vet school won't be easy."

Claire replied, "Beth and I talked too. Did you know they are planning on going into Grand Rapids for New Year's Eve?"

"No."

"Beth prepared me that they probably wouldn't be home... back up here, I mean, for New Year's. I think they are planning on going to her condo after they have finished celebrating. She asked if we wanted to join them. I hope you don't mind, but I declined for us."

"No, not at all. To tell you the truth, I can't think of anyplace I'd rather be than up here with you and the two dogs on New Year's Eve, if that's all right with you?"

"It's a dream come true," she murmured.

Rock pointed to the one unopened package leaning against the wall near the Christmas Tree. "So what's in that big package over there?"

"I promised Beth and Josh we wouldn't open it until they got back. Can you wait?"

"Really? Do I have to?"

"Yes, you do. They helped me with it," and she gently punched him on the arm.

Dusk had changed to full dark by the time Beth, Josh and the dogs got back. They swooped in the slider door, the dogs damp from having romped at the water's edge, Beth and Josh complaining about how bitterly cold they were.

"You shouldn't have stayed down there so long," Claire chided them. They blamed the dogs, but Rock and Claire knew the two had relished their time alone. The four winter-beachcombers settled in front of the fireplace while Rock and Claire made some hot chocolate for them and tea for themselves.

"You've acquired quite a taste for my tea," Rock commented.

Claire retorted, "Along with quite a taste for your company as well. So are you ready to open your last present?" As Claire picked it up, Rock settled into a leather chair. She placed it on his lap. "Pretty heavy," he commented. "What is it?" He looked around the room at the three of them. Claire and Beth's face were etched with excited expectation, but he thought Josh appeared a bit worried.

"Open it up and see, Rock," Beth prodded.

The first thing he saw was a perfectly-folded American flag in the upper left corner of the beautiful wood box. Next to that was a brass plaque on which a letter was inscribed. The plaque was affixed to the red felt background that covered the entire interior of the box. He didn't take time just yet to read it in its entirety, but the gist of it was that the flag had flown over the nation's Capital Building. He also saw that the letter was signed by Senator Debbie Stabenow. He pulled the rest of the wrapping down over the box to reveal a magnificently mounted Navy Cross, his Navy Cross. Directly underneath it on one side was the original citation. Next to it, the original certificate given to him thirty-nine years ago at the Battle Creek Veterans' Administration Hospital, where he had spent nearly a year going through painful physical therapy as he recovered from his wounds.

Staring blankly at it, he demanded, "Where did you get this?"

Beth, unfamiliar with his tone, cheerfully piped up, "Josh and I went to the loft..." she stopped as Josh put his hand on her arm.

Claire could see the distress in his face. "Rock, we didn't mean to..."

He set the display box down, got up and walked to the slider, wordlessly staring out into the darkness.

Josh was prepared. He grabbed the phone from its holder and punched in Russ's number, hoping he would answer immediately. On the second ring, he heard, "Hello."

"Uncle Russ, I need you to talk to Uncle Rock."

"Let me guess. He didn't handle the present well."

"Exactly."

Russ let out a sigh, "OK, put him on. Let me talk to him."

Josh walked across the room to his uncle, who was still staring out into the darkness. "Uncle Rock, it's Uncle Russ. He wants to talk to you."

Almost as if he didn't hear him, Rock made no move to take the phone Josh was trying to hand off. Josh repeated, "Uncle Rock..."

"I don't want to talk to him."

"That may be, but he wants to talk to you. You've been friends for a long time and... well, it is Christmas, Uncle Rock." He thrust the phone in front of him. He could hear Russ telling him to take the phone.

"Hello." It was flat, emotionless.

"Rock, if you want to blame somebody for this, then blame me dammit! Lay off of Josh and whoever else is there. They got nothin' to do with this. Josh is a good kid. He called me about this idea of theirs to put your Navy Cross in a proper display case for Christmas. The more I thought about it, the more I thought it would be a good idea."

"I don't want to remember a damn thing about that night, Russ. You of all people should know that."

"Yeah, I know, Rock. You blame yourself for every Marine that died in that ambush, but what you don't know is that no one blames you at all. Shit, man, it was so fuckin' dark that night that no human being could have seen those bastards laying there waiting for us." He gave that a minute to sink in, then continued, "You know you saved my ass that night?"

"No I didn't. I was nowhere near you."

"You are exactly right!" You were nowhere near me and, if you had been, we both probably would have died right then and there."

He forgot where he was and cursed into the phone, "What the fuck you talkin' about Russ?"

"You know what I did when they sprang that ambush?" Russ didn't wait for an answer. "The bullets all of a sudden were flying everywhere. Two guys on either side of me went down immediately." There was a brief silence and then, "I shit my pants, Rock," shame evident in his voice.

"Russ..."

"Shut up and listen to me, Rock. I really shit myself."

In all the years they had known one another, this was a new piece of information for Rock.

"I'd have climbed in a hole if there had been one big enough, but it wouldn't have done any good, the bastards would have smelled me. I froze. I couldn't pull the trigger on my M-16, much less aim at anything." Another long silence punctuated what Russ had to say. "Then all of a sudden, some crazy son of a bitch on the other side of the kill zone starts firing a machine gun and the enemy shifts their fire from us to you, Rock. That gave us just the time we needed to get our shit together and start returning fire. Once we got them in that crossfire, those little bastards didn't hang around long. You saved us, Rock and every guy that was there that night knows it. None of us would ever blame you."

In the great room all one could hear was the faint noise from the flames in the fireplace. Rock wasn't talking and apparently neither was Russ until, finally, Russ asked, "Rock, you still there?"

"Yeah."

"When Josh called me to ask what I thought about this, it took me a while to come around to it, but I told him it was a good idea. You think that medal came from the Marine Corps. It didn't, Rock. That medal came from Marines just like you and me. I know it didn't always happen that way. Sometimes guys got medals for shit reasons. Yours wasn't given for a shit reason. You earned it. All of these years it's just sat there collecting dust. I think they did the right thing in getting it all spruced up. You don't have to make a big deal out of it. In fact, I know you won't. But dammit, Rock, it should see the light of day, because there are a lot of Marines walking around today enjoying the light of day because of what you did that night. I'm one 'em. So put it on one of your bookshelves in the loft. Look at it once in a while and know that there are a lot of guys that thank you for what you did."

Rock didn't know what to say. He'd suppressed so much for so long that words were hard to find.

Russ thought he'd said all he could. He'd admitted things tonight that he never had before. He needed to go someplace and process what had just happened to him, so he said, "Hold on. Patti wants to wish you a Merry Christmas."

"Russ, no..." but it was too late.

"Merry Christmas, Rock. I've been listening to the one side of this conversation and for what it's worth, I couldn't agree more with Russ." She paused for a minute and then added, "And you know how damned rare that is."

On the other end, Rock cracked a slight grin. "Yeah, thanks, Patti. Merry Christmas to you guys too." He paused for a second. "Listen, tell the big guy he gave Josh good advice. Tell him I said thanks."

"You got it, Rock. Give Josh a hug and tell everyone else there that Russ and Patti look forward to meeting them."

He took the phone down from his ear. The others were in front of the fireplace and he could sense that none of them knew exactly what to say or do. "I'm sorry about this. It's just that some of the memories are..."

"Uncle Rock, we've all read that citation. None of us can believe what you did that night."

He had carried guilt around for nearly forty years, blaming himself for missing any signs that the enemy lay in wait for them that night, blaming himself for leading his platoon into that ambush. He hadn't done his job, and then he had to make that terrible choice to give up on Billy Riley, taking his machine gun from him and letting him bleed out there on the jungle floor. Why had he survived when kids like Riley and half a dozen others had not? His guilt was like a big, heavy bag that he'd carried around for all these years, never opening it because he feared what he might find inside. All these years he thought he had been right never opening the bag. Tonight, Christmas 2008, their gift gave him the opportunity to unpack at least some of the load. He began to cry. Claire, Beth and Josh encircled him. No one said anything. There was no need to. Unpacking this bag was best done in silence comforted by the loving touch of those he loved.

Chapter Thirty

Opulence

It was during the week between Christmas and New Year's that Rock started to get a true picture of Claire's wealth. On December 29th they departed Little Point Sable mid-morning and stopped in Grand Haven about 11:30 a.m. at the Kirby House for a light lunch. The view from their table was of the Grand River just before it flows into Lake Michigan. The bright blue sky and brilliant sunshine belied a bitterly cold outside temperature of nineteen degrees with a fifteen- to twenty-knot wind driving the wind chill temperature to a frosty ten degrees or less. From there they went to Holland and Claire's home. As they pulled into the semi-circular driveway, past the five-car garage, Rock whistled and said, "How many people live here?" He meant it to be funny, but it rattled Claire.

Inside the house, his eyes couldn't move fast enough to take in the opulence. The place must have been six or seven thousand square feet. By comparison, his loft in Flint was about twelve hundred square feet. As he stood at the windows and slider that extended across the back of the home's living room, he looked out at Lake Macatawa and saw the deep water dock. "Do you have a boat?"

A note of embarrassment in her voice, Claire replied, "Yes."

It was at some distance, but the dock appeared to be at least six to eight feet, maybe more, above the water. "Must be a pretty big one, huh?"

Claire felt embarrassed but also sensed something in his questions that gave her pause.

"Yes. It was Alan's. I have to admit that it doesn't get much use, but I have it put in every year about May 1st and then Captain Tim takes it to the marina for winter storage every October."

It's big enough that it has its own captain, he thought. He had to ask, "Captain Tim? Exactly how big is it?"

"It's fifty feet or so. I can't remember exactly. Once in a while Beth uses it. She and her Dad loved to take it out. When the girls were younger, Alan and Beth would sail it up Lake Michigan to Pentwater. Ingrid and I tended to get sea sick, so we would meet them at the marina. Alan would keep it there all summer, but it was one of those things that really didn't get used a lot because he was gone so much. I couldn't operate something that big." She chuckled, "Beth would say to me, 'C'mon Mom, I'll show you how,' but I knew that was a recipe for disaster. Then, after Alan died, I found Captain Tim. He lives just a few doors down. He's a retired Coast Guard Captain, knows a lot about boats and helps me with mine."

Claire disappeared upstairs and while she was gone, Rock discovered the library. She found him there, reading. "Find something interesting?"

"That would be hard not to do in this library. How many books do you have?" he asked. Rock was usually a pretty sensitive guy, especially when it came to Claire, but he was completely missing the signals she was sending him.

"I don't know," she responded with an edge to her tone.

And then his thoughtlessness got away from him, "I'll bet you have to have a librarian to keep track of all of them."

Claire didn't respond. She simply turned and left the room.

He sat there finally realizing the hole he'd dug for himself. *What the hell is the matter with you? You knew she was from money. None of this should surprise you.* It was the sheer magnitude of the home's opulence that had overwhelmed him. He took a minute to compose himself, returned the volume to its shelf and went to find Claire. She was in the kitchen, making herself a cup of tea. When he came in, she didn't offer him any. Now he was reading her signals loud and clear.

"Claire..."

She avoided eye contact.

"Claire, I'm sorry."

This time she looked at him. "I should have realized that you might not be prepared for all of this." She paused, searching for the words to try to explain it to him, when there was a knock on the kitchen door. It opened and in trudged Maria and Jesus, carrying cleaning supplies.

"Ms. Claire," Maria said, "We weren't expecting you. You should have called. I would have..."

Claire smiled at the two of them. "Maria, it's OK. We're not here for very long. I just needed to stop and get ready for the symphony this evening. I didn't have the proper clothes at the lake house. We were just about to leave, but I want you to meet my friend, Rock Graham. Rock, this is Maria and Jesus Chavez, two wonderful friends of the family."

Maria extended her hand, "Mr. Graham, so nice to meet you. I have heard some very nice things about you." She smiled at him and nodded her head toward Claire.

"Mr. Graham, very nice to meet you," Jesus said.

Claire excused herself, saying she had to get dressed. Rock thought that she might still be miffed at him, but there was little he could do about that now. Maria and Jesus took the cleaning supplies and busied themselves putting things away. The three of them made small talk until the Chavezes politely excused themselves, asking Rock to say goodbye to Claire for them.

At about 4:00 p.m. she came down. Rock had had at least an hour to consider the error of his ways, but when he saw her he was lost in the spectacle of her beauty. She was wearing a sequined evening gown that stretched to the floor and slit up both sides revealing her long, slender legs to mid-thigh. Sequined straps flowed over her shoulders and the neckline plunged tantalizingly. Wrapped around her neck were several strands of pearls. Of course they were genuine, Rock knew. Adjusting to the opulence, he refrained from mentioning them and smiled with approval at what he saw. The contrast between the natural beauty she exhibited at the lakeshore and the exquisite glamour that now stood in front of him was striking.

"Claire, you... you are beautiful."

She liked the way he looked at her, but she was still miffed at him. There was air that had to be cleared. "Are you ready? We have to get going."

He could tell she was still upset. He couldn't blame her. He had been insensitive; overwhelmed, but nonetheless insensitive. "Let me get my suit out of the car and..."

"You don't need to change."

He looked at her, not understanding. He was in jeans, a long-sleeved T-shirt and hiking boots.

"Just trust me, OK?"

He had begun to stride toward the Range Rover they'd driven down from the lakeshore when Claire said, "Let's take another car." She led him to the second bay of the five car garage, punched in the code and as the door rolled up Rock stared disbelievingly at a shiny Rolls Royce Silver Shadow.

"You... you want me to drive that?" Never in his wildest dreams had he ever imagined himself driving a Rolls Royce.

"Do you mind?"

"Uh, no…no, not at all."

They drove into downtown Holland, not far from The Styles of Holland, where Claire pointed out a parking spot almost in front of a tuxedo shop. When they entered, she was greeted by name by a man she called Peter. Claire said, "Wait here just a minute, Rock," and she and Peter retreated to a spot in the back of the store. When they returned, Peter said, "Mr. Graham, if you'll come with me, I will get you fixed up." Thirty minutes later, when Rock returned to her, he was outfitted in a black tuxedo, cummerbund, heavily starched and nicely fitted tuxedo shirt with gold studs and cuff links and a black silk bow-tie. The tie was not a clip-on, but one that Peter had hand-tied himself with much fussing to get it just right. Claire nodded approvingly.

Rock looked at Peter and asked, "How much do I owe you?"

Peter cast a questioning glance toward Claire, and Rock saw her shake her head almost imperceptibly. He then said, "It's been taken care of, Mr. Graham."

Before Rock could protest, Claire took his arm and said, "We have to get going, darling. Our dinner reservations are for 6 p.m." Rock let her lead him out of the shop and to the car.

The trip from Holland to Grand Rapids took about thirty minutes.

Just outside Holland, Claire decided it was time for her to get some things off her chest. "Rock, I know a lot of this is making you uncomfortable, but you must understand something. The Claire Van Zandt that you know at the lake isn't the same Claire Van Zandt that lives in Holland. Don't get me wrong, I love the lakeshore and the person that I am up there, especially since I met you. But down here, things are..." she had to think about this for a moment and couldn't come up with anything better than, "Well, they are just different."

He hesitated and then asked, "May I ask you a question, and if it ticks you off, then you don't have to answer?"

"If it's about how big something is, or how many do I have then I'd prefer you not ask."

Again he paused, not wanting to anger her again, but he wanted her to confirm something he already thought he knew about her. "It's about the Chavezes."

"Jesus and Maria? What about them?"

"You introduced them as friends of the family, but they really work for you, don't they?"

She shot him a withering look, but he stared straight into her eyes. Her voice held an edge, "They have worked for my family for a long time. Our kids grew up together. Beth and Ingrid learned to speak Spanish from the Chavezes and their children. When Alan died, I would have been lost without them. If you want to know how much I pay them, then you can go to hell." Claire's temper was showing. He'd never heard her swear. "If you want to know how much they mean to me, then I can tell you, the Chavezes are priceless."

He looked at her and smiled.

"What?" she shot back at him.

"You may be different in some ways when you are down here, but in the ways that matter, you are still the same Claire Van Zandt that I met at the lakeshore. I can get used to the things that you have in your life. It may take me a while because they are so many more than I am used to. What I like about you, Claire... no... make that, what I love about you, is the way you treat the people that are in your life. That's what matters the most."

He took his right hand from the steering wheel and offered it to her. She took it.

"I love you, Claire."

Dinner at Ruth's Chris was elegant and delicious. The symphony overwhelmed him with its sights and sounds. They took it all in from the middle of the center section, 10th row back. It seemed to Rock to be the perfect spot to see and hear everything that was happening before his eyes. He was close enough to fully appreciate the power-fully athletic form of the dancers as they moved about the stage in effortless grace. And then there was the orches-tra. The music ebbed and flowed to crescendo heights to match every wonderful emotion he was feeling that night. As they waited in the warm foyer for the valet to bring the Rolls around, he whispered in Claire's ear, "I can't thank you enough for this evening. I've never seen or heard any-thing so beautiful."

As the valet pulled the car to the curb and got out, he headed toward Rock to give him the keys when Claire intercepted him. Handing him a ten dollar tip, she said, "I'll take those."

It surprised Rock, who said, "I don't mind driving."

"I've got this, Mr. Graham," she said confidently.

"Yes, Ms. Van Zandt," his surprise still evident. This was her night. She had planned everything, and if her plan called for her to drive home to the lake, then that was the way it was going to be.

He assumed they would take the Rolls back to Holland and then return to Little Point Sable in the Range Rover they had driven down. As beautiful a car as the Rolls was, it would be out of place on the barely-more-than-two-track-sometimes-gravel-sometimes dirt road that led into their lakeshore homes. It did not, however, take him long to determine that they were not headed to the lake-shore that evening. Instead, Claire drove them to the valet entrance of the Amway Grand Plaza Hotel in the middle of downtown Grand Rapids. As they got out of the car, the valet called Claire by her name. At the door, the hotel's General Manager met them and handed her a pass card, "Your suite is ready, Ms. Van Zandt." She was on Rock's arm as they walked through the lobby. He could feel the eyes of other hotel patrons on them. Claire led them to a private elevator, where the pass card opened the elevator's door that did not reopen until they had reached the penthouse. A lavish suite stretched before them. A floral arrangement dominated a magnificent, round table in front of them as they stepped from the elevator. On one side was an assortment of cheeses, fruits and a bottle of champagne on ice. He helped Claire off with her coat, which he laid across the other side of the table. Claire placed her gloves and purse on top of the coat. Beguilingly, she took a few steps ahead of him after motioning for him to follow her. In front of him now, she reached behind her for the zipper on her dress. At the bedroom's door she let the dress fall to the floor. The silver high heels lifted her calves and made her legs appear endless. She was wearing black, sheer silk stockings held up by a black garter belt. She turned to face him. Skimpy black panties and a black bra cupping her breasts completed the picture.

Rock was standing looking at her and a slight smile crossed his face.

As if reading his mind, Claire looked at him and said, "Don't worry. Flotsam's not here and, if she were, she wouldn't bark. She likes me."

Laughing, he came to her.

Chapter Thirty-One

Ann Arbor

After their return to the lakeshore from Grand Rapids, Far-Far-View was put into a kind of cold storage. Rock turned off the water heater, the water pump, closed the damper on the fireplace after assuring himself that every ember had burnt itself out, and turned the thermostat down to a cool forty-five degrees. For the most part, December had been milder than either of them had expected it to be, but it looked like January was going to make up for it. Snow was piled six or eight inches deep and ice had started to build along the lake's edge. Claire had told him, "Watch this over the next couple of months. You won't believe how the ice builds up along this coastline, mounds of it, some of the mounds ten, fifteen, twenty feet high. It's the wind, you know. You can't believe how strong it can be."

Claire had waited until Monday, January 5th of the new year to make her appointment at the University of Michigan. Partly because her doctor didn't seem to be in a rush and partly because of her own reluctance, she scheduled herself for three days of tests beginning January 14th. In the meantime she and Rock spent every minute together, day and night.

When Claire made her appointment at the U of M Medical Center, it triggered an entire series of events. For Rock this trip would prove to be another exercise in learning about the extent of Claire's wealth, influence and power.

"Do you have a particular place you'd like to stay while we are in Ann Arbor?" Rock had asked.

"It's taken care of," she had said, with a smile on her face reminiscent of the trip they had made to Grand Rapids for the symphony. He did not inquire further.

The night before they were to leave, he was packing when Claire told him, "Be sure to take a suit and tie." He had not planned on doing that, but he didn't ask questions, dutifully packing the one suit, one shirt and one tie he'd brought with him to the lakeshore last September. At the time he'd wondered why he should waste that precious space in Green Girl. Now it seemed providential.

Claire's first appointment was at 1:00 p.m. on January 14th. Rock had asked if she needed to arrive early for paperwork and in-processing. He had not had experience in hospitals since his days recuperating after Vietnam. But he did remember that at the Lakeshore Hospital in Shelby, after getting treated for his cracked head, he had spent as much time in the administrative offices settling his bill as he had waiting on and getting treatment. Claire had explained that she didn't think it important to arrive much before 1:00 p.m.

As they approached the city, Claire directed him into the heart of Ann Arbor and The University of Michigan's Central Campus. As Rock drove, she looked around and warm memories flooded back to her. When they were courting, she had visited the campus many times to see Alan. Nearing their destination, she could see the Engineering Arch, which at one time gave way to the College of

Engineering's main building. Some time ago, the College of Engineering had moved to the newer North Campus. Nonetheless, the landmark and its name endured. She remembered the evening Alan had maneuvered her under it at midnight and kissed her. "There," he'd said to her, "We're going to be married." She remembered her puzzlement at the time. He told her of the Arch's lore, "If you kiss at midnight under the Engineering Arch, you will marry the person you kiss. So, I hope you love me as much as I love you, because it's a done deal now." Claire was able to wipe away a tear without Rock noticing.

At her direction, he pulled the Range Rover into a parking spot with a sign in front of it that read, *Reserved for Guest.* Behind the sign was a beautiful, vine-covered stucco cottage. Upon entering, a bubbly young woman introduced herself as So-and-So, Rock didn't catch her name, who told Claire she was a student in the College of Engineering and it was her privilege to welcome her back to the U of M. She turned over a set of keys to the cottage and a parking pass to Claire. The pass, she explained, entitled them to park anywhere on campus without fear of receiving one of the hundreds of parking tickets the campus police issued daily. Then she asked Claire if there were any questions. When Claire said no, she handed her an envelope with their names and excused herself.

"I thought you went to MSU," Rock said quizzically.

"I did."

"But she said welcome back?"

She averted her eyes from his, "Rock, listen, they insisted that I... I mean, that we..." She was searching for the way to explain all of this, then it hit him.

"Wait, let me guess, Alan graduated from here?" She nodded. "Of course, from the College of Engineering. That young woman... from the College of Engineering..."

"Don't be upset. They were so nice when they called. They think they owe this to my family."

Now she was losing him. "Claire, I'm not upset. This place is beautiful. They really know how to make you feel welcome, but they don't do this for every graduate of the University's engineering program do they?"

Sheepishly she looked at him and said, "No." She paused for a minute and then decided she owed more. "About ten years ago Alan established an Endowed Chair at the University's College of Engineering. Among other things it pays the salary of a full professor in the College in perpetuity."

He bit back the temptation to ask what something like that must have cost. It of course wasn't of true importance to him, but the question would be on the tip of anyone's tongue unaccustomed to wealth. Instead he merely nodded and pointed to the envelope in her hand. "What's that?"

She opened it and then said to him, "This is the reason you had to bring a suit," and she handed the contents to him. The card stock was of high quality. At the top was an embossed block M in blue with a maize border around it. The raised black lettering jumped off the page at him.

The President of the University of Michigan
requests the pleasure of your company
at dinner on the evening of Thursday, January, 15th, 2009
at seven o'clock in the evening,
at the President's House

He managed to hide his intimidation well.

At the Medical Center, they were greeted by the hospital's Chief of Staff. Everywhere they went over the next two and a half days, they perceived that their visit had been long expected and anticipated. Dinner on the fifteenth had been a wonderful evening spent with the University's President, the Dean of the College of Engineering and the current holder of the Van Zandt Endowed Chair and their spouses.

As they departed Ann Arbor on the afternoon of the 16th, the only downside was that they knew nothing more about the cause of Claire's episodes than they knew when they had arrived. She had been through test after test, but no results were available, nor were they likely to be for a month or more.

Rock's cell phone rang. Normally he would not answer it while driving, but he handed it to Claire and asked her to look at caller ID and see who it was.

"It's Josh. Would you like to me answer it?"

He nodded and said, "Yes. Maybe he's heard something."

"Josh, it's Claire. Your uncle's driving and asked me to answer. How are you?"

He could hardly contain himself, "Claire, I just got some great news..."

"Wait," she said, "I'll put you on speaker phone. I think I know what it is, but I want your uncle to hear it at the same time I do." She pushed a button. "Can you hear me?"

"Yes. Uncle Rock?"

"Hey, Josh, how's it going?"

"Couldn't be better, Uncle Rock. I got my acceptance letter today."

A broad smile broke over Rock's face. Claire did a fist pump. Both of them chimed in at exactly the same time, "That's great!"

The next month or so was going to be an anxious one for them. The medical tests and all the questions associated with those were one thing, but the complete silence from Ingrid since her visit before Christmas was another. She was apparently so miffed at Claire, Beth and Rock that she hadn't bothered to call on Christmas Day, causing Claire and Beth to form a pact mirroring Ingrid's stubborn silence. Though Claire assured him differently, Rock felt that he was tearing Claire's family apart. Good news like Josh's had come at a time when it was much needed.

Chapter Thirty-Two

The Price of Inattention

If January was cold, February was brutally so; short days, long nights, snow. And then there was the wind, the ever present, bone-chilling wind. All of this conspired to keep them penned in far more than any of them wanted. The two dogs in particular suffered from cabin fever. Even though they would have bouts of play in the house, tugging with one another or chasing around, it was not the same as being able to run, jump and play on the boundless stretch of beach that was just steps away, but unbearably cold.

Despite the fact that there had been no word yet from the doctors in Ann Arbor, nor had there been communication from Ingrid, Rock and Claire's life had settled into a comfortable familiarity. They also took joy from the fact that the relationship between Josh and Beth seemed to continue to blossom. Though the four of them had not been together since Christmas, Josh and Rock kept in close touch, as did Claire and Beth.

Claire suffered another bout of shortness of breath. She'd been alone and had not mentioned it to Rock, rationalizing that it would do no good to alarm him. Competent doctors were looking into the matter. She would find out soon enough. In the meantime, she was determined to enjoy her new life with him.

Early in the evening on Thursday, February 5th, the phone rang. Rock was closer, so Claire waited for him to pick it up. He looked at the caller ID, then at Claire, his face expressionless, and said, "It's Ingrid." Handing her the phone, he asked, "Would you like me to leave?"

"Absolutely not," Claire said emphatically and took the phone.

"Hello." She delivered that word well. It didn't sound short as if to say *It's about time*, nor did it sound overly excited like, *It's been so long since we talked, I'm so glad you called.*

"How are you, Mother?"

"Fine, dear, and you?" Claire looked at Rock and shrugged her shoulders.

"Sorry I haven't called. I've just been so busy at work..." If Ingrid was looking for Claire to forgive her lack of communication, Claire wasn't going to provide it. After an awkward pause, Ingrid continued, "The reason I'm calling is that I was thinking that perhaps Brian and I might drive up this weekend. Ethan is out of town Friday on business and can't get a flight home until Saturday. Brian has been asking to see you."

Claire and Rock had no plans, but after her last visit, Claire couldn't help but be skeptical of her daughter's true motive. With an ever-so-slight hint of caution in her voice, Claire said, "We'd love to see you and Brian." Claire was sure the use of the pronoun we was not lost on Ingrid.

"Well, then, we will be up tomorrow evening after work. Don't hold dinner for us. We will stop along the way for something."

"Fine, dear. Will it just be you and Brian or should I make up a bedroom for the nanny?" Claire suffered no illusion. She knew a lot of the day-to-day duties of motherhood were being handled by the nanny. She'd met her several times and didn't like her.

"No, it's just Brian and me. I've given Karla the weekend off. Her sister is getting married, and she's off to Colorado tomorrow afternoon."

Claire, could not help but become inwardly pessimistic. *So you've decided to come up here so Rock and I can entertain Brian while you do what? Work?* But she surprised herself with her civility. "OK. Drive carefully, and we'll see you tomorrow evening."

Rock, inferring what was going to happen based on Claire's side of the conversation said, "Well that's a surprise. What do you think it means?"

Claire disclosed her pessimism.

Rock, though still stinging from his last encounter with Ingrid, thought Claire's take on it a bit harsh. "Maybe she's extending an olive branch." Claire gave him a skeptical look. Rock smiled at her and then said, "Well, I guess I'd better get over to Far-Far-View and turn on a few things."

Claire said, "Why? You don't have to do that. We're old enough."

Rock looked at her and said, "Claire, let's plan on the worst. I'm pretty sure Ingrid doesn't like me and, if she found me living here, dislike would turn quickly to hate. Let's not make matters worse than they already are."

"I'm not going to let her run my life, Rock," Claire told him defiantly.

"I'm not suggesting that you do, but this visit might be a chance for the two of you to talk. Let's face it, if you can't get through to her, then who can?"

Reluctantly Claire nodded in agreement.

Ingrid and Brian arrived as scheduled on Friday night. Rock had just let the two dogs out the back door and was standing in the driveway as their guests pulled in. While

Ingrid retrieved their overnight bag from the trunk of her car, Rock went to the door and called to Claire. Ingrid greeted her mother perfunctorily. To Rock she offered an insincere, "Hello," which he interpreted to mean, *What are you doing here?*

The five-year old grabbed his grandmother around her legs and hugged her tightly. "Oh, my gosh, look at you. You've grown just since I saw you last," Claire said, bending down to hug the boy back. "How tall are you now, Brian?"

Without hesitating he answered, "Mama says I'm big for my age, almost four feet tall, Grandma."

Still hugging him, Claire responded, "I thought so. I'm going to put a book on your head to slow you down."

Brian giggled, but Claire wasn't sure if he got what she was trying to say. She introduced the boy to Rock, who was surprised by his maturity and confidence. Extending his hand, Brian said, "Nice to meet you, sir."

Smiling, Rock bent over, took his hand and said, "I've heard a lot about you, Brian. It's nice to meet you, too."

Claire beamed at the two of them.

Brian spotted Flower and called to her. The two dogs were standing together just a few feet away from them. Claire said, "Brian, the other dog is Flot..."

Before she could finish, Ingrid intercepted her son, grabbed his hand and headed for the door. Rock, Claire and the two dogs were left standing in the driveway.

"I'm so sorry," Claire said, the frustration evident in her voice.

"It's OK, Claire, but I think Flotsam and I should skedaddle on out of here and let you two talk."

Saturday morning dawned bright, sunny and beautiful, albeit cold, at the lakeshore. At about 9:00 a.m. the phone rang at Far-Far-View. "We're going into Shelby for breakfast, and you're invited. We'll pick you up in fifteen minutes." There was a certain prickliness to her tone and, from this, Rock surmised that it had not gone well after he'd left them the night before.

"Claire, are you sure..."

"Positive. See you in fifteen," and she was gone.

Nothing had changed. Ingrid refused to acknowledge Rock's presence unless he asked her something directly. Her answers were short, clipped snippets delivered as if to ask, *Why am I even bothering to talk to you?* Normally this kind of an attitude would have encouraged him to engage her, just because he knew it would piss her off, but this was Claire's daughter. He didn't want to make matters worse for Claire, nor did he want to widen the already vast chasm between Ingrid and him. So for over an hour he talked mostly to Claire, to Brian and smiled occasionally in Ingrid's direction to find that he was being ignored. As for Claire, he believed she would have bitten Ingrid's head off if it weren't for the presence of her grandson. When they arrived back home, Rock excused himself by saying he needed to check on Flotsam. Claire was nearly in tears, but not wanting to make a scene in front of Brian, she kissed Rock softly on the cheek, took her grandson by the hand and said icily to Ingrid, who'd paid at the restaurant, "Thanks for breakfast. C'mon Brian, let's go check on Flower."

Once he got back to Far-Far-View, Rock busied himself building a fire and making a mug of tea. He tried reading, but his mind was next door, thinking of Claire. While he had to give Ingrid kudos for her cunning, Rock despised her. Ingrid was intentionally using her son as a shield against Claire's anger. As long as the boy was around, Claire wouldn't get angry and so Ingrid could continue to make it clear that Rock was little more than gum on the bottom of her shoe. He asked himself, *What kind of a person uses a little boy like that?*

"Mommy," Brian said, tugging on her pant leg, "Can we go down to the beach?

"It's too cold, Brian." Ingrid told him.

He'd been sitting at the slider studying the ice formations that stretched from the shoreline out at least the length of a football field. At the furthest distance from the shore was a line of ice mounds, some of them as high as fifteen or twenty feet. Directly in front of their house was one that had a blowhole. The wave action under the ice would occasionally send a gusher of water spouting into the air and cascading down the mound's slope.

From the kitchen, Claire heard Brian ask his mother again if they could go to the beach. Through the window, she looked at the outside thermometer. It was twenty-five degrees Fahrenheit, moderate for early February temperatures. She looked at the dune grass just as Rock had taught her. It was barely moving. "Why don't you take him outside, Ingrid? It's not that cold. The wind isn't bad."

"Please, Mommy, we brought winter clothes."

Ingrid was preoccupied reading, but broke away long enough to cast a manipulative smile toward her mother. "Can you take him? I have to get through this brief before court on ..."

Claire had anticipated her. "I can't, honey. I'm fixing meatloaf for dinner," and seeing a chance to assert herself, Claire added, "It's Rock's favorite. He's coming for dinner at 5 p.m. and I have to get started." She could almost see Ingrid rolling her eyes in disgust.

"Please, Mommy. I want to go. I want to take Flower with us."

Ingrid turned to him and impatiently relented. "OK, OK. I can see I'm not going to get any work done until you've had your way." Impatiently pointing in the direction of his room she directed, "Go get your winter clothes on." On her way out of the house, Ingrid grabbed the legal brief she'd been reading. Flower and Brian ran down the steps toward the lake's frozen edge, while Ingrid trailed behind, trying to find the place where she'd left off.

The dog led Brian to the frozen edge of the lake, but stopped there. Playfully Brian ran up behind her. Patting her on the head, he said, "C'mon, Flower, let's go out there," pointing at the distant blowhole which had just spouted a fountain of water.

Ingrid stopped at the top of the steps, brushed the snow from the stone wall that surrounded the patio and then sat down, her head still buried in the brief.

As the boy stepped onto the solid ice at the lake's edge, Flower whimpered first, and, then, barked. Ingrid looked up, but chose to ignore Flower's warning. Brian had stopped only a few feet from shore and knelt down to examine the peculiar sand-snow-ice mix that was the surface on which he now found himself. Ingrid turned her attention back to the brief and in the next crucial, several minutes failed to notice her son's progress further out onto the ice field, toward the mound and the blowhole.

Flower, who was more attuned to the creaks and cracks of the ever-shifting ice than her fearless young companion, followed him. Every now and then she would stop and twist her head from side to side as if trying to determine if it was wise to continue. But she would start moving again as Brian would distance himself from her, never letting that distance grow to more than ten or fifteen feet. When they reached the bottom of the mound that was the blowhole, she whimpered and barked again, as the boy ascended the side of the mound. This time the distance between them and Ingrid was too great and Flower's bark was swept away by the light southwesterly wind long before it could ever reach Ingrid, whose head was still in the brief.

While the trip to the mound had been over jagged, uneven sheets of ice, the more steeply sloped side of the blowhole's mound was fairly smooth, the result of the fountains of water cascading down the slope and then freezing in February's cold temperatures. Brian found it difficult to scale, so he began jabbing his feet into the slope, trying to find a foothold. His body was splayed on the side of the mound at about a forty-five degree angle relative to the flat surface of the ice field he'd walked out on. He had managed to poke and claw his way nearly to the mound's summit when the ice under him began to splinter and crack. In the next instant, the boy splashed into the freezing water at the bottom of the blowhole. Fully immersed, he couldn't determine up from down as a wave banged him into the ice at the interior of the mound's base. It hurt, but it also got his attention. He managed to get his feet under him and realized the water was up to his shoulders, but wasn't over his head. Another wave banged him into the ice wall that surrounded him. Frightened, he slapped at the ice cold water. Too afraid to cry, he began panicked calls, "Mommy! Mommy! Help me! Help me!" but the thick walls of the mound proved an effective sound insulation. On the surface of the ice, at the base of the mound, Flower began to go crazy, frantically barking at the top of her lungs.

Ingrid heard one or two of the dog's louder barks, looked up from her work, saw only Flower, far out on the ice field and immediately felt a sudden jolt of panic-induced adrenalin. *Where is he? Oh, my God! Where's Brian?* Tossing the brief onto the steps, she scrambled down from the patio, screaming, "Brian! Brian! Brian!" Only Flower and one other soul heard her plaintive calls.

Inside Far-Far-View, Flotsam, from her perch at the sunroom's window, suddenly erupted in a fusillade of long, shrill barks. Rock looked up from his book and went to the window to see Ingrid running toward the lake and

Flower at the base of a mound about a hundred yards from shore. Though he couldn't hear the dog, he could see breath each time she lunged and barked at the base of the mound. He knew something was desperately wrong. As he pulled on his boots and coat, Flotsam barked furiously at the cottage's back door. When he opened it, she spilled out past him. He wished he could be only a fraction as fast as her. Turning to head to the steps leading to the beach, he caught sight of her old rope leash, lying on a bench next to the cottage door. He grabbed it, running as fast as his limp would allow.

By the time he reached the lake's edge, both dogs stood barking at the base of the mound. Ingrid, who'd already fallen twice in her haste to reach the spot where she could only hope to find her son, was nearly at the base of the ice mound. Rock yelled at her, "Ingrid, wait..." he was waving the rope above his head. "Wait, you'll need this."

Though she heard him, there wasn't time to wait. *He's been in the water too long already. I've got to get him out of the water.* Ignoring him, she continued toward the ice mound and the two barking dogs.

Rock moved ahead out onto the ice field. He could hear the creaking and cracking of the ice and at first, feared it was breaking beneath him. But then he realized it was the sound the ice made as the ever-present wave action underneath drove the ice in and out and from side to side. He cursed his limp, but he remembered the last time he'd been in a tough situation. He slipped and nearly fell, but caught himself. He pushed through it and managed to increase his pace.

When Ingrid reached the mound, she started to crawl up its steep slope just as her son had done only a few minutes earlier. From inside the mound, faintly she could hear Brian's cries for help. "Mommy's coming, honey. Hang on! Mommy's coming." She had no idea if he could hear her or not, but took encouragement from the boy's continued calls for help. Looking up the side of the mound that loomed in front of her, she could see a place about ten feet above her head where it looked as if a piece had broken off. As she began to ascend, she experienced the same difficulty as Brian, so she began to kick and claw at whatever foothold or handhold she could get until she was able to reach the jagged edge of the break and pull herself up to it. Just as she was nearly high enough to peer into the blowhole, she heard the crack first, and then, felt the ice break under her just above her waist. All she could think was that it was going to fall directly onto her little boy. She screamed, "Brian! Watch out!" She felt sick to her stomach as she slid the five feet or so back down to the base of the mound. She began to cry as she turned to re-ascend the side of the mound. Then she felt something draw tight around her waist.

Brian had been looking up at his mother when he saw the piece of ice break from under her. Instinctively he'd put his hands up over his head, moved as close to the mound's interior wall as he could and bent down, shielding himself from it. Only its trailing edge scraped the back of his head, near the crown, as it fell into the water next to him. His thick winter hat had helped to pad the blow and prevent bloodshed.

Ingrid screamed at Rock as he put the finishing touches on a knot, "I have to get to him! I have to get him out of there!"

Rock didn't say anything. Instead he cinched Flotsam's old rope leash down tighter around her waist. Though he felt nearly as panicked as she did, he realized more panic wasn't what was needed.

Screaming, she turned away from him and back to the slope, "Mommy's coming, Brian!" As she scrambled back up the slope, handholds and footholds more familiar this time, Rock could hear her say that again and again, only softer and softer each time, as if she were saving her energy, but needed the words to compel her back up the slope.

He coached her as she climbed, "You're doing just fine, Ingrid. That's it. Good!"

She managed to get her head and shoulders back to where the ice had cracked out from under her, but when she stuck her arms down into the hole, despite her best efforts to reach down and the boy's best efforts to reach up, they were still about six inches away from one another's grip. "OK, honey. Hold on. Mommy's going to get you out," she said to him in her most reassuring voice. Ingrid pulled herself up further on the slope. Her waist was now at the jagged edge where the ice had broken from under her. She bent over, her entire upper torso reaching down into the hole. She heard another crack, but the expected fall did not come. "OK, honey, grab Mommy's hand."

It was awkward. She had little leverage and, later, she could not determine where she'd found the strength to lift his soaking wet, nearly fifty-pound frame out of the hole. But she managed to snatch him cleanly up to her. Their faces just inches apart now, in one movement she twisted onto her back, rolling Brian completely clear of the blow-hole. He landed solidly on top of her. Wrapping him firmly in her arms, she let gravity take over and the two of them slid down the side of the mound just as the ice on which she'd been lying, seconds earlier, fell into the water below them.

The boy was crying and Ingrid could feel his shivers. Realizing that time was still not on their side, she struggled to get up. Rock helped her and quickly untied the rope from around her waist. She held the boy tight against her. He was crying. Ingrid's eyes were fixed on Claire's house and Rock could see that she had begun crying. The ice field, jagged and uneven, was difficult for them to navigate. When Ingrid fell, he bent down to help her. She was fatigued, he knew that, he'd experienced that kind of fatigue before. "Let me carry him, Ingrid."

"No," she shrieked and tightened her grip on her son and pulled away from him. She struggled to her feet and they began to move again, toward the house, the dogs following on their heels. When she fell again, she sat sobbing. It was only thirty or forty more yards to the beach, then fifty or so yards to the dune, then another fifty yards to the steps... she tried to stand. Rock helped her.

The boy was crying harder now. "Mommy, I'm so cold... help me..." his voice was thin and raspy.

She was on her feet again, but her steps were short and tentative. She knew she was adding time, time they did not have, to the trip to the warmth of the house. When she slipped and fell yet again, Rock was right there, but he remained silent. He knew she would have to come to her own decision. For a few seconds, she sat on the ice, cradling the boy against her, sobbing and rocking back and forth. Rock was about to say something to her, but he didn't need to. She knew she had no energy left. As she sat sobbing, Brian crying in her arms and shivering, she looked at Rock and said, half screaming, half pleading, "Just get him inside!"

Rock nodded and took the boy in his arms, surprised at how much weight she had pulled from the hole, at how much weight she had managed to carry this far. He struck out toward the house, peering back occasionally to make sure she was coming. She was. Both dogs stayed with her, replacing Rock. He comforted the crying boy in his arms, "It's OK, Brian. You'll be back at Grandma's house in a minute and we'll get you warm again."

Claire came around the corner of the kitchen when she heard the slider open, "Well, how was..." and then she saw her cold, wet grandson in Rock's arms. "My God! What happened? Where's Ingrid?" She could hear the boy sobbing and see him shivering. "Is he all right, Rock?"

"I need to get him out of these wet clothes. Could you get..." He looked up, but Claire was gone. Rock laid the boy gently down on the sofa in front of the fireplace and began removing his gloves, hat, coat, winter pants.

Just as Claire returned with an armful of blankets, Ingrid rushed in the open slider. "Is he...?

Rock looked up at her. "He's OK. He's been asking for you."

Ingrid removed the rest of his wet clothing, wrapped him in several of the blankets Claire had brought to them, then picked the boy up in her arms and settled into an easy chair closer to the fireplace. She sat rocking back and forth, murmuring things to him until they both stopped crying.

In the kitchen as Claire made Rock a mug of tea, he told her what he knew. Claire wondered, but didn't ask how the boy wound up so far out on the ice. The important thing, at this point, is that he appeared to be all right. When they walked back into the great room, Brian, snuggled in his mother's arms, no longer crying, was asleep.

Rock whispered to Ingrid, "It's probably best to take him to the emergency room in Shelby and let them check him out."

Ingrid couldn't look at him, but nodded.

Rock continued, "You did a good job out there, Ingrid." Again, she avoided eye contact, but he could see the tears starting to flow down her cheeks. "I'll drive you in."

Claire piped up, "I'm going, too."

A long moment passed. Both Claire and Rock thought that she might be considering not taking the boy to the hospital. Finally, Ingrid looked back and forth between the two of them and said, "No, I'll take him in. We'll be just fine."

"But, Ingrid," Claire said.

"Mom," the word Mom wasn't lost on Claire, Ingrid had not called her that in a long, long time, "It's OK. He's OK.

It's just a precaution." Then she repeated, "We'll be just fine."

Claire sat in the easy chair holding her grandson tight against her, while Ingrid rounded up a dry change of clothes for the trip into the emergency room. When she returned, mother and grandmother gently woke the boy up. As Ingrid dressed him, Claire said to Rock, "Ingrid told me a piece of ice may have hit him when he was standing in the water. Do you think he might have a slight concussion?"

Rock whispered back to her as he pointed to his own head, "Don't worry, they have excellent concussion protocols at the hospital."

Claire nodded.

After Brian was dressed, Ingrid wrapped him in a dry blanket, picked him up and headed for the door. Claire asked, "Are you sure you don't want at least one of us..."

"Thanks, Mom, but we'll be fine. I'll call you."

Claire, Rock and the two dogs stood in the driveway as Ingrid drove away. Claire was crying.

Rock put his arms around her. "He's fine. They'll be back before you know it."

About two hours later, Rock was setting the table for dinner when the phone rang. Claire answered it.

"Mom..."

There it is again, 'Mom', Claire thought. "Yes, dear, how's Brian?"

There was a pause that gave Claire some concern, and then Ingrid said, "He's fine. No concussion, no frost bite, temperature is normal, just some jangled nerves."

"Thank God. How are you? Are you on your way? Dinner's almost on the table."

There was a longer pause this time and then, "Uh, Mom, I'm taking Brian home..."

"But, Ingrid..."

"I know this seems really ungrateful, but Ethan was terrified when I told him what had happened. He wanted to drive up. I told him no, that we would come home."

"Well, OK. I suppose you're right. A boy needs his father." Even as she said them, the words sounded trite to Claire.

"Yeah, well, there's that and..." she paused as if reflecting on something, "I need some time alone to think about what might have happened today. Sorry, Mom. I hope you understand."

Claire didn't, but told her she did and added, "Give us a call when you get home."

After dinner, Claire and Rock were sitting in front of the fireplace reading when Flotsam began to growl at something outside the slider. Flower immediately joined her, and the two let out a couple of anxious barks. Rock looked at Claire and wordlessly got up to see what had them so spooked. In the darkness he couldn't see anything. He switched on the outside light. It had started to snow and he could see by the way it was swirling around that the wind had come up as well. Then he saw what had disturbed the dogs. He stepped outside and retrieved the brief Ingrid had thrown to the ground. Its pages were fluttering in the rising wind and, while he hadn't been able to see it in the dark, both dogs must have heard the pages rattling. Claire heard him open the slider and felt the cold rush of wind as he stepped outside. When he walked back in, he closed the slider behind him and turned to her, "This must be Ingrid's?"

Claire nodded, "It's a brief she was working on. She must have forgotten it in all the excitement."

Rock said, "Surprised she hasn't called about it. If it had been left out there all night, it would have been ruined. It's snowing like crazy."

The next day, after walking the dogs, while having a bite of lunch, Rock asked Claire, "Did Ingrid ever call about her brief?"

Claire looked at him a bit oddly, "You know, she hasn't. She said something about needing it in court on Monday, but, not a word. That's not like her."

"Should we call? Maybe tell her we have it?"

Claire thought for a moment, shook her head and said, "No. She knows where it is. If she needs it, she'll call.

Chapter Thirty-Three

Gulf Breeze

"I have an idea."

Rock had come to like those words. He liked Claire's spontaneity. It was one of those endearing qualities that he'd grown to love about her. At first, he'd been reluctant to accept it, because it wasn't something that he was used to. Work on the production lines at GM did not promote spontaneity. You were expected to be at work at a certain time, work steadily until a certain time, and when the call for overtime came, it usually wasn't optional. Sometimes her spontaneity meant that they were going to spend an extravagant amount of money on something. However, as it usually turned out, Claire allowed him to contribute. Now, into the third week of a miserable February, he was ready for one of her ideas. "I'm all ears."

Claire had called Ingrid a few days after Brian's accident to reassure herself that her grandson was all right. At the time, Ingrid had apologized again for leaving so abruptly, but assured her that her grandson was perfectly OK and was telling everyone how his mother had rescued him, making her out to be some kind of superhero. Despite Claire's urge to do so, she'd made no other calls to Ingrid, nor had any come from Ingrid. From this Claire had concluded that Ingrid had not changed her mind about her relationship with Rock or Beth's with Josh.

The other person she'd not heard from was her doctor and with each passing day, Claire was inwardly becoming more anxious. She needed a change. "Let's go to Florida for a couple of weeks."

"I'd love to, but it might be hard to find..."

"A place to stay?"

Rock just looked at her and said, "Let me guess, you have a place?"

Sheepishly Claire nodded, "On Manasota Key, near Englewood. Do you know that area?" He didn't, so Claire filled him in briefly.

"Do you want to drive or fly?"

"We'll fly."

Rock didn't get it. "OK. I'll see what I can find." He paused, "There might be a cheap flight out of Flint. We could drive over the night before, and I could show you my etchings," he said in his most lecherous voice.

Claire laughed and replied, "I'd love to see your loft," and then there was a pause. "We can fly out of Flint. I'll just make a call."

He sat for a minute. *No! No way!* He scratched his head and said, "Let me guess again. Corporate jet?"

"Yes," she replied unapologetically. "They've been very kind about allowing me to use it. Basically all I do is call and they haul."

Shaking his head, he asked with a certain amount of resignation in his voice, "Rental car?"

"Tom or Rita Metz will meet us at the airport in Punta Gorda. It's the closest to the house. They watch the place for me. There are two cars there. The Metzes will have everything ready for us. All we have to do is show up."

It was what he'd come to expect from Claire, but he had another thought. "Listen, Russ and Patti Sluwinski, my best friends..."

Claire nodded, "Of course, I remember."

"Well, the Sluwinskis are down there right now, and they were talking about looking at places around Fort Meyers. Would you like... I mean, maybe I could give them a call..."

"Rock, I'd love to meet them. They can stay at the house with us for as long as they'd like. There's plenty of room. This is going to be so much fun." She had come over to him and put her arms around him. He kissed her and said, "Thanks, Claire. You're going to like them. They're great people."

They had arrived late at his loft. The dogs piled out of the back of the Range Rover and did not go far before each squatted. Rock let himself into the garage and lit an outside light as the dogs sniffed around their new environment.

As the dogs were finishing up their work, Rock grabbed an overnight bag from the rear of the Range Rover and then the four of them headed up the stairs to the loft. Rock unlocked the door, reached in and flipped a switch just inside the door. Three drop lights over the kitchen counter emitted a soft, warm light in the loft's approximate center. Claire stepped in just behind him and looked around. In the low light her sense of smell seemed stronger than her sense of sight and she took in a masculine scent of wood and leather. As Rock switched on a floor lamp between two leather easy chairs in the living area, Claire could see the bookshelves lining the walls. Walking over to the one directly in front of her, she ran her hands over a row of books. "You've read all of these?"

"Yes. A few of them, the special ones, a couple of times."

"Special ones?" she inquired.

"I really like Roots. On days when I think it's a struggle, I'll pull that off the shelf and read a little of it and realize I hardly know the meaning of the word. When the company gave me the boot, I pulled this off the shelf," he lifted

Dicken's *Tale of Two Cities* and showed her the spine. "I thought it interesting that when we first met, you were reading this too."

"The opening really resonates with our times, don't you think?"

"He had it right," Rock agreed, slightly modifying Dickens' famous lines, "It is the best of times, it is the worst of times."

"How did you become such a reader?"

"My Mom and Fitz get the credit for that."

Fitz was a new name to her and Rock detected a puzzled look on Claire's face. "Fitz?"

"Yeah, I grew up in a pretty rough part of town. Mom worked several jobs, so my sister and I were alone a lot of the time. The only place outside of the apartment we were allowed to go without her was the library, which was only about two blocks away. There was a lady there that kind of took us under her wing. Her name was Mrs. Fitzgerald, but she insisted my sister and I call her Fitz."

Claire had never known a man quite like him. *He could have been anything he wanted, but he doesn't care about what might have been. He's perfectly happy with who he is.* She knelt down to look at her reflection in the hardwood floor and then walked over to the kitchen area and rubbed her hand over the granite countertops. "Did you do all of this?"

"Russ and I. It took us a lot of years, but we were persistent, worked on it when we could. It came together pretty well, didn't it?"

She walked over to him, put her arms around him, kissed him and then said, "It's lovely, Rock. Absolutely lovely!" The dogs were asleep on the deeply padded area rug in the living area. She led him to the bedroom, placed a finger over her lips suggesting they be quiet, and then made love to each other. Afterwards, with Rock sound asleep next to her, Claire thought to herself, *I wonder how many women he's had up here?* She chided herself for the thought, but quickly rationalized her curiosity was only natural. She could hear the click of toenails on the wood floor. One of the dogs wandered into the kitchen area and drank from the bowl Rock had put down for them. *What does it matter? Until four months ago, you didn't even know him.* The toenails clicked again, back toward the sitting area and the loft fell silent except for Rock's slow breaths. *Nothing either of us did before we met really matters. What matters now is that you love him and he loves you.*

The Gulfstream 450 was waiting when they arrived at Flint's Bishop International Airport. They followed the signs for the civil aviation terminal, showed identification at the gate. Then Rock drove the Range Rover directly planeside, where the co-pilot loaded their luggage into the storage compartment while Rock and Claire exercised Flotsam and Flower.

The flight to Fort Meyers took about two and a half hours. The dogs were fine until the descent into Punta Gorda. Like babies, they began to wail as their ears clogged. Despite Claire and Rock rubbing them, they were still shaking their heads and flapping their ears as the plane rolled to a full stop at the civil aviation ramp. Upon deplaning, the captain asked Claire if she knew when they would be returning. Rock heard Claire say that she did not. As he stood in the seventy-degree sunshine, he liked the sound of that very much.

They were greeted by Tom and Rita Metz. Claire hugged each of them, introduced Rock and then Rock and Tom loaded the luggage into a gleaming black Toyota Land Cruiser, along with the two dogs. Claire and Rita climbed into a red, two-seater Mercedes Benz SLK. "Can we put the top down?" Claire asked.

Rock heard Rita say, "We can do whatever you would like, Ms. Van Zandt. Probably nice to see the sunshine, isn't it?"

As they rolled away from the plane, Tom Metz said to Rock, "It's good to see Ms. Van Zandt again. It's been a long time. Two years or more I think."

"We've had a tough winter up north. It's nice to see the sunshine and feel warm air again," Rock said.

"Are the Chavezes coming down later?"

Rock gave him a puzzled look, "Not to my knowledge. Do they usually?"

He cautiously replied, "The Van Zandts bought Gulf Breeze about ten years ago. Their kids were grown. I think Ingrid was in law school and Beth was a senior in high school or maybe a freshman in college. They said the place was a winter getaway, but they hardly ever made it in the winter. When they did come, the Chavezes were always with them. I know Jesus and Maria work for them, but Mr. and Ms. Van Zandt treated them like family."

"The place is called Gulf Breeze?"

"Sure is. Won't take you long to see why, once we get there."

The trip from Punta Gorda to Gulf Breeze was a quick one, almost all on high-speed, four-lane highway, but in Englewood, when they turned toward the Gulf and headed toward Stump Pass Beach, things slowed down considerably. At the beach, they turned north down a road that bisected the north-south length of Manasota Key. Huge trees, decorative hedges and shrubs and elaborate gates and fences lined the road and obscured the Gulf of Mexico from view, except for occasional brief glimpses. For about five miles on the trip northward up the key, traffic was moderate as beachgoers were coming from or going to the three public beaches that lay along the key's western edge. As they passed the third public beach, traffic reduced to virtually zero. "Pretty quiet down here," Tom remarked.

Rock swiveled trying to take in the natural beauty of the passing landscape on either side as well as the huge estates he could glimpse every now and then. About two miles past the last public beach, Tom pulled the car into a driveway, stopped at a keypad and punched in a code. Rock watched as two massive iron gates swung open. The gate on the left held the word *GULF* in its intricate iron-work near the top, the other contained the word *BREEZE*. A circular drive led them to a stop at the bottom of a set of semi-circular steps that led to two magnificently carved mahogany doors inset with beveled-glass in the upper half. Rock's view through the doors was obscured by the intricate beveling, but he could see through to the glass wall on the other side and knew the blue-green was the Gulf of Mexico. Flotsam and Flower had followed him up the stairs and patiently sat waiting for the doors to open.

Claire and Rita were a minute or two behind. While Tom and Rita took both cars around to the garage for unloading, Claire climbed the steps toward Rock. At the top she took his hand and opened the door. "Let me show you Gulf Breeze," she said.

Rock's only comment was, "Holy smoke! Russ and Patti aren't going to believe this place."

Chapter Thirty-Four

Claire and Patti

"Russ, write this down." Rock paused, giving him a chance to get a pad and pencil.

"OK, Rock, go ahead."

"9-5-2-9. Got it?"

"Yep. You must be in one of those what they call gated communities."

"Uh, yeah, you might call it that. Just punch those numbers into the keypad and the gate to Gulf Breeze will open for you. Then just come up the drive. We'll be here watching for you and Patti."

"So Gulf Breeze is the name of the condos?"

"Uh, well, not exactly. It's a surprise. You'll see when you get here. You've got the address and the gate code, so drive carefully, and we'll see you tomorrow."

Rock and Claire had had two marvelous weeks at Gulf Breeze together. In that time they had been chased off the beach only one day by foul weather. They had taken endless walks up and down the beach along Manasota Key, which is known for its sharks' teeth. When they were finished walking, they would take their specially designed baskets with handles about four feet long and wade in the warm waters of the Gulf. Dipping their baskets into the sand just at the water's edge, they would dredge up a dripping load of sand, shells and the occasional coveted shark's tooth.

Most of their meals were pool-side. Rock was truly torn between the beach and the pool, which featured an infinity edge that appeared magically level with the surrounding deck's surface. From the deck the view of the beach was breathtaking, and Rock liked that he could take it in while reclining on a comfortable chaise lounge perfect for napping. Usually the beach won out, though, because that was where the dogs were the happiest. Outside nearly every waking hour, he and Claire managed to avoid sunburn. But that was only through the massive use of spray-on sunscreen, their purchases of which Rock thought surely must have put an upward spike in the local economy.

On Monday, March 9th, they stayed close to home waiting for Russ and Patti to arrive. Over a cup of tea, Rock said, "Uh, you know they are going to be stunned by this place."

"Stunned?

It was awkward, but he knew Russ and Patti. "A little like I was when we went to Holland that first time. It takes some time for people like me..." he paused again and then continued, "And Russ and Patti, to get used to it."

She smiled at him, "Should we have warned them?"

Rock thought and then said, "I suppose we could have, but I'm not sure it would have done much good. It's a different world, Claire. That doesn't mean that there's anything wrong with it; it's just different, really different."

"I understand. So we, make that I, will have to work hard at making them feel at home."

"You were right the first time, Claire, we will have to make them feel at home."

At about 1:00 p.m., the dogs heard them first and ran barking toward the front door, followed closely by Rock.

By design, Claire hung back and would wait for Rock to make introductions. As he opened the door, both dogs barking and tails wagging, dashed out toward the new arrivals. Over the racket Rock heard Patti scolding Russ. "I told you we should have dressed better than this," as she held out her sundress and pointed to her flip-flops. Russ, in Bermuda shorts, a well-worn T-shirt and sandals, was down on one knee greeting the dogs and ignoring her.

"Welcome to Gulf Breeze," Rock said above the commotion as he stepped toward Patti for a hug.

"You should have told us," Patti said.

"How? How do I describe this to someone? Wait until you see it. But there's someone I want you to meet first."

She stepped away from him and squeezed his hand, "I can't wait."

Mischievously he smiled at her and said, "Patti, meet Flotsam," and he pointed to the border collie, "And Flower," and he pointed to the lab.

Russ was still playing with them. Patti looked at Rock and said, "Go to hell. Where's Claire?"

"Oh, yes, Claire. Then right this way, my dear," he said, laughing, and motioned for her to follow him up the steps.

"Russ, let those dogs alone. Come on and meet Claire," Patti commanded. Russ dutifully followed them up the stairs, the dogs at the side of their new-found friend.

As they walked through the house to the pool area where Claire had busied herself setting up a light lunch, Russ was uncommonly quiet. Patti was looking around, trying to take it all in, but Rock could tell from her expression she was on visual overload. As they stepped out on the deck where Claire was waiting, Rock said, "Claire Van Zandt, I'd like you to meet my two best friends in all the world, Russ and Patti Sluwinski."

Patti, happy to have a single point in front of her to concentrate on, stepped toward her, "Claire, Rock should have told us. We would have dressed better."

Claire simply said, "Then you would have been over-dressed." Claire offered a hug. "Welcome to Gulf Breeze. It's so nice to meet you." Claire stepped back, held out her sun dress and pointed to her flip-flops and said, "We're both dressed just right."

Patti liked her immediately.

Russ stepped forward, extended his massive hand and said, "Very nice to meet you, ma'am."

Claire took his hand in hers and said, "Oh, no, you don't." Russ had one of those startled looks on his face as if he'd done something wrong, then Claire put him at ease, "None of that ma'am stuff. Call me Claire."

"Yes, ma...er, uh, I mean Claire. Thanks for having us."

"We didn't know if you'd eaten or not, so I fixed a little tuna salad and some lemonade. Let's sit down and talk. I've been dying to meet you both. Rock has told me so much about you." Thus began perhaps the quickest week that either couple had spent all winter.

On days when the four of them were together, breakfasts and lunches were taken at Gulf Breeze and dinners were eaten out. It wasn't fancy, but they all took a liking to Café 776, agreeing that for the best food, cold beer and relaxed Florida atmosphere, it was their favorite. Claire added it was also the most affordable, a comment that endeared her further to practical Patti.

There were several days when the boys went their way and the girls went theirs. For Claire these were her fondest memories of the week. The two of them, Claire and Patti, had spent time looking at real estate listings and become intrigued by a listing in Old Englewood Village, a bungalow that was a fixer-upper. Only a couple of blocks off the beach, it was reasonably priced. But it had been on the market for well over a year, so the girls thought they could offer less and still have the offer seriously considered.

Today, Thursday, they were meeting the realtor, but had decided to stop at Café 776 for lunch first. After the waitress brought them two iced teas, Claire said to Patti, "You know Russ's talk with Rock at Christmas has helped him."

"That damned war," Patti said shaking her head. "I met Russ just after he got home. He was a real mess, couldn't sleep at night, wouldn't talk about it. I remember one night, just after we'd first met, we were at a restaurant and someone in the kitchen dropped something, I dunno, a bunch of plates or pots or pans or something like that. I'll never forget it. It made a helluva racket, even scared me, but I thought Russ was going to jump out of his skin. We had to get up and leave. Rock was in rehab down in Battle Creek back then. Russ worried constantly about him, more than he worried about his own damn self. They go all the way back to high school, ya' know. Has Rock told you how they came to be such good friends?"

Claire shook her head, "Just that they were in the Marines together."

"Well, it goes back a lot further than that. Russ tells people that Rock was his tackling dummy in high school," and she gave a laugh. "Rock was a running back and a pretty good one, I'm told. Russ was a middle linebacker. He was All-State his senior year. When you can get the two of them to talk about those days, it's hilarious. Russ claims he never missed a tackle his entire senior year. Rock says it's because he got to practice against the best running back in the league. Anyway, they were inseparable in high school. Both of them were offered scholarships. Rock's was partial and he couldn't afford college. Russ's was a full-ride, but he hated school and knew college would kill him. So they joined the Marines together."

"He loves the both of you, you know," Claire said.

Patti smiled and nodded, "Oh, yeah, I know, but that connection between him and Russ..." she paused, looking for the right word, "No way to describe it except maybe simply special. When they came home from Vietnam, I always had the feeling that Russ felt that he owed Rock something. He busted his ass to get Rock on at the plant. A couple of good old boys in the union had been Marines, and Russ went to them. As soon as they found out what Rock did to earn the Navy Cross, they got him on the job. I think Rock getting that job and Russ being able to work side-by-side with his best friend really helped both of them cope with what they'd been through. Good God, Claire, we were all working our butts off back then. I'll bet our average work week was sixty hours, and more often than not, more. It took their minds off of it."

"Wasn't there some way to get them help? Claire asked.

Patti shook her head, "Not back then. Not when they really could have used it. Then when the Veteran's Administration finally recognized PTSD as a legitimate ailment, neither of them felt like they were really suffering from it. They don't like to talk about it, not even to each other. I think both of them consider themselves lucky that they have other things in their lives that takes their minds off of it, the war, I mean, and what they had to do over there. Russ has never suffered some of the violent outbreaks of rage that you hear about today. Neither has Rock, as far as I know, and I think I'd know. The three of us have been pretty close for a lot of years."

Claire told her, "I've read the citation that goes with Rock's Navy Cross. What he did... I mean, I can't imagine any man being able to do something like that. I just don't understand why he should feel guilty about it."

Patti was quiet for a minute while the waiter brought their lunches. After she'd unwrapped her silverware and put her napkin on her lap, she looked at Claire and said, "You know the mind is a powerful thing. The only problem is that it's a sealed unit. When you won't talk to anyone else about what you are thinking, all you're getting is one opinion. After they talked on the phone at Christmas...

mind you, I could only hear Russ's side of the conversation... I said to him, 'You never told me that... I mean about messing yourself'." She looked at Claire who had a puzzled look on her face and said, "You don't know what I'm talking about, do you?"

Claire said, "No. I could only hear Rock's side of the conversation, but whatever Russ said, it helped Rock. I thought I'd really screwed up with the Navy Cross gift. I knew there was some concern. I'd spoken to Josh, and I knew he'd spoken to Russ, but I never thought that just seeing it would affect him like it did." Claire was gesturing with her hands as if she were unwrapping a package, "He pulled the wrapping paper off and his anger was almost immediate. I felt so bad. I didn't know what to do. Thank goodness, Josh was there and called Russ."

Patti nodded, "After the phone call on Christmas, Russ came to me. He was crying. I can tell you I've been married to that man almost forty years, and that is maybe the second time I've seen him cry, but that night he was babbling like a little baby. He went through it with me, each and every minute that he could remember about that night in the jungle. Some of it I'd heard before, but he told me some things that were new, things he'd kept buried inside of himself all these years. I let him talk, and when he was finished I just held him while he cried. Claire, I love Rock Graham. If it weren't for him, I really think Russ would have been killed that night. If that would have happened..."

There was a long silence as they picked at their food. Then Claire said, "Well, Rock is better. He talked a little bit about it at Christmas. He hasn't mentioned it since, but the Navy Cross sits on the mantle above the fireplace, so he sees it every day we're there. It has to serve as a reminder of what he tries so hard to forget, but he doesn't seem to mind. We still keep a light on all night..."

Patti interrupted, "Good. You know about that then."

"Yes. Josh had told me, but Rock also told me after he and Russ had talked at Christmas. You know, too, then?"

"Yeah. Russ told me years ago. The Army nurse at the hospital in Saigon apparently told him about it when he visited Rock there. Russ swore me to secrecy and for better, or worse, I kept the secret."

"Did you know he accidentally turned the lights off at his cottage when he first moved to the lake? The darkness caused him to have a panic attack. He fell, hit his head and had to have stitches. He told me he couldn't sleep after that without waking up in a cold sweat."

"My God," Patti replied. "Is he still not sleeping? He looks great, by the way."

"It's better. First Flotsam came along. He loves that dog." She blushed bashfully, "Then, he says, I came along."

"He told me how the dogs introduced the two of you. Great story!" Patti paused for a moment and then continued, "Claire, he's never had..." Patti was searching, *The words... what are the words?* "There's never been anyone in his life like you." She fell silent again as if carefully choosing her words. "He was married once." She paused with a stricken look on her face. "Claire, I'm sorry. I assumed he's mentioned that."

Reassuringly Claire said, "It's OK, Patti. He's told me."

Relief evident in her voice and in her face, Patti continued, "I knew that would never work out. After that, I vowed that I would be more assertive with him. He would bring women around for dinner, a movie, something. Most of them didn't last more than a month or two, a few hung on for six months maybe, but I can't remember a single one of them lasting any longer than that. I'd tell him what I thought, and it was never good, but Rock is stubborn. He'd have to find out for himself that they weren't right for him. When it comes to women, Rock Graham, for all his good qualities, has not, in my humble opinion, been a good judge of them," Patti looked up and into Claire's eyes, "Until now."

That night before dinner, the girls took the boys back to the little bungalow in Old Englewood Village. The realtor let them in and, obviously in a hurry to be someplace else, asked them to make sure the lights were out and the doors were locked when they left. The girls went their way through the house, and the boys went theirs. Later, over dinner at Gulf Breeze, their ideas converged. Friday, on their way out of town, back to their rental near Ocala, Russ and Patti put in an offer on the bungalow.

Friday morning after saying good-bye to the Sluwinskis and securing a promise that Russ or Patti would call as soon as they found out anything on the listing, Rock, Claire, Flotsam and Flower took a walk on the beach. When they returned to Gulf Breeze, there was a message on the answering machine from Claire's doctor in Holland asking her to call... as soon as possible.

Chapter Thirty-Five

We Thought I Should Ask You

Claire pointed out that they'd gotten her diagnosis on Friday, March 13th. Van Zandt Engineering's corporate jet returned them to Flint on Saturday. Tuesday morning, March 17th, they sat in the admissions area of The Cleveland Clinic, looking for a second opinion. The appointment had been arranged by Claire's doctor in Holland, but in doing so, her office had given no indication of the diagnosis received from the University of Michigan Medical Center. If it was what the U of M doctors said it was, her doctor wanted it confirmed independently with no prior knowledge that Claire had already been diagnosed.

The tests took three days to conduct, as they had at the U of M. Some of them were more painful than others. The spinal tap and muscle biopsies were the most invasive and painful. While they were there, Claire had a shortness-of-breath bout in the presence of one of her doctors. When he began to ask some elementary questions regarding frequency, length and severity of these attacks, Claire began to lose patience with him. Fortunately, Rock was there to smooth things over before Claire, out of both stress and frustration, nearly blurted out the University of Michigan Medical Center diagnosis.

They returned to the lakeshore with no results, just as they had after the U of M testing. The Cleveland Clinic, it seemed, could not promise results any faster than the U of M could. Under these circumstances, four to six weeks was an eternity for them both.

Shortly after their return, Russ called Rock to tell him that their offer on the bungalow in Old Englewood Village had been accepted by the seller. They would close on the property before returning to Flint at the end of April. When Rock told Claire, she smiled and nodded her head, but then became morose. "You OK?" he asked her. She began to cry. He went to comfort her and said, "Claire, darling, it's going to be OK. We will get through this." He held her close to him, and he could feel her sobbing subside. "It'll be fun helping them fix that little place up. You've seen what Russ and I can do with a place," he paused and then added, "And Patti and you will have fun picking out the furnishings for it."

"You're right," she acknowledged, "It will be fun."

The two held an ongoing discussion about the U of M's diagnosis, but had reached no conclusion. Then, on Friday, April 3rd Beth called and said that she and Josh would like to come to the lakeshore over the weekend, that there was something that they wanted to discuss with them. While Claire had a hunch what it was they wanted to discuss, Rock and Claire had not reached a decision on when to disclose her diagnosis. Claire's daughters did not know, in fact no one knew about the visits to the U of M or the Cleveland Clinic. Rock and Claire had covered these trips with lies. However, Friday evening over dinner, they decided they would not tell anyone until they heard from the Cleveland Clinic. There was always the chance that the U of M doctors had gotten it wrong.

Beth and Josh must have left East Lansing or Grand Rapids at the crack of dawn. It wasn't clear where they had spent the night before. But Rock and Claire were pretty sure the two of them had been together. Based on their bubbly greeting at 8:00 a.m. on Saturday, it was evident to Rock and Claire what was on their minds. But they kept their thoughts to themselves, allowing the young couple to tell them in their own way.

Claire fixed breakfast and while they ate, Josh filled them in on his acceptance to vet school. He was one of three in contention for a prestigious scholarship. If he got that, his tuition and fees would mostly be covered. He was also going to be employed by the university as a graduate assistant working in the microbiology department a maximum of fifteen hours per week. While this was not many hours, paid at near minimum wage, he reasoned that he would not have more time to give them even if they offered. Becoming a veterinarian was his focus, his priority.

Beth shared her work on a Grand Rapids community project dubbed, *Art Prize.* For the last couple of years, Claire had heard bits and pieces, most of it from Beth. But Beth was now able to say it was going to happen and quickly, in just a matter of a couple of months. Art projects from around the country would start popping up at strategic locations in the downtown area of Grand Rapids. The winner would be chosen by a vote of the visiting public, and the winner would receive $100,000. "My gallery," she announced proudly, "Is sponsoring three entries that will be on exhibit. Two of them will be in the shop. The third one will be on the sidewalk in front. No one can predict how much business this will bring to downtown, but people who come to see the art will have to eat, drink and shop somewhere. It might as well be in downtown Grand Rapids."

After breakfast, Claire and Josh did dishes. Rock and Beth took the dogs down to the beach for exercise. This division of work, though it struck Rock and Claire as a bit odd, was suggested by Beth, so he and Claire went with the flow.

"Claire, may I ask you something?" Josh said, tentativeness obvious in his voice.

"Of course, Josh. What is it?"

"Do you think Beth is over..." pausing, still unsure, "Do you think she is over Nathan?"

Claire continued to clean the skillet she had fried bacon and eggs in as she looked over at him, "Josh, I think you'd know the answer to that better than me. But OK, since you've asked, I think she's been over him since Thanksgiving Day, when she first met you."

Smiling now, relief obvious on his face, Josh said, "Well, then, there's something I have to ask you. Beth and I have discussed this, and we decided that if her father were here, I'd ask him, but since he isn't and she..." he hesitated for just a moment, "Well, she loves you so much, we both thought I should ask you."

Claire was smiling now, too, but she played the innocent, "Ask me what, Josh?"

"You know Josh thinks of you more like a father than an uncle."

Rock knew that, but it was nice to hear it from someone else, "He's a great kid, always has been."

"He's told me about his mother, about how you helped her."

"Yeah, well, some would say I helped her, others would say I enabled her. She had her demons. We all do, but she never could come to grips with hers. Finally the alcohol and the drugs took their toll."

"His biologic father..." This was awkward for her, "Josh doesn't even remember him?"

"No. He's probably best described as a one-night-stand." Now it was Rock's turn to contemplate for a moment. "That's probably not very fair of me, Beth. He was around for a year or two after Josh was born. But for every demon my sister had, he had three. To be honest, I don't know whatever became of him. When he stopped coming around, my sister stopped talking about him. If she didn't talk about him, I sure wasn't going to, so he just... well, it's like he evaporated."

They were quiet for a while as they both watched the dogs play in the frigid edge of the lake. The ice field that had once stretched a hundred yards or more from the shore was now gone. The huge mounds of ice, in the spring-like temperatures of early April, were reduced to much smaller floes of ice that floated here and there, eventually directed to the shoreline by the incessant wind.

"Josh says he doesn't know what he would have done after she passed without you."

"He was a senior in high school. My loft was too small for the two of us. I'd paid for the house he and my sister lived in, and I figured it might be good college prep if he could stay there for the rest of his senior year of high school and get the hang of being independent. Since he wasn't quite eighteen, I had to work with social services, but it turned out to be a good plan. Then, after he went to MSU, I sold the house and put the money away to pay for his education. He's a smart kid. Most of the money is still there."

"I want you to know that I support his dream of becoming a vet."

He looked at her and smiled. "I know." He paused and then added, "But that's not the reason you're down here on the beach with me, and he's up there in the kitchen with your Mom, is it?"

She raked the toe of her shoe in a wide arc through the sand and looked sheepishly at him. "No. We decided he should ask Mom for her permission, and I should ask you for yours. I know it's a bit old fashioned, but we both feel like it's the least we owe the two of you."

Rock smiled at her, "That's extremely kind and thoughtful of you, of the both of you."

"Josh and I would like your permission to marry. We won't set a date right away. He needs to get into vet school and get his routine established. I'm extremely busy right now with *Art Prize,* but we love one another."

He looked at her. She stepped toward him and gave him a hug. It was difficult for him because of the emotions he was feeling, but he managed to say to her, "I couldn't be happier for you both."

Above, Josh and Claire looked down on them. "Well, I guess there's your uncle's answer, Josh," she said to him and gave him a hug.

At dinner that evening, the elephant in the room finally came up.

"Mom, have you heard from Ingrid?" Beth asked.

"Not one word," Claire said.

"I stopped and saw her and Brian a week or so ago. Ethan was out of town on business. I asked her if she'd called you since Brian's accident. She said she had called you once. Then she said she was working on something and didn't want to talk to you until she had it 'firmly in hand,' those are her exact words."

"What is she doing?" Claire asked.

"No clue, Mom. She and Brian seemed fine. Whatever it is, her home office is a mess, books and papers piled everywhere. I asked her about it, but she wouldn't tell me. All she said was that she'd be in touch."

"How did she look?" Claire asked.

"That's just it. She looked more relaxed than I can ever recall. There was no nanny anywhere to be seen. Brian was parked next to her desk, sitting on the floor, playing with his toys. She looked," Beth paused for a second, "She looked at peace, Mom."

"Well, that's comforting. I'm not going to bother her. When she wants to talk, she knows how to reach me. Until then, I'm glad to hear she's all right."

Sunday afternoon, after Josh and Beth departed, Claire asked, "So what do you really think?"

He answered with a question, "Is she over Nathan?"

"Josh asked me the same thing." She threw her hands up in the air, "Heavens yes, she's over Nathan. To be perfectly honest, I don't think she ever truly loved Nathan. She was doing what she thought she needed to do as a Van Zandt. However, Beth was smart enough to know that she needed more than social status and wealth. She wants someone that will love her, and to her that means sharing his time with her."

Nodding, Rock said, "It's going to be hard. They are two busy people, and it will be kind of a long-distance relationship with him in East Lansing and her in Grand Rapids. But I think they are both mature beyond their years. They'll work it out."

The visit had taken their minds off of Claire's diagnosis. It was just the two of them now and the reality of their lives together returned. The weather forecast predicted a winter storm bearing down on the western side of Michigan, threatening to turn spring back into winter for at least the next forty-eight hours. They clung to the hope that somehow the U of M Medical Center had gotten it wrong. Claire's disease had killed one of the greatest baseball players that ever lived and it did it in a hideous, slow, painful way. The U of M diagnosis hung over them like a dark cloud. Lou Gehrig's disease had one prognosis. It was terminal.

Chapter Thirty-Six

Mood Swings

They made the best of April they could. The month's weather lived up to its northern Michigan reputation, one day beautiful, the next with winter charging back as if avenging spring's intrusion. Rock had anticipated life with Claire might be much like April's weather. He was prepared for dynamic mood swings, but by month's end and seeing none, he said to her as they were walking on the beach, "You are the strongest person I have ever known."

She picked up a stick Flotsam had dropped at her feet and threw it into Lake Michigan's chilly waters. Both dogs pursued it, splashing first and then diving into the waves. Laughing at them, she turned to him and said, "If I didn't have you, I would be desperate." She paused. He knew there was more, so he took her hand as they continued their walk. "It bothers me, Rock. I think about it. I think about how unfair it seems. I keep hoping that they find something else, something not so bad. But it never fails that just as I am about to sink into a sad state, you say something to me, you suggest we do something or you just come and sit beside me." She held up their joined hands, "Or you hold my hand. You have no idea how much comfort I take from these things. I'm not afraid, you know."

He looked at her, wonderment in his eyes. *How can that be?* he thought. Instead he said, "I know."

"No. Truly I'm not afraid of this damned disease. When I start to get afraid, I step up to the mantle and read the citation accompanying your Navy Cross."

"Claire, I ..."

She held up her hand and said firmly, "Let me say this to you, my darling. If this disease is the thing that is going to take my life eventually, then that is the way it is meant to be. Nothing you and I can do will change that. You, on the other hand, my handsome Marine," she stopped, turned toward him and laid her hand along his face, "You, almost single-handedly, changed the course of a lot of lives that night in the jungle. If you hadn't done what you did, when you did, a lot more would have died, including your best friend." They both had tears in their eyes as they started walking again down the beach, their dogs running ahead of them tugging over a stick. "Whatever strength I have, I draw from you. This disease, if it's going to kill me, won't take me easily. Like you did all those years ago, I'm going to fight, and I will fight every day I am alive because, my darling, with you in my life, I want those days to be many."

He stopped and pulled her to him. It was one of those bright, sunny, late-April days with the temperature approaching sixty degrees. The wind was light. Seagulls swooped up and down the beach. The dogs, when they noticed the two of them had stopped, returned to their sides. While tears stained his cheeks, Rock suppressed any sobbing that might alarm her. He buried his face into the light scarf she wore around her neck. He could smell her perfume. He could feel the ebb and flow of her breath against his chest. He wondered, *What will I ever do without you?* He whispered into her ear, "We were meant to be together, Claire. We make each other better, stronger. I love you so very much." As always, it was exactly what she needed to hear at exactly the moment she needed to hear it.

They returned home to find a message on the answering machine from, of all people, Ingrid. "Mom, call me when you get this. I want to invite you and Mr. Graham to dinner. I love you."

Rock had stepped into the bathroom, but when he returned to her, Claire said, "Listen to this, Mr. Graham."

It was the way Ingrid had said *Mr. Graham* that had caught Claire's attention even more than the *Mom* or the *I love you* at the end. Claire's training as a counselor had taught her to read tone, inflection, volume in a person's speech pattern. Ingrid's voice qualities were almost reverential as she spoke Rock's name.

"I wish she'd call me Rock."

Claire nodded as she dialed Ingrid's number.

"Mom, thanks for calling me back. I was wondering if you and Mr. Graham would join Ethan and me for dinner this Friday night? I've been working on something that I want to talk to you about, and Brian has been asking about Grammy."

Again, Claire measured her voice qualities and could detect only sincerity. She put her hand over the mouthpiece and said to Rock, "She wants us to come to dinner this Friday." Rock smiled, shrugged his shoulders and gave her a thumbs up. "Rock and I would love to see all of you. What time would you like us there?"

"How is six o'clock?"

"Yes, that would be fine, dear."

"Uh, Mom, I should warn you. It's a celebration. There will be some others here as well."

She quickly ran through the events-to-celebrate in her memory and couldn't remember any birthdays or anniversaries she had missed. *Damn,* Claire thought, *that stuffy bunch she works with.* Cautiously she asked, "What are we celebrating?"

"It's all a surprise, Mom," Ingrid said conspiratorially, "But don't worry, it's not the partners. Everyone coming loves you very much."

Now her curiosity was piqued, she could not help herself, "Ingrid, what's going on?"

"Mom, you and Mr. Graham are just going to have to trust me. It's a surprise. Please say you'll come."

There was an excitement in her tone that Claire had not heard since Ingrid was a little girl. Abandoning for the moment her concerns over Ingrid's past behavior, she said, "All right, dear. I trust you. Rock and I will see you Friday evening."

"I love you, Mom."

"I love you, too, dear."

As she cradled the phone back into its charger, Claire looked at Rock and said, "Well, Mr. Graham, we are expected at dinner at Ingrid's on Friday at 6 p.m. Others will be there, but I'm not sure exactly who. She says she wants to talk to us about something, but it's all a big surprise."

Rock asked, "Claire, do you think..." He stopped himself. He was trying to be delicate, but couldn't find the words, "Do you think she's on the up and up?"

Claire shrugged her shoulders. "It's been years since she's called me *Mom* and a long time since she's said, *I love you.* And you... well, I don't know what to make out of this Mr. Graham-thing, but I can tell from her voice that she's not meaning any disrespect. I think the only way we are going to find out what's really going on with her is to go to dinner."

He smiled. "Then that is what we shall do. Coat and tie?"

"I think we should be a little more casual. I'm going to wear slacks. You could do an open-collar shirt and sport coat."

"I don't have a sport coat with me."

"Then let's make a day of it tomorrow and go into Grand Rapids. I know a nice men's shop there."

Her spontaneity was alive and well.

Chapter Thirty-Seven

Ingrid

Wednesday, April 30th found Rock and Claire in Grand Rapids for a leisurely day. Mumford was checking in on the dogs to make sure they got at least one good walk on the beach. While the day was overcast, the temperature was a balmy fifty-five degrees with virtually zero wind, at least in Grand Rapids. They parked in a central parking garage and walked from there, holding hands, laughing, two people seemingly without a care in the world.

Claire led them to an exclusive men's store. Rock was not a fashionista, but he was impressed with their selection of all things for men. It took him awhile to make his choices, but Claire was pleased with what he found.

"While you try those on, I'm going to call Beth and see if she would like to meet us for lunch."

"Sounds great." Rock took shirt, sport coat and slacks he'd picked out along with a new pair of shoes and socks and headed to the dressing room at the rear of the store.

"So, you've been shopping for the big evening on Friday?" Beth asked as they sat down at the table.

The waitress took their drink order, and then Claire asked, "Yes. Are you going to be there?"

"Uh... Mom...uh, I'm..." Beth laid her hands flat on the table leaned forward toward Claire and said, "I'm sworn to secrecy."

"But you're going to be there, aren't you?" Claire prodded. Beth nodded. Claire could tell she was nearly bursting with excitement; that she really wanted to tell them what was up. Claire prodded some more, "She told me others besides Rock and I were coming. Who else?"

"Mom, I can't..."

"Bethie," Claire thought endearment might break down the security system, "What can be the harm in letting us know who's going to be there? You know how much I detest going into a room without any idea of who is in there. Give us a clue, at least." The waitress took their meal order. Beth thought that the diversion might have thrown her mother off the scent, but she was wrong. When the waitress was gone, Claire said, "OK, so who else is coming?"

"Mom, listen this thing that Ingrid has been working on..."

Claire interrupted, "You know what this is all about?"

Shut up Beth, a voice in the back of Beth's head told her. Ruefully, Beth nodded and then added firmly, "But there is no way you are going to get that out of me. This is all Ingrid's idea, and I can tell you I've never seen her so excited about anything. You are going to be so surprised."

Claire didn't know what to say. Rock sat, smiling, looking back and forth between them, completely clueless. "So this is all good, in your opinion?" Claire asked her.

"Mom, this is beyond good. What Ingrid is doing is... well..." Claire leaned forward, anticipating that Beth was going to spill the beans. "Well, you'll just have to wait until Friday and see, but I can assure you, the two of you will be among friends."

Rock asked, "Is Josh invited?"

Beth paused before she answered. She'd already told them more than Ingrid would have wanted, but answered,

"He is…" she paused for just a moment, for effect, "And it was Ingrid who called him." She knew that would shock both of them. "Now, that's it. If you are going to keep asking me questions about Friday night, I'm going to have to leave. I can't tell you any more than I already have. If I spoil this for Ingrid, she'll never speak to me again." And then Beth added, "You know how she can be."

That was the point, both Rock and Claire knew how Ingrid's behavior had been. But this was a new Ingrid, and all the way back to the lakeshore they discussed what she might be up to. Later, as they sat in front of the fireplace sipping on wine they had bought in the city, both had to admit that they had no idea.

Eager anticipation had the two of them ready to leave home by mid-afternoon on Friday, May 2nd. Ingrid's home was a two and a half hour drive. It was entirely too early, but Claire's spontaneity had come through. "I can call Bob again. He can feed the dogs this evening and let them out. We can stop by the Country Club and have a cocktail before going to Ingrid's."

Rock had learned to express little surprise by now, but inwardly wondered, *What Country Club?* He didn't ask, knowing that whatever one it was, it would be exclusive.

May marked the month that life returned to Little Point Sable. They had to pull over to the side of the road three times to make room for oncoming traffic, other homeowners returning from their winter respites and opening up their summer homes. At the farm stand, which had just reopened after being closed for the winter, Rock stopped and bought a cherry strudel, something he'd missed after discovering it last fall. While the cherry filling was from preserves put up last year, the strudel was fresh-made. Rock said it was for their breakfast Saturday morning, but both knew he would eat the lion's share.

Over cocktails at Claire's country club, they continued to speculate on what was up with Ingrid. Rock offered, "I don't know what she's working on, but whatever it is, I think Brian's accident was the trigger. Remember, she called you *Mom*. What was the word Beth used to describe her? '*Peaceful*'."

Claire agreed.

"I've met Ingrid." He made a gesture with his eyes that made Claire laugh. "But I've not met her husband. What's Ethan like?"

She thought for a moment, then a smile crossed her face and Claire laughed again, "He is to the law what Alan was to engineering. U of M, *summa cum laude* undergrad. I don't remember his major. Went to Harvard Law, where he was President of the *Law Review*. Did an internship with one of the US Supreme Court Justices and, last I heard, he is soon to become a partner in his law firm. I think he loves Ingrid and Brian, but his work keeps him away from them a lot of the time. I don't think Ingrid minds, though. She is as much like her father as Beth is like me. So they cope. They share calendars, resolve conflicts where they can, talk more about their work than their family, hire nannies to care for Brian, and, like Alan, miss out on a lot of the stuff that really matters. The difference is that they are both so driven. At least with Alan and me, I was around to raise the girls..." she paused reflectively, "And I had the Chavezes. That reminds me. I have to call Maria this weekend. I haven't talked to her in a month or more. I wonder how James and Mary are coming along with finding work."

"But it sounds like maybe Ingrid is changing," Rock said optimistically.

Claire looked at her watch. "Maybe. We'll see. We should probably start heading that way. Their condo is in the middle of downtown, and traffic this time of evening in Grand Rapids can be killer."

Claire had been right, traffic was miserable. Rock pulled the Range Rover up to the doorway in front of the high-rise condo at precisely 6 p.m. His intention was to let Claire out so she would be on time while he parked the car. As Claire swung the door open, the doorman stepped up and said, "Ms. Van Zandt, Mr. Graham, Ms. Hoffman has made arrangements for you to leave the car parked here this evening. I will keep an eye on it. Everyone is expecting you," and he held the door open for Claire.

The Hoffman's penthouse had its own elevator. Claire punched in the code on the keypad, the door slid open, and they stepped in. As it rose the thirty floors to the top, Rock looked at Claire nervously and said, "So how do I look?"

She squeezed his hand and kissed him lightly on the cheek, then wiped off the trace of her lipstick, "Handsome as ever." As the doors slid open, Ingrid, Ethan and Brian were there to greet them.

Ingrid and Brian went first to Claire, Ingrid hugging her high and Brian grabbing her just above the knees. "Mom, I'm so glad you and Mr. Graham could come tonight," she whispered into Claire's ear. Claire thought she could see Ingrid's eyes welling up, as were hers. Then Ingrid stepped forward to Rock, put her arms around him and whispered into his ear, "Thank you."

The two of them were overwhelmed, Claire on the edge of tears and Rock, simply bewildered. Before he could say anything, he felt Brain's arms around his legs. He put his hands on the boy's head, knelt down and smiled at him. "You doin' OK, Brian?"

Brian stuck his little hand out, "I sure am, Mr. Graham." Rock thought, *What is with this Mr. Graham-thing?* Rock smiled, though, and shook the proffered hand.

Claire hugged Ethan and then introduced Rock. In the other room, they could hear voices. Taking her mother by the arm, Ingrid pointed in the direction of the others, "Shall we? There are a lot of people here who are anxious to see the two of you." Without waiting for a response, she led them into the vast living room with a wall of windows that looked out over the lights of the city that were just starting to come on.

And there everyone was. Beth next to Josh; Jesus, Maria, James and Mary and their spouses; Natalie Perkins; the senior partners in Claire's accounting firm, Arthur DeBoer, Stuart Klassen and Bart Formsa and their wives; Jan Fremeyer and Madeline Murphy were there. And, freshly returned from Florida, looking tan and relaxed, perhaps the biggest surprise, Russ and Patti Sluwinski. Nearly in unison, the greetings came, "Hello! Great to see you! There they are! The couple of the hour!" and all of it blending together in a jumble of noise that bubbled with warmth, delight and the true happiness that comes when people who care about one another come together. Over cocktails and a delightful array of appetizers, Claire and Rock caught up with their friends. But despite Claire's best efforts to pry out of them Ingrid's secret, no one broke their pact.

Dinner was served buffet style, a concession to formality by Ingrid that surprised Claire. Dinner affairs with her in the past had always been so stuffy, with business usually being the primary purpose for everyone coming together. Tonight Claire did not hear any business discussed during either the cocktail hour or dinner. When everyone was properly stuffed, Ingrid announced, "There's coffee, port, brandy, whatever you might want for after dinner. Please help yourselves, but if I could ask all of you to move to the living room and find a seat, it's time to tell Mom and Mr. Graham about the idea."

Everyone was smiling as they moved in that direction. Claire, as she was pouring herself a cup of decaf, suddenly found Maria at her side. "Ms. Claire," Claire looked at her and noticed she was crying.

"Maria, what is it. Are you all right?"

"Oh, Ms. Claire, I am so happy. What Ms. Ingrid is doing is such a wonderful thing. You will be so proud of her."

This was Claire's chance to find out. "Maria, I am proud of her, but you can tell me," she urged her, "What is she up to?"

Through her tears Maria smiled and wagged a finger at her. "Oh, Ms. Claire, I can't tell you, but you will be proud. I promise you will be proud."

It took about ten minutes for everyone to get what they wanted and to find their spots in the living room. They clumped themselves together in groups that made sense. The accountants and their wives were all together. Claire noticed that the three partners were all holding their wives' hands, a softer side of them that she had not seen despite their nearly three decades of working together. Beth, Josh, Ethan, Brian, and the Chavezes were another group as were Natalie, Jan, Madeline, Russ and Patti. Ingrid led Claire and Rock to two chairs arranged next to one another that were in the center of the room facing the windows, which gave a panoramic view of downtown Grand Rapids after dark. As Ingrid stepped in front of them, her back to the windows, the room fell silent.

"First of all, let me begin by thanking each and every one of you for coming tonight and for the assistance you have been to me personally over the past several months. Your support means that this idea has a chance, and God knows the people it will serve deserve a chance."

Claire searched the room with her eyes. Every head was nodding. She looked at Rock. He nodded, smiled at her, but gave a slight shrug of his shoulders. It was obvious that they were the only ones in the room that didn't know what Ingrid was talking about.

"Mom, Mr. Graham," Ingrid's voice breaking a little as she said Rock's name, "I have spent a lot of time over the last few months doing much soul-searching and thinking." She looked at her mother, "I owe you an apology..."

Rock squeezed Claire's hand. She said, "Ingrid, you don't need to..."

"But I do. I owe one to Beth as well. I treated each of you very badly for a very long time, and I'm so very sorry for that. Beth, Josh, I'm so happy for the two of you." She had to pause to wipe away tears and when she looked back at all of them, she was smiling again. "A lot has happened over the last few months. It took a while for me to put it all together, but as I started to take stock of the people in my life, the ones who have been there for a long time, the ones who have loved me and my family, the ones who have been there for us over the years, I realized what a great team we could make and what a great difference we could make in some lives that could really benefit from a leg up. That's when the idea came to me, and everyone in this room has been a part of it."

She turned to the Chavezes, "Jesus, Maria, James, Mary, you have been such a help to me getting to know the community." Looking at James and Mary she added, "Thanks so much for the help with the language. I know when we were kids all we did was babble to one another in Spanish, but that has been all too long ago and, unfortunately, I didn't keep up with it very well over the years. That's something that is going to change."

Turning to the accountants and their wives, "How can I thank the three of you for all the work you did in figuring out the finances?"

Arthur DeBoer held up the hand not gripping his wife's and said, "Ingrid, it has been our pleasure. What you are doing is phenomenal and we," he waved his free hand toward his partners and their wives, "Well, let's just say we feel privileged to be a part of it."

Natalie Perkins, Jan Fremeyer and Madeline Murphy were seated next to one another. "And you three... what can I say? I needed some help understanding the education bureaucracy. My God, I thought the law was complex, but we lawyers are just novices when it comes to creating complexity." There was nodding and laughter around the room. Ingrid let the humor run its course and then added, "It's important that we all realize that this endeavor will be entirely funded with private money. I have looked at the complexities of trying to use state and federal dollars to assist in financing." She turned to Ethan. "Ethan has spent even more time on this than I have. Thank you, darling."

Ethan smiled and nodded.

"The strings attached to even a dollar of government money make it impossible for me to recommend taking any of it. As far as I can tell, all it would do is require us to create a bureaucracy that would not add a single bit of value to what we are trying to do."

From the corner of the room, Natalie Perkins raised a fist above her head and shouted, "You go, girl!" which brought the house down again.

Ingrid turned to Russ and Patti. "So having said that, everyone, I want to announce that we have our first major contributors. Russ and Patti Sluwinski have pledged $50,000 over the next two years as we go about the process of site selection and construction."

Patti had her arm around Russ. She and Rock locked eyes across the room. Patti smiled and blew Rock and Claire a kiss. Russ pawed at his eyes.

Turning back to Claire and Rock, Ingrid smiled and asked, "So are you ready to hear my idea?"

Both nodded.

"We would like to open a school that is, as far as I can tell unlike any other in the state or in the country. The Chaveses and I have spent a lot of time talking with people who are migrant workers. Up and down the western side of Michigan, these men and women work in asparagus fields, they pick cherries, apples, peaches, grapes... suffice it to say, if it grows in Michigan, it wouldn't get to market without these folks. A major part of Michigan's economy would die right where it grows. It is a sad reflection on our society that they do all of this for minimum wage and live in conditions that are substandard at best. As a mother, I searched my soul. How would I feel if my child spent every school year in two, three and sometimes more schools as we moved from harvest to harvest? How would I feel if my child would never have a shot at anything better than what I was doing in the fields? That's when the idea for the school came to me, a school for migrant workers' children here in Michigan. It will be a residential school, where they will live and learn for eleven months out of the year. The twelfth month will be spent with their families, working in the fields alongside them.

Ingrid paused here for a moment and then walked over to the Chavezes. "Maria, Jesus, James and Mary have given me an insight into our migrant worker community that for me has been rare and beautiful. They are a proud people, a subculture of America, with their own set of family values and traditions. The twelfth month is meant to honor these things, and to honor the sacrifices these families will make as they give us their children for the other eleven months of the year." Ingrid had placed her hand on Jesus's shoulder as she talked. With tearful eyes, he patted her hand.

She moved back to the center of the room, facing Claire and Rock, and continued. "Of course, parents can visit their children whenever they want, or perhaps better said, when they are able to take time off from work, which, from what I'm told, is very rare. When the parents visit their children at school, we will provide them with accommodations in the dormitories and meals in the school's cafeteria." She paused here and looked into her mother's eyes, trying to get Claire's reaction so far. All she could discern were tears. Ingrid smiled at Claire, "Mom, we need to create a Foundation. I propose we start it with our family's money and, at least, for the next few years, use that money to open the school. Everyone here has already said yes. Arthur, Stuart and Bart will work the business end. The Chavezes will be a liaison into that community. James, Mary and Natalie will be employed by the school. Jan and Madeline have offered to volunteer at whatever they can do, and so far that has been an immense help. I've already told you about Russ and Patti. I know as we move this forward there will be others, individuals, corporations, foundations, all of them willing to put resources towards our school. So what do you say? Are you in?"

Claire was in tears as she looked around the room. There was no doubt in anyone's mind what her answer would be, but when she nodded and in a raspy, emotion-filled voice said, "Yes," the room erupted in shouts and applause. Rock put his arm around her. Everyone gathered near the two of them.

Before either of them knew, it was 10:00 p.m., and the evening was ending as quickly as it had begun. As people filed out, Claire went with Ethan to say good bye as their guests boarded the elevator. Ingrid pulled Rock by the arm and led him into the kitchen, which was piled high with dirty dishes.

Standing there and surveying the mess, Rock said to her, "You did all of this yourself?"

Ingrid smiled, "Brian and me... well, mostly me, but he was right with me through all of the preparations."

"It was a delightful evening, Ingrid. Your mother and I will help you clean up."

"You will not. I'm so excited right now that I won't sleep for the next day or two. This will give me something to do." She paused and stepped in front of him, her eyes locked on his, "That day on the beach," she paused, remembering it, "I'm not sure what might have happened if you hadn't been there..."

"Ingrid, I didn't..."

She held up a hand, "Yes, you did. I was exhausted after I pulled him out of that hole. He was so heavy from the water, the ice was so jagged." Tears came to the corner of her eyes. "You saved precious moments that we didn't have to spare. You were there for me... you were there for Brian. You helped me realize what was important."

Neither of them noticed Claire standing in the doorway.

Ingrid stepped closer to him and took his hand in hers, "Mr. Graham, please understand that my mother and father raised me better than I have behaved toward you." She paused as if collecting her thoughts. "This is hard to explain, but my entire life has been one of privilege. I can't remember ever experiencing any adversity that couldn't be solved without throwing money at it. Well, that day on the ice at Lake Michigan, changed that for me, forever. I almost lost the most important person in my life that day. No amount of money could have made that better." She gently placed her other hand over his and smiled, "But we saved Brian and I learned a lesson that will last the rest of my life. This school is my way of paying it forward."

She stepped forward into a hug which Rock returned as he said, his voice breaking softly, "Ingrid, I don't know what to say. Your idea... it's wonderful... it's exactly the kind of thing that's needed right now. Your mother and I..."

"I could see the excitement in Mom's eyes. She really likes the idea, doesn't she? I know this was a lot tonight and, I must admit, I don't know where it is all going to lead, but I know now that I have to try. I know now what is truly important. I can never repay you."

Claire backed out of the doorway. Neither of them knew she'd been there.

Before letting go of her, he pushed her back to arm's length and said, "Ingrid, there is a way."

She gave him a puzzled look.

"There is a way you can repay me."

This surprised her, but she asked, "What can I do, Mr. Graham?"

Quietly and ever so calmly he said, "Any debt you feel you owe me is repaid a thousand times over if you will stop calling me Mr. Graham. Call me Rock."

Laughing she buried her head in his shoulder and said, "It's a deal, Rock!"

On the ride back to the lakeshore, they were silent, but their joined hands resting on the center console of the Range Rover spoke volumes. One or the other would smile occasionally remembering a moment, something that someone said, a gesture someone had made and recall it to the other. Finally, near Rothbury, a short distance from their exit off US 31, Claire turned to him and said, "Rock, I heard you and Ingrid talking in the kitchen?"

He looked over at her as she wiped at a first tear.

Keeping his eyes on the road ahead, nonchalantly he replied, "Yeah, I think your eldest daughter and I might be good."

Claire looked over at him and thought, *Heroes. We love them, but the real ones move among us silently*. She leaned over the center console and kissed him delicately on the cheek and said, "I love you, Mr. Graham."

Epilogue

Saturday morning, June 17, 2017, broke magnificently clear, calm and sunny at the Lake Michigan shoreline along Little Point Sable. With a mug of tea in one hand and the invitation in the other, Rock opened the slider, took in a deep breath of cool, morning air, stepped onto the patio, and made his way to one of the two Adirondack chairs that sat facing west, toward the lake. The Adirondacks were considerably lower than most chairs and leaned back more than most. His was the one on the left and even though he'd been in and out of it a thousand times, it wasn't easy for him. Awkwardly he lowered himself into it, muttering something unintelligible about his leg. Looking out at the vast blue-green in front of him, he caught a chill from the cool northwesterly breeze and pulled the hood of his sweat shirt over his head.

Flotsam and Flower settled themselves on either side of him. Neither moved as quickly as they used to. Flower had developed arthritis in her back legs. Her vet, Dr. Josh Graham, told Rock it was a fairly common condition in older dogs of her size and had prescribed a mild medicine to slow its onset. Rock watched her as she laid down heavily. When she turned her head to look at him, he took her now-gray muzzle in one hand and petted the top of her head with the other. She closed her eyes as if shielding them against the rising sun, but when she gave a little groan of pleasure, Rock knew she was simply enjoying his touch and attention. Flotsam, ever the vigilant one, sat with her haunches under her as if ready to spring, as she once had, at anything that moved on the beach in front of her. In her old age, however, she had become more discriminate, content now to watch the seagulls strolling the beach below. Rock smiled at her lying there. "It's OK, girl, let them go this time," he said. Flotsam turned her head toward him, and he thought he could see a look of relief on her face that she didn't have to chase them away. He glanced at his watch, *8:03 a.m.* They would need to leave in an hour. He took a sip of the hot tea and let it slide down his throat, its warmth feeling good in the chill air. This was *their* favorite spot. He looked over at the empty chair beside him, closed his eyes and remembered.

Claire's diagnosis had been confirmed by the Cleveland Clinic sometime around mid-May, 2009. For a while it stopped everything. His eyes still closed, he smiled as he recalled how she'd put a halt to the pity party. She called together everyone who had been at Ingrid's party that night in April, 2009. Rock's job had been to reserve a private dining room at Ruth's Chris Steakhouse at the Amway Grand Plaza Hotel. Claire took over from there. When everyone arrived, she directed the several waitresses to take everyone's drink order. Once cocktails had been taken care of, Claire asked the wait staff to excuse them for a while, close the door on their way out and she would let them know when they were ready to order their meals.

Still smiling, he chuckled to himself. He'd never seen a woman more fired up. It was a one-way conversation, Claire transmitting and everyone else in the room, receiving. Rock remembered it like it was yesterday. *I'm not dead yet, so stop treating me like I am! They say five to eight years, I say more. I intend to live well for whatever time I have remaining on this earth. Each of you should make that same choice, and you can't do that if you're mourning me.* He remembered she singled Ingrid out then, *You must get on with your work. It's too important to let it wait any longer.*

From that point on, no one ever mentioned her illness to her. If they wanted an update, Rock got the questions, but never in Claire's presence. No one wanted to risk her wrath.

The school became Claire's passion, but she deferred the details to Ingrid. He remembered the trip when Ingrid took them to Augusta, Michigan. Ingrid's exact words were, "This is the perfect place," the former estate of a prominent doctor who'd made his fortune in pharmaceuticals. At some point it had become the property of Michigan State University, which operated it as a conference center for a few years before it became too much of a financial drain on the university's coffers. And so it was just sitting, in caretaker status, as if asking them to turn it into something useful. The only downside, it was a little too far removed from the migrant population the school would serve, but Ingrid had already thought of a work-around for that. The school would provide transportation to and from for both students and their parents. "Mom, don't you know a couple of the university's regents?" Ingrid had asked. That was all she needed to say. Claire made some calls, and the sale was final in only a few months.

From 2009 through 2012 the property was remade. Most of the existing buildings were converted into classrooms. New construction included dormitories, a dining facility, a gymnasium, an aquatic center, an auditorium, a library and faculty housing. The plan for the school called for teachers and counselors as well as their families to live on the campus. Ingrid's logic was simple. "If we are going to pull our students away from their families and have them live on campus, then the people who teach and advise them should live there as well. The students will become a part of the school family and we will become a part of their family," she had said.

James Chavez, his wife, and two children lived on the campus, where he served as the Chief Information Officer. Mary Chavez Humphrey and her family resided there as well. With a master's degree in curriculum development, paid for entirely by the Van Zandt Foundation, Mary led the design of the school's academic curriculum. Natalie Perkins led a robust group of ten counselors. Both Claire and Natalie had been adamant about this. It wasn't going to be like a typical public school where the student-to-counselor ratio might be 500:1. No, if these children were going to be separated from their families for most of the next five years of their lives, they were going to need access to trained staff, counselors that could listen, hear what they were saying, and help them with the travails that their new life at the school would certainly throw at them.

One hundred eighth grade students arrived in the fall of 2012 and each year since then. There were currently four hundred seventy-five students enrolled. Each was carefully screened. Rock remembered how he and Claire had talked with Ingrid about the selection process. It was the hardest part. Claire wanted to take anyone that wanted to attend, but that simply was impossible. There had to be a process, and Ingrid's training as a lawyer paved the way for one, a good one, but still a very difficult one.

Working with local school districts up and down western Michigan, Ingrid developed relationships with school counselors, administrators and teachers to help her identify those children of migrant workers who were the best and the brightest. Once that was done, Jesus and Maria Chavez got involved. First, they provided a bridge to the language barrier. Ingrid was working on rebuilding her Spanish-speaking skills, but Jesus and Maria were a welcome and often needed backup. More than anything, Jesus and Maria lent an easy, familiar sense to the visits that Ingrid, herself, would make with the families of prospective students to see if there was interest in applying for their school. There almost always was. Then Ingrid, Natalie Perkins, Mary Humphrey, and a handful of teachers from those local schools poured over applications, grades, and anything else they could find to make the selections. For Ingrid's idea to work, the students needed to be at the school for five years. So, if they didn't make it then, at the beginning of their eighth grade year, their chance was gone forever. If there was anything unfair about Ingrid's idea, it was that. Each applicant had just one, single chance. Make it or break it. Everyone shared in the joy of those who made it. Everyone wept with the families of those who didn't. It was so very difficult.

Once accepted, everything was free and no one more than the families of those who had made it knew what a leg up on life their children had been given. There was only one stipulation to maintain eligibility for enrollment. At least one of each student's parents had to work a minimum of two months in the State of Michigan each year the student attended. In the five years the school had been open, no one had failed to maintain eligibility.

Rock could feel the warm sun on the back of his hoody now. He opened his eyes, took a sip of his much cooler tea and studied the invitation in his hand. Today was a milestone. To say the school had been successful would be like saying landing on the moon was easy. Ninety students out of one hundred who had started five years ago were about to graduate. All of them were bound for college or tech schools. One was attending West Point, one, the Air Force Academy, one, the Naval Academy, one, the Coast Guard Academy, and one was going to the Merchant Marine Academy at King's Point, New York. Another ten had been accepted into Ivy League schools, one of which was

Harvard. Every graduate was at least bilingual; a few were fluent in three languages. Average SAT and ACT scores, across the board, were on par with the scores coming out of the country's most exclusive boarding schools. That was remarkable considering this was from kids, who five years earlier, had little to no hope of succeeding at life, much less school. In the last five years, word of the school's success had spread. For the last three years, educators from around the world visited the school to see for themselves how such success was being achieved. Ingrid's idea had turned into a model for other residential academies to emulate.

Rock took a sip of lukewarm tea and recalled the scholarship campaign Claire had seized on about a year ago, when she first realized that every student graduating in this first class was college-bound. She argued loudly in front of the Van Zandt Foundation's Board of Directors, that they had to provide last-dollar scholarships to any college-or-tech-school-bound graduate. The board had resisted her because no one knew how much that might cost. But Claire never forgot why Rock had not gone onto college. These migrant worker families, like Rock's mother, would not have the funds to pay for any balances that partial scholarships might not cover. Claire believed so strongly in this point that she told the Foundation's Board that she'd pay out of her personal accounts if need be, but the board needed to step up and set some money aside for these kinds of possibilities. Claire Van Zandt was still a wealthy individual even though the vast majority of her holdings had been turned over to her foundation and used to fund the school. With her underwriting any shortfall, the board approved up to $250,000 in last-dollar-scholarship money. Now, with this first class graduating, as it turned out, it was much ado about nothing. Though figures weren't yet final, it looked like nearly every graduate of this first class had gotten a full-ride scholarship.

These last-dollar scholarships would amount to less than $50,000. Claire had missed the last quarterly Van Zandt Foundation Board meeting three months ago, but Ingrid carried a message to them on her behalf. It simply was, *See, I told you so!*

He looked out across the lake. He and Claire had traveled extensively for six out of the last eight years, even though her condition had made it increasingly difficult. But they always liked getting back here to the Lake Michigan shore. Their hearts were here. He glanced at his watch; it was time to get going.

He hoped to be early so he could have some time before the festivities to visit with Josh, Beth and their two-year old daughter, Claire. She called him Grandpa, and no one wanted it any other way.

Jan Fremeyer and Madeline Murphy were driving and he was supposed to be next door, at Far-Far-View, at 9 a.m. These two women had become great patrons of the school, giving of their money, time and talents over the past eight years. Well-off, but not fabulously wealthy, each of them had given a $50,000 gift. In return for their gift of money, their talents, and endless time, the media center at the school was named the Fremeyer-Murphy Center.

He was also looking forward to seeing Russ and Patti Sluwinski. All of them had been together last winter in Englewood, he and Claire, Russ and Patti. Russ and he had finished renovating the second bathroom in the bungalow in Old Town. Patti and Claire had finished their decorating touches to the place. The four of them had been inseparable for most of January and February of 2017. Russ and Rock took turns pushing Claire up and down the beach at Manasota Key in her specially-adapted beach wheelchair. He and Claire had come back early in March after she'd taken a turn for the worse. Russ was driving

Green Girl down from Flint. He'd argued that she needed a road trip. Rock agreed. Patti really didn't like folding herself up into the sports car; she detested the stiff ride and, while she would have gone anyway, she was smart enough to bargain a shopping trip out of Russ, in exchange for her discomfort. The Sluwinskis had given a $50,000 gift to the school, but more importantly, their wills, without children of their own to leave their estate, identified the school as their sole beneficiary.

Rock glanced at his watch. *8:45 a.m.* Getting out of the Adirondack was equally as awkward as getting into it. As he stood, so did both dogs, who shook themselves from head to toe as dogs will after first getting up from a nap. The invitation, which had been lying in his lap, fell onto the patio. Bending down, he picked it up and thought, *who would have ever imagined it would come to this?* The invitation read:

The Governor and the First Lady
of the State of Michigan
request the pleasure of your company
at a reception
following the first graduation of
The Michigan Academy for Migrant Workers' Children
where we will honor the graduates, their families
and the memory of Claire E. Van Zandt
on Saturday, June 17th, 2017

At the bottom were instructions to *RSVP: Ms. Ingrid Van Zandt Hoffman, Head Mistress.*

He went into the house, put his mug in the kitchen sink, went to the bedroom, traded the sweat shirt for a dress shirt, a tie and suit jacket, and headed for the door. He thumped his leg and Flower and Flotsam followed him. At Ingrid's invitation, they would attend as well. She'd told

Rock, "It only seems fitting. If it weren't for them, you and Mom might never have met."

On his way out, he stopped for a moment at a picture of all of them; Claire, Beth, Josh, Baby Claire, Ingrid, Ethan, Brian and him taken on their beach. A brass plate on the frame read, **Frog Farm Memories, July, 2016.** He picked it up and touched Claire's face. She had passed just over a month ago after a valiant fight. *I miss you so much. I wish you were with me today.* He wiped away a tear. As he carefully placed the picture back in its place, he smiled at her. *Your legacy surrounds you, my darling, and it will grow by ninety today.* He followed the dogs out of the door, the weariness of the last month, at least for this day, behind him.

ACKNOWLEDGEMENTS

I would love to sit down and write a book from start to finish without any help. It's a nasty streak of pride and independence that dwells in me. The fact is, though good characters, settings and plots may come out of me unassisted, turning all of that into a good book requires the help of many others. So the first person I have to thank is my wife, Diane. She always had time to listen to a chapter and her comments were always spot on, even though it might take me time to come to that realization. Without her steadfast love, I'm not sure I would have finished this book. Next, is my dog, Sydney, a border collie. In retirement, she has become my shadow. She keeps me moving, she motivates me, she makes me more patient, she makes me a better person. Third, Sally Ginter helps me with the big pieces. The characters, the setting, the plot's organization have to have Sally's approval before I can call the words a manuscript. Then, a special thanks must go to Marie Showers, Rolla and Liliane Baumgartner, and our daughter, Brynn, who were "beta readers". They got the first glimpse of *Winter's Bloom*. Their positive comments were motivational; their criticisms, priceless.

Now, there is the entire group of professionals at Mission Point Press. Let's begin with John Pahl, who line-edited *Winter's Bloom*. John is a masterful teacher of creative writing. I would liken his work more to a college course than an editing. I learned so much from him during our nearly four month collaboration. Jennifer Carroll copy edited the manuscript. John's help made the book shine; Jennifer made it sparkle. Heather Shaw created the beautiful art work for the book's cover and has helped me through the process of making the book available in the market place. Finally, a sincere thanks to Doug Weaver, Mission Point Press's business manager. We met for lunch and I told him I was looking for a different publishing experience than I had the last time. I wanted to publish a quality product rather than just push another book out there. He listened, planned, presented and most importantly, followed through. As an author, I was looking for support to do things right. At Mission Point Press, I found what I was looking for.

To you, the reader of *Winter's Bloom,* I hope you enjoy the read as much as I have enjoyed the entire process of writing.

John V. Wemlinger
March, 2016

John Wemlinger is a retired U.S. Army Colonel with 27 years of service. He lives now in Onekama, Michigan, with his wife, Diane, close to the Lake Michigan shore where *Winter's Bloom* takes place. When he and their border collie, Sydney, aren't roaming the beaches or nearby hiking trails, he is playing golf, pickleball, working on his next novel or creating an unusual piece of original art from the driftwood, rocks and beach glass that he finds along the shoreline. One of the true joys of his life is talking with people about his books and his art. He can be contacted at www.JohnWemlinger.com or on Facebook.